LOVING HER COWBOY BEST FRIEND

TEXAS LONGHORN RANCH, BOOK 1

EMMY EUGENE

CHAPTER
ONE

Regina Barlow pushed her shopping cart out of the grocery store, the familiar sight of the huge trees only paces away reminding her of where she lived now.

Back in her parents' house.

"Only for now," she told herself for the tenth time that day. She'd given herself the same caveat at least a hundred times since returning to Chestnut Springs five days ago.

As she pushed the groceries past the trees and toward her car, she muttered, "You have to find a job. Today."

A job would mean she could afford an apartment. A job would mean she wouldn't lose her car and her dignity. Yes, she had a little bit of money from the severance package from the high-end restaurant in Dallas, but not enough to support herself independently for longer than a couple of months.

She pushed her hair back, semi-disgusted she'd let Ella

talk her into all the highlights. Her sister loved getting her hair done, and she'd been shocked at the state of Gina's upon her return to their small, Texas Hill Country town.

Truth be told, Gina had been somewhat shocked she'd let her hair get as frayed and as dim as it had, and she did feel better now that the blonde shone, and the sun caught on different hues of color. It was just a little too much, and it had cost her a small fortune.

With the groceries all loaded in her truck, she pushed the cart over to the return. A couple of men stood there, both cowboys of course, with a woman. In Chestnut Springs, Gina could throw a stick and hit a cowboy.

"Excuse me," she said, her voice taking on some Texas twang she'd left behind a long time ago. Confusion ran through her at the same time the three people turned toward her, one of them edging out of the way so she could return her cart.

She pushed her cart into the chute, but her body froze immediately after that. Her arms fell to her sides like lumps of ice.

"Regina Barlow?" one of the men said. Calvin Rowbury. Of course she'd run into the most popular boy from high school, the one who'd known everyone, who'd come to Gina's eighteenth birthday party fresh from his win in the state rodeo.

Before she could even offer a forced chuckle and a whispered hello, Cal engulfed her in a big hug. Of course. His spirit had always been as big as the Montana sky, and he would know, as he'd traveled all over competing in the rodeo.

He laughed and twirled around, all while Gina stayed still, her arms pinned to her sides by his. He set her down and backed up, his face aglow with life and love and laughter. Gina wondered what it would be like to feel those things again, actually, and her heart pinged out a twist that hurt.

"Hello, Gina," the woman said. Tawny Grossburg. The way she linked her arm through Cal's, it was obvious she was Tawny Rowbury now.

"Hi," Gina said, looking to the other man. Todd Stewart. Her heartbeat knifed through her body, and she couldn't look away from those dark hazel eyes. He didn't look exactly like his older brother, but close enough.

Too close.

"Gina," Todd said formally, with a nod of his cowboy hat. "Well, I best be goin'." He looked back to Cal and Tawny. "My daddy has a whole bunch of interviews today, and he hasn't been feelin' the best. Needs this ginger ale."

"Yeah, go," Cal said. "We'll pray for him." He still grinned like he'd been deemed Santa Claus, and Todd started to walk away.

Gina couldn't help her interest in him. Not because he was handsome, though he was. Not because she'd known him real well growing up, though she had. She had spent countless days and hours out at his family's dude ranch, because she'd dated his older brother for quite a long time.

Yeah, she told herself. *Back in high school.*

Which was almost twenty years ago now.

No, the reason she was interested in Todd was because

he'd said his daddy was interviewing, and well, Gina needed a job.

Not at the Texas Longhorn Ranch, she thought. Immediately a war started within her. *Why not there? You don't even know if Blake is still there.*

There certainly wasn't anywhere else in this small town, and Gina was done with big-city living.

She looked at Cal, who grinned on back at her. "You should come to dinner," he said. He glanced at Tawny, who clearly didn't share his same sentiments. "Shouldn't she come to dinner, baby?"

"Sure," Tawny deadpanned.

Gina wasn't sure what she'd done to Tawny, but she shook her head. "No, I can't," she said. "Thank you, though." No reason to make Cal's light dimmer. "What are the Stewarts hiring for?"

"A chef...something or other," Cal said, turning away from the cart return too. "I guess they've been in a real hurt."

"I can't imagine they have that many people applying," Tawny said, going with her husband.

Gina couldn't either, and she watched as Todd swung himself into a huge pickup truck the way men did to get in saddles. Without thinking too hard, she started jogging toward him. With any luck at all, she might be able to flag him down.

Turned out, luck and the Lord were on her side, because he backed out and pointed his truck right at her. Needlessly, she waved both hands above her head, hating herself and what her life had come to in that moment strongly.

He took care of that truck, because she could clearly see his eyebrows lift through the impeccably clean windshield. *Can't back out now*, she thought, and she continued over to his window. "Hey," she said breathlessly. She hadn't been in a kitchen in a month now, and she didn't subscribe to exercising all that much. "What job out at the ranch?"

This time, Todd's eyebrows shot toward the sky. "You want a job at the ranch?"

"I need a job," she said, not appreciating his attitude. "Cal said it was for a cook."

"Pastry chef," Todd said, reaching to rub the bridge of his nose. "Does Blake know you're back?"

"No," Gina said. "Listen, Todd, you know *I'm* a pastry chef, right?"

"I've heard," he said wearily.

"Would your daddy interview me?"

Todd appraised her, and wow, the Stewarts had always had eyes that could dive right into a person's inner-most secrets. Blake had done that to her countless times, but his whole family could achieve the same thing. "I'm not going to keep this a secret from my brother."

"But you don't need to tell him right this second either," Gina said. Desperation clogged her throat. "Listen, what about this?" She put one foot on the runner of his truck and boosted herself up so she was more eye-level with him.

"I come interview. If your daddy likes me and my

résumé and I get the job, then you can tell Blake. Or I'll tell him." She swallowed, her fear and all of the past she shared with Blake and his family lodging in the back of her throat. "But if I don't, then…no big deal. He'll find out I'm back in Chestnut Springs when he comes to church or…something."

Both Todd and Gina knew Blake didn't make the trip to town for church. Or much of anything. He had brothers and sisters who brought him his groceries and took care of his errands. He ran the family dude ranch, at least if his daddy had started thinking about retiring.

Maybe she was wrong, because Max Stewart was obviously conducting the interviews.

Todd cocked his left eyebrow, but he was considering her proposal.

"Please, Todd," she said, stopping herself from adding a plea that she needed a job. She'd take one almost anywhere, but if she could get something that actually utilized her education skills? That was the job she wanted.

"Fine," he said with a sigh. He scanned her down to her toes, though he couldn't possibly see below her chest. "Can you come out this afternoon? I know Daddy wants to get this done today."

"What time?"

"Come on out any time," Todd said, and discontent wove through Gina. She didn't want "any time." She didn't want to show up and wait for an hour while others got interviews.

"I have my mama's groceries," Gina said, stepping down off the runner. "I'll come after that?"

"Should be fine," Todd said, looking out the windshield. Another car came their way, and Gina fell back to the parked cars so it could pass.

"Thanks, Todd," Gina said, and Todd nodded his hat at her and eased down the row.

Gina took a deep breath and looked around. The wind blew across her face, and Gina shivered in the late winter weather here in the Hill Country. She didn't even know what she was doing, standing here in this parking lot.

"Car," she muttered, finally spotting her father's semi-old truck and striding toward it. "Groceries. Job interview."

———

AN HOUR LATER, GINA TURNED AND WENT UNDER THE massive arch that announced her arrival at the Texas Longhorn Ranch. "That's new," she said to herself and all the perfume that had come with her in the car.

There'd always been a sign here at the Longhorn Ranch, but not one that nice, and never with hand-carving. She wondered if one of the Stewarts had done it, or if they'd hired it out.

The roads, which had always been dirt, seemed nicer. They were still dirt, but it was packed and dark, and almost as smooth as the asphalt she'd driven on from town. Twenty minutes it had taken her to get from the house where she'd grown up to this ranch, and that hadn't changed.

The lampposts along the quarter-mile stretch between the entrance and the lodge had, as had the hanging flower pots which actually boasted colorful blooms. The parking lot was still dirt, but at least three more buildings had been added to the epicenter of the ranch, which was the lodge itself.

An ice cream shack sat to the left, and two big barns took up quite a bit of land on her right. *The south,* she heard in Blake's voice. His hearty, deep chuckle accompanied the words, because he did everything in proper directions, and she used her left and right. For him, things were universal. For her, it was her perspective.

Her stomach swooped as she pulled into an available parking space, one of only a few. Things seemed very busy at the ranch today, and she hoped with everything inside her that all of these cars didn't belong to prospective pastry chefs.

She wasn't sure how that was possible, as Chestnut Springs wasn't exactly a hotspot for the culinary arts. She'd left this small town for precisely that reason in the first place.

Still, her legs shook as she went up the steps—again lined with flowers attached to lariats—and to the big, heavy double-doors of the lodge. Those hadn't changed either, though someone had stained them a different color since the last time she'd been here.

She didn't need to knock, and she didn't. She went right inside, the scent of coffee and chocolate meeting her nose. Blake had joked that his daddy never went anywhere without a coffee mug in his hand, and it was obviously someone's birthday today, because a small card table had been set up several paces inside the building. It bore two

LOVING HER COWBOY BEST FRIEND 9

half-eaten pans of brownies, and three melting cartons of vanilla ice cream.

Definite life and activity buzzed here, but no one sat at the desk just inside the door. It wasn't quite check-in time, and it wasn't even close to mealtime, which she knew were two of the busiest times here at Longhorn Ranch.

She didn't see a row of chairs with people waiting in them, their legs bouncing nervously while they held a manila folder with their life's credentials. Gina swallowed as she gripped her folder tighter, wishing she had more directions than just "come on out anytime."

Out where? The interviews could be happening somewhere else, and Gina wouldn't know. She hadn't gotten Todd's number, and she glanced around nervously, the war inside her raging.

She wanted to see Blake.

She didn't want to see him.

She wanted to hear his voice.

She'd rather bury herself alive than hear his voice.

"Ma'am?" someone asked, and Gina blinked her way out of her inner struggles. "Can I help you?" A cowboy stood there—where he'd come from, Gina would never know—his smile genuine and soft at the same time. He wasn't a Stewart, and that only added a gold star to his stature.

"Yes." She cleared her throat. "I'm here for the pastry chef interviews?"

"Oh, sure," the cowboy drawled. "They're in the back, by the kitchen. I'll take you." He started weaving past the huge dining hall on the right, where the lodge fed their guests two square meals each day. On her left sat a variety of desks, some with cowboys at them, but most without.

They were probably all outside at this time of day, tending to cattle or fields, because while the Texas Longhorn Ranch was first and foremost a dude ranch, it was also a functional cattle ranch. Just on a very small scale compared to others surrounding Chestnut Springs.

No one seemed concerned about the dripping ice cream, and Gina wanted to rescue it. She told herself to ignore it as she followed the man in the red plaid shirt.

Blake would never wear red and black. He was more of a blue and yellow type of cowboy, and Gina schooled her thoughts. She really had no idea what kind of cowboy Blake Stewart was anymore.

"Thank you," a man said, his voice diving deep into Gina's chest. "We'll call you." She knew that voice. She'd heard that voice whisper her name right before the man it belonged to kissed her, and she'd heard that voice beg her to come back to him here in Chestnut Springs.

Around her, or maybe beside her, a woman moved.

"That's the last one," Blake said from somewhere beyond Gina's sight. He stood in front of the red-plaid-shirted cowboy, a sigh slipping from his lips. "No one good. Daddy's not gonna be happy."

"I've got one more," the man who'd greeted her at the door said.

Before Gina could yell that she'd made a mistake and run for the exit, he stepped out of her way.

"You do?" Blake asked, his words warping in her ears.

Their eyes met, and the whole world froze. Gina took in the glorious cowboy in front of her.

Blake Stewart. He still had deliciously dark hair, with long sideburns that connected to a full beard. He stood tall and tan and trim, and wow, he'd bulked out a lot in the shoulder department over the years.

His thick eyebrows drew down, breaking the spell over time. "Regina Barlow," he said, not forming her name into a question.

Her heart thundered through her chest, sounding like the hooves of a hundred horses sprinting over dry ground.

"What are you doin' here?"

"She came to interview," the other cowboy said.

Blake settled his weight onto one cowboy booted foot. He wore jeans too—Gina had never seen him wear anything but jeans—but he'd paired his with an equally denim shirt in a light blue that made his dark features even more handsome.

Her mouth watered, and it wasn't for the brownies and ice cream out front.

He folded his arms, and she cleared her throat to speak. "Is that right?" he asked. "Well, I think the job's filled." He held her gaze for one more moment, turned toward the other cowboy, and said, "Thanks, Baby John." Then Blake turned and headed down a hallway Gina hadn't seen yet.

Baby John turned toward her, surprise and confusion on his face simultaneously. "Oh-kay. I guess the job's filled?"

Gina watched Blake until he disappeared, and then her muscles thawed enough for her to move. "No," she said, her vocal cords tight but functional. "He just said there was no one good for this job." She smiled up at Baby John, though by the look on his face, it wasn't a happy gesture. More like terrifying.

"*I'm* good for this job," she said. "I'm just gonna head back and see what he thinks of my résumé, okay?" She started after Blake, her step as sure as his now. She'd driven all this way. He couldn't just dismiss her like that. Not after everything they'd been through.

He'd been her best friend for years. Her boyfriend. Her everything. So she hadn't come back. All that sentence needed was a *yet*, and she wasn't going to let the stubborn cowboy close the door on this opportunity she needed so badly.

In the hallway, several open doors greeted her, and Gina took a deep breath. She'd poke her nose into all of them until she found the one with Blake inside. Then... well, then she'd deal with whatever she had to in order to leave the Texas Longhorn Ranch as its newest employee.

CHAPTER
TWO

Blake Stewart's pulse leapt through his body like some sort of jackrabbit. The big kind. The kind that had just seen a coyote and run for its life.

"You can't hire her," he said to his reflection in the mirror on the inside door of the coat closet in his office. He turned away from it, the other side of the room his goal now. He paced in front of the open doorway, his breath coming in spurts.

Regina Barlow. Gorgeous, flirty, fun, kissable Regina Barlow.

He'd been in love with her once, even if he was only eighteen years old. He'd told his mother a bunch of times that love didn't have age boundaries. Of course, Gina had fled Chestnut Springs by then, and she'd written him for the duration of her culinary education.

He really thought she'd come back.

He'd been a fool.

"A darn fool," he whispered to himself when he reached the lamp in the corner. A recliner sat there too, and Blake didn't think he'd ever actually reclined in it. Todd would sit there while Blake would rant about something from the safety of his desk. Sometimes Kyle would text from the recliner while Blake went over the finer points of their meeting.

His sisters sat there and told him about the problems out on the ranch or in the lodge, and it was up to Blake to solve them all. All of his brothers and sisters came in and out of his office at-will now, especially since Daddy had announced his partial retirement at the New Year. He'd be out of his office and living duty-free by June first.

The weight of the world sagged onto Blake's shoulders, the fire Gina had relit inside him burning up against it. He turned and rolled his eyes as he started striding toward the other side of the office again.

On one step, he was alone, and on the next, he'd collided with a very solid, warm body. A grunt and a grumble escaped his mouth, and his hand slid down cloth and over bones as he tried to steady himself and the curvy woman in front of him.

He and Gina came to a standstill, his hands on her waist and hers braced against the outside of his biceps. Dang it if his pulse didn't turn into a jackhammer then.

"Blake," she said, the word mostly breath. "There you are."

He could only blink at her. It was definitely her, with all that shiny blonde hair, and those deep, gorgeous, ocean-blue eyes. She even had the freckles dashed across her nose she used to cover up with makeup.

She wore makeup today, especially on her eyes, but she hadn't used anything to blot out those freckles. Blake wanted to kiss them the way he once had, but just as quickly, his desire to get away from this woman shot through him.

She seemed to get the same idea, because they backed up simultaneously, his hands falling back to his sides. They knew the shape of Gina's body though, and his nose understood the scent of her perfume.

She'd changed over the past couple of decades, but she was still herself too. Stunningly beautiful, full of fire, and completely confident. Who else would've followed him down this hallway and started poking her head into every room until she found him?

Along with the makeup and perfume, she wore a pair of jeans, sneakers, and a sweatshirt in a shade of purple that made her eyes almost seem violet too. It was a tie-dye actually, that started out purple, and faded into blue near the hem.

He sure did like it, and Blake curled his fingers into fists to keep himself from grabbing onto her again.

Friends, whispered through his mind. Gina had been his best friend since the fifth grade, when they'd been paired in a science experiment. She had the brains, and he had the fearlessness, and they'd taken first in the district fair.

They'd been inseparable since, even when she started dating Tony McCollins in ninth grade, and he'd had a fairly terrible stint with dating Veronica Turnby. After that, Blake had only had eyes and feelings for Gina, and it had taken him all of his sophomore year to tell her about them.

They'd gone from friends to more, and he'd sure enjoyed their last couple of years of high school. He'd known about her wings from the age of ten, and he wasn't sure why he'd thought he'd be able to clip them.

He cleared his throat and headed for his desk. "When did you get back into town?"

"Four or five days ago."

He sat and shuffled some papers around his desk. He couldn't switch them around too much, because they had to be signed and given back to Lindsey before the end of the day. He picked up his pen to get his signature on the lines where it belonged. "And? Just visiting?"

If she was here about a job, she wasn't just visiting, and he knew it.

"No," she said, coming closer.

Blake steadfastly refused to look at her. He could resist Gina for several seconds, but if she stayed in this office for much longer than that, he'd look at her and fall for her all over again. He practically scribbled his name as she sat down.

"Do you run the ranch now?"

"Not entirely," he said, sliding the now-signed paper behind another one. "Daddy's semi-retired." She didn't need to know more than that.

"Todd said you need a pastry chef," Gina said, her voice like warm, pleasant music in his ears.

Blake lifted his head then, his pen point coming to a halt. "Todd did?"

"I ran into him in the grocery store parking lot," Gina said with a small, single-shoulder shrug. "Blake, I have a bachelor's degree in pastry arts."

"I'm aware," Blake said, his shock still waving through him in pulses. Todd had run into Gina? When? Why hadn't he said anything to Blake? Out of all the siblings, Todd alone knew how broken Blake had been when Gina had taken her first job in New Orleans instead of coming home.

"When did you talk to Todd?"

"About an hour ago," she said.

The fire licking through Blake quieted. "What happened to your job in Dallas?"

A flicker of a smile touched her mouth, which she'd painted a light pink. Blake tore his eyes from those lips he'd kissed before and went back to signing papers. He didn't care about her previous job. He didn't care about her.

Lies, he thought, but his pen scratched out another signature.

He looked up when she remained quiet. That was new for her, and he caught the hint of apprehension in her gaze.

"The restaurant went out of business," she said. "Sort of." She licked her lips, her tell that she was about to say something hard. Blake paused, because he found he wanted to hear it. "The previous owner was doing something illegal. Embezzlement or something? He sold the restaurant, and that's when it was discovered. Of course,

Paulo is gone, off to some South American country or something, and the rest of us—"

She cut off, her eyes widening. She gave herself a little shake and ground her voice through her whole chest. "I got a small severance package. We all did, but the new owners wanted to start fresh."

"Makes sense," Blake said. He didn't believe for one second that Gina would do anything like embezzlement. She didn't even know what that was. Heck, Blake barely knew. "So…you want to make desserts at a dude ranch?"

A smile brightened her whole face, extending way down into her very soul. He loved that look on her, as he'd seen it several times in years gone by. *Not for a while,* he told himself, but that didn't make her any less shiny to him.

"I would literally sacrifice a goat to make desserts on a dude ranch," she said.

Blake blinked, then burst out laughing, all of the tension gone between them. *See?* his mind whispered. *Friends.*

"All right," he said, reaching for her folder. "Let me see your résumé."

She dutifully handed it over, then sat back, her hands clasped in her lap. Blake just needed her to think she might not get this job. Gina wasn't stupid, though, and she'd heard him tell Baby John there wasn't anyone good.

She'd be perfect here, and his heart started making plans to ask her to dinner too. He shut those down real fast when he saw the four premier restaurants she'd worked at over the years.

"Hmm," he said, keeping his voice real neutral. "This last place was only for two years." He flicked a look in her direction and went back to her credentials. "Why'd you leave...The Tall Texas Grande?" He looked up then, surprised he'd been able to keep his tone so even.

The Tall Texas Grande was a five-star resort-hotel in Corpus Christi, and somewhere he'd never even *dream* of visiting. Families who never got dirty went there. Billionaires and politicians. Gina had probably met celebrities while they dined spa-side and presented them with upscale caramel cheesecakes, all fancied up with chocolate curls and strawberry sauce she'd labored over for hours.

"Are you kidding?" she asked.

"No, ma'am," Blake said, clearing his throat and snapping the folder shut. He set it on his desk, making no move to give it back to her. Their eyes met, and Blake determined he'd win this time. She'd speak first, and she'd tell him what he wanted to know.

"They weren't paying you enough?"

Gina's eyes narrowed. "The head pastry chef quit. He was my mentor, and I followed him to The Parisian in Dallas."

"Was he the embezzler?"

"No," Gina bit out.

"He must've lost his job too."

"Yes."

"Where did he go?"

"Miami."

"You didn't go with him?"

"Obviously." With every answer, her shoulders had

lifted a little higher. Finally, she exhaled out. "I know where you're going with this."

"Do you?"

"I dated him once," she said. "Five years ago. But after it fell apart, we were just colleagues."

"And he didn't take you to Miami." Blake leaned forward, steepling his fingers. "So you left your job at a resort-hotel on the beach for him...but he didn't have a place for you when you needed it."

Gina's eyes blazed with blue fire, and oh, Blake had missed that so very much in his life. He held up one hand. "Never mind." He took a big breath and looked down at the paperwork on his desk. Daddy would be thrilled with the addition of Gina to their staff. Heck, everyone would. He couldn't even imagine the culinary delights she could put on the table here at the Texas Longhorn Ranch.

"Do you want the job?"

"Is that a real question?"

Blake bent to get the hiring paperwork out of the bottom desk drawer. "I asked it, didn't I?" So she'd made a long-lost joke about sacrificing a goat for something she wanted. They'd been doing that since they were twelve.

"Yes," she ground out through clenched teeth, though he couldn't see her. "I want the job."

"Great." He plunked the paper down on top of her folder and slid everything toward her. "I need this filled out, and I think you should come out in the morning and meet with the head chef. She does her weekly meetings on Tuesdays as we gear up for the weekend, and you'll get a feel for how the two of you will work together."

Gina took the folder and simple tax paperwork. "Is she hard to work for?"

"Depends on how you define that," Blake said, standing with a smile. "I'm used to her, but our last dessert master *did* quit because of Starla..." He clucked his tongue like that was just too darn bad, and he chuckled at the horrified look on Gina's face.

"Starla Masters is the head chef here?"

Blake could've been imagining it, but he thought he saw her swallow. More like a gulp, in all honesty.

"Yes," Blake said, drawing the word out. "Is that a problem for you?"

Gina looked like she might throw up, but she shook her head. "No," she said, her voice somewhat tight. "No, sir."

Blake took a step around the desk and then kept going. "Gina," he said quietly. "You don't have to call me sir." He stood in front of her now, and he might as well have been naked for the way she looked at him with such a sharp edge in her eyes.

"We were friends once. We can be friends again." He took a breath, because he'd nearly choked on the word *friends*. Twice. He wasn't thinking of her in a strictly friendly way, that was for certain. The longer he looked at her, the further she pulled him in with those ocean-y eyes and the more he thought about kissing her. "Right?"

She simply gazed up at him, and Blake thought for sure he'd just made the biggest mistake of his life, but whether that was saying he and Gina could be friends or hiring her to be the ranch's pastry chef, he wasn't sure.

Why wouldn't she answer him?

"Listen," he said, sighing. "If we can't be friends, I'm not sure you should take the job." He couldn't stand to watch her walk out of his life again, not when she'd only been back for ten minutes. Working with her when they couldn't have a conversation would be torture, though.

"Well?" he asked, unsettled by Gina's long silence.

CHAPTER
THREE

Gina's skin tingled with the chemistry between her and Blake. That hadn't changed about this place, about this man. He'd changed over the years, sure, but his eyes were still deep and dark, like the night sky full of stars. His beard had grown long, as had his hair, and she wondered if he still did that to irritate his mama.

When he let it get long, it curled around his ears and across his forehead, and she watched as he pushed his hand through that hair and sighed.

"Yes," she said, finally finding the word in her vocabulary. "We can be friends." She put a smile on her face and semi-lunged at Blake. He grunted as he caught her, and her arms went around him easily, the way they always had.

He eventually settled his hands on her lower back, and his chest expanded as he breathed in deeply. Gina pressed her cheek to his heartbeat and breathed too, maybe completely and fully for the first time since she'd learned her job in Dallas was no more.

"Thank you," she said, stepping back, a keen sense of awkwardness filling her. Friends didn't hug and breathe in deeply together, swaying slightly. That behavior existed in a living room prom, with a fake disco ball throwing rectangles of light onto the walls while a cheesy eighties ballad played.

This was an office—her boss's office.

"I'm not your boss," he said gruffly, as if he could read minds. "Starla is, and you'll be reporting to her. She reports to me, so I'll know if there's any problems."

"There won't be any problems," Gina promised, even reaching up to cross her heart. Instant embarrassment heated her face, and she turned away from Blake so he wouldn't see. He used to tease her relentlessly when she blushed, and she'd already inserted herself into this office and basically demanded he give her the job. Not only that, but she'd questioned his right to interview her.

She pressed her eyes closed and breathed in through her nose as she reached the doorway. She looked left and then right before moving, and she'd barely lifted her foot to step before Blake said, "Right, Gina."

She twisted to look at him, her foot coming down on the floor while she wasn't watching. Her ankle decided that was a great moment to give out on her, and her knee and then hip buckled too. She scrambled to find a grip on the doorjamb, but that thing might as well have been polished with butter.

Gina hit the floor as a cry left her mouth, and Blake

LOVING HER COWBOY BEST FRIEND 25

arrived at her side in less time than it took for the pain to flash through her body.

"You're okay," he said, his voice tender and soft, as it had been many times before when he'd spoken to her. One hand went around her back to support her, and the other held onto her forearm. He lingered so close, she could smell his cologne and the Ashe juniper—bitter, fresh, and sappy.

She looked up at him, and suddenly everything was okay. "Sorry," she said.

"Still a bit directionally challenged," he said with that trademark smile. That hadn't changed. Gina wondered if she'd be categorizing what had changed and what hadn't here at the Texas Longhorn Ranch forever. She hoped not. "And klutzy."

"That's why you're around," Gina said, leaning into him and using him to stand. He went with her, finally pulling his hands back to himself. She cleared her throat, the moment turning heated and intense quickly. "So what time in the morning?"

"Starla does her staff meetings before breakfast is served," he said.

"And that still goes from seven to nine?" Gina asked. "Right?"

"Still does, yep." Blake pocketed his hands and rocked back onto his cowboy boot heels. "So six." His eyes glittered with those stars, clearly asking her if she got up that early.

Gina swept her stick-straight hair over her shoulders and said, "Great. I'll be here at six." She stepped around

Blake and went down the hallway toward the room where she'd left Baby John. He wasn't there anymore, and as there was only one hallway leading out of this room, besides the one she'd just come down, Gina knew the way back to the front of the lodge.

A few more people worked in the big main room, but none of them paid Gina any mind. She didn't want to talk to anyone anyway. She just needed to make it back to her car, and then she'd come up with a plan for how she could be at the lodge by five-forty-five in the morning.

———

"YOU'RE UP EARLY."

Gina turned toward her mother's weathered voice and found her in her fluffy red robe and slippers. Fox trotted in front of her and went straight to the back door, his master following.

"So are you," Gina said as she returned to filling her travel mug with coffee. She'd need the whole thing to make it through breakfast, and she was sure the day held a lot more for her than that. "I could've let out Fox."

"Oh, we have our routine," her mom said. "You're dressed and everything." She reached the back door and let out the dog.

"Yes, Mom," Gina said as gently as she could. "I'm starting my new job this morning, remember?"

"Of course I do," Mom said, but Gina didn't think she did.

She sighed and capped her coffee. "Yeah, it's a twenty-

minute drive to Longhorn, and I don't want to be late."
The sun had not peeked its head over the horizon yet, and
Gina told herself that the life of a pastry chef was often
lived in darkness. Most people who worked in restaurants
or bakeries had to endure interesting sleeping and eating
schedules.

For example, she'd have her coffee on the drive in to
work, but she wouldn't eat until breakfast closed for
guests at the lodge. After that break, she figured she'd
work on the evening desserts, then be done for the day in
the early afternoon.

"I'll be back by three to take you to your pedicure." She
stepped over to her mom and kissed her on the cheek.
"Okay? You're going back to bed?"

"Yes, after Fox comes in." Mom smiled at her, and Gina
could see Ella in her mother so easily. She wondered if
others could see her in her mom, but she wasn't sure.
Everyone, for her whole life, had commented about how
Mom and Ella looked like sisters. Then they'd look at Gina
and just smile. The black sheep's wool she'd been carrying
for decades definitely fit her, but Gina gave her mom a
smile.

"Good luck with your new job," Mom said. Gina's eyes
caught on the clock, and she nodded.

"Thanks, Mom." She ducked out the back door, didn't
see Fox, and went down the few steps to the yard. She
parked on the side of the garage, and she'd been tromping
through the gravel and dried weeds for several days now,
so a path had been forged.

She adjusted the heater to blow and turned off the

radio. She just wanted to be alone with her thoughts as she drove, and once she got on the road, she realized just how good the Texas countryside was at taking a person's thoughts and echoing them back to them loudly.

She'd hated that as a teenager, but now…she found it peaceful and calming. She sipped her coffee and thought about the person who hadn't left her mind for much longer than a few seconds since yesterday.

Blake Stewart.

Friends.

She scoffed out loud, because they'd been so much more than friends. She told herself the past didn't matter. What mattered was her being able to move out of her parents' house and having some stability so she could figure out what she wanted to do next with her life.

Chestnut Springs had never been part of Gina's plans, but the world had an odd way of shifting so early in the morning.

She made the turn to drive onto the ranch, and the lodge lights lit up the darkness like a beacon calling her home. She immediately resisted the idea, but her heart softened at the same time.

The Stewarts didn't spare any expense when it came to their grounds, facilities, and buildings. The roof boasted lights every few feet, with the whole front porch flooded with a cheery golden glow.

Starla Masters had texted Gina instructions last night, and she made another turn after the first barn before reaching the lodge parking lot. That was for guests and visitors, and Gina was now neither. She pulled around to the back of the lodge, noting how wide and tall it was before parking next to a pick-up truck. A man got out of it as she cut the engine, and she took a deep breath and then opened her door.

After reaching back for her purse, she went around the truck.

"Good mornin'," the man said, and Gina yelped.

"Whoa, whoa, it's just me." He held up both hands, but Gina had no idea who "me" was. She held her purse in front of her like this guy dressed in gym shorts and a T-shirt with a faded palm tree on the front would attack.

"You must be new," he said.

She nodded, glancing toward the door Starla had said would lead right into the kitchen.

"I'm Nash," he said, grinning. "Blake's brother."

Gina's heart pounded with adrenaline, but not because Nash might rush her. "What?" came out of her mouth. "You're like...old."

He laughed, the sound filling up the Texas sky. "So are you, Gina." He came toward her, his face all lit up like the lodge. "Blake said he'd hired you." His eyes slid down to her sneakered feet. "I sort of didn't believe him, but here you are."

"You were eight the last time I saw you."

He chuckled again and said, "I'm twenty-eight now." He gestured for her to follow him. "Come on, Starla doesn't like it when we're late."

"I left early," Gina said, falling into step with him. "She's not as bad as she seems, is she?"

"Sometimes she's worse," Nash said under his breath.

"Don't tell her I said that."

She crossed her heart again, asking, "You work in the kitchen?" She didn't think the Stewarts did things like that. They held administrative roles around the ranch, didn't they?

"I'm the morning manager," he said. "So I have to know what's going on for breakfast, morning activities, et cetera." He made his job sound so casual, but Gina had a feeling it wasn't. He opened the door for her, and she slipped past him into the belly of the beast.

Heat filled the kitchen, as it does in all good kitchens. Someone had been here working for a while already, and Gina's stomach trembled. She looked around, trying to take everything in at the same time. She couldn't do that, of course, but her eyes did catalog the fancy appliances, the steaming pots, the warmers full of food.

"All right," a woman bellowed, the voice clearly belonging to Starla. She couldn't weigh more than a hundred pounds, but everyone working in the kitchen—Gina estimated there were probably eight of them there—stopped what they were doing and turned toward the dark-haired woman. "Staff meeting in five," Starla said, her eyes settling on Gina as she stood next to Nash. She wanted to cower into him, but she didn't. She lengthened her neck and looked right back at Starla.

They'd worked together once, at a cupcakery back in the first year of their culinary education. Gina had gotten a promotion when Starla hadn't, and that had started a tiny rift between them. Starla had left the pastry arts to focus on kitchen management after that, and while they hadn't been besties, Gina certainly wouldn't categorize them as enemies.

Starla smiled at her as she walked closer. "Come with me, Gina. We'll get you outfitted before the meeting."

"Okay," Gina said. She nodded to Nash and followed Starla into a microscopic office just inside the back door. A messy desk had been wedged into the corner, and it held everything from a small bag of flour, to folders, to loose papers, to someone's breakfast. Starla's presumably. She hadn't finished it, which didn't surprise Gina at all.

"Apron," Starla said, opening one of the cabinets built in to the wall and tossing something white in Gina's direction. She closed her eyes and flung up her hands, managing to fist the fabric before it fell to the floor. "I'll get you a name tag. I have to put in a special order."

"Okay," Gina said, looping the apron around her waist. Even with the activity in the kitchen behind them, it felt silent and awkward inside the office.

"We haven't had a pastry chef here in a while," Starla said, and she looked exhausted though it was only Tuesday. "We've had people who can make good desserts, but I expect you can conjure up pastries for breakfast, lunch, dinner, and snacks." Her perfectly sculpted eyebrows went up, and despite her likely hours of work this morning, her makeup hadn't budged a centimeter.

Gina swallowed, her pride sliding right down her throat. "I can do whatever you need me to, Starla."

The other woman nodded and said, "Today, I want your best desserts for dinner tonight. The lodge isn't full, but we need seventy-five units of something."

"Something all the same, or could I do twenty-five of three different things?"

Starla's eyes sparkled as she smiled. "Up to you, Gina. Just make sure we have seventy-five desserts for dinner tonight."

"Yes, ma'am," Gina said.

"You know what?" Starla said, her eyes flickering to something behind Gina. She too turned that way and found Blake standing there, his arms folded. She shrank back, though they were supposed to be friends.

Friends.

An internal scoff burned in her throat, because the way her heartbeat fluttered at the mere sight of him didn't speak of friendly things. *Boy*friendly things, yes.

"Make it eighty," Starla said. "Blake and I would like to have a taste-test before we serve the desserts to paying guests."

"Yes, ma'am," she said again, her voice scraping her throat this time.

Starla moved past her and patted Blake's shoulder. "Taste-test at two, Mister Stewart?"

"Sure," he said smoothly, and Gina barely dared to pull in a full breath because of that fresh, minty cologne.

"All right," Starla called, answering Blake as well as getting the rest of her staff's attention. "Let's go over this morning. Gina here is new."

Blake stepped out of the way, and Gina exited the office to have nine pairs of eyes on her. She lifted her hand in a pathetic wave, noting that only a couple of people smiled.

"She'll be running this morning, and then Stasia, she's

going to need the oven station for her evening desserts."
Starla looked at Gina, her eyebrows raised as if to ask if
that was good. Gina nodded, because she didn't know all
the stations in this kitchen.

Yet, she told herself. She didn't know how things
worked here at the Texas Longhorn Ranch yet, but she'd
figure it out. She'd started in a half-dozen kitchens over
the years, and this was just number seven.

Starla started going over menu items and what needed
to be finished in the next fifty-five minutes, but she never
came back to what "running" meant. Blake hadn't moved,
and Gina stood slightly in front of him. When it was clear
Starla wasn't going to detail the job for her, Gina bent her
head toward Blake and asked, "What does running
mean?"

"Running?"

She turned toward him, the meeting over, and said,
"She said I'm going to be this morning's runner. What does
that mean?"

A smile curved that strong mouth, and oh, that nearly
undid all of Gina's defenses. "It means you're going to be
taking food from here out to the buffet," he said. "Running. Back and forth."

She looked down at her shoes, seeing how they didn't
quite fit with his cowboy boots. Upon meeting his gaze
again, she said, "At least I wore the right shoes."

"Yeah." He chuckled and shook his head. "Now, let's
hope you don't get lost in between."

CHAPTER
FOUR

Blake had no sooner sat down behind his desk, ready to orient himself to the work he needed to accomplish, when his brother said, "Blake, I need you for two seconds."

He looked up to find his brother Jesse standing in the doorway. Halfway, at least. He nodded down the hall and disappeared. Blake sighed as he got to his feet to follow Jesse. He couldn't just ignore his request. Jesse—and it was always Jesse, not Jess—ran the customer-facing side of the lodge.

He handled all their guest relations and bookings. Now that they had a functional and beautiful website for the lodge, Jesse's workload had eased slightly. He still worked with Becks, their cousin who'd come to the Texas Longhorn Ranch to get them online, as did Blake. In fact, he had a meeting with her about mid-morning.

When they held their big monthly meetings, where

new activities and ideas were presented, Blake or Adam always acted as voice for Jesse. He had a mind Blake couldn't comprehend, but he didn't want any of the accolades. For as grumpy and closed off as he was, he managed to handle the guests and their complaints like a champion.

If things got really bad, Jesse and Blake referred disgruntled customers to their sister, Holly. She was the charmer of the Stewart family, having gotten all of the charisma that Jesse lacked from their mother. There wasn't any problem that Holly couldn't fix, and both Blake and Jesse tried to only send her their most difficult customers.

Jesse handled everyone else, and the moment he stepped into the public spotlight, he shone like all the lights over a football stadium. Behind closed doors, though, and Jesse only spoke in growls and grunts.

Today, he led Blake into his office, which he shared with another of their brothers, Nash, and Holly. The three of them ran the lodge from morning to night, while Todd, Adam, and Sierra ran the actual ranch side of their land. Blake oversaw it all, and he couldn't remember the last time he hadn't worked seven days in a week.

Jesse picked up a card and showed it to Blake. "I'm thinking a caramel tasting for our April Spring Break event."

Blake took the card, which didn't have even a hint of caramel on the front of it. He frowned, trying to put together dots that didn't exist. In fact, the card was a birthday card with some well-known cartoon characters which Jesse happened to love.

"Who is this from?" He flipped open the card only to have Jesse rip it from his hand.

"No one," he growled. "What about caramels? We just got that new ritzy pastry chef." His eyebrows went up, but Blake rubbed his fingers together, the skin still burning from the speed with which Jesse had taken the card from him.

"How did you get caramels from Winnie the Pooh?" Blake tilted his head at his brother, trying to see past the dark look on his face. Jesse always operated with that look, and Blake wasn't alarmed.

Jesse turned and dropped the card on his pristine desk as if he didn't care about it. Blake wouldn't be surprised to find it magneted to his fridge—with perfect ninety-degree angles between it and other appliance decorations—in his cabin. He turned back to Blake and folded his arms. "The card came with caramels."

"What flavor?" Blake asked.

"Sea salt," Jesse said. "Which is so boring. I think your fancy girlfriend-chef could come up with some amazing flavors, and we can have guests taste-test them. Guess the flavors. Sell the winners in the front shop."

Blake's brain filled with so much from what Jesse had said, which wasn't unusual. "First," he said, holding up his palm. "She's not my girlfriend."

"Yet," Jesse said without moving his lips.

Blake didn't argue with him. "Second, you're talking about having Gina make a lot of caramels that we give to guests for free."

"Right."

"And then we start selling the winning ones in the store."

"Yes."

Blake looked over to Holly's desk, finding more comfort there. She organized things into trays, but at least it looked like someone worked at the desk. Jesse was so neat, and so square, and while Blake knew why, it still unsettled him if he spent too much time in his brother's space.

"That's a lot of work for a pastry chef," he said. "She might not be able to make caramels every day."

"She doesn't have to make them every day," Jesse said, as he loved to argue. The man could argue that horses didn't have four legs, for crying out loud. "Just during the taste-testing event, which won't be more than a few days. Then, according to her schedule, she can make them and we'll stock them in the store."

"Let me talk to Starla."

"Okay." Jesse nodded at him, and Blake turned to leave. Nash came through the door in that moment, and the two of them almost collided.

"Whoa," Nash said, chuckling as he stepped to the side. He loved to laugh, and he hardly ever said a sentence that wasn't accompanied by a chuckle. "Things are lookin' good in the kitchen."

"Really?" Blake asked, which caused both Nash and Jesse to peer at him more closely. Instant heat flushed through him, and he wasn't even sure why. "I mean, yeah, of course. I didn't think she'd be a problem."

"Not for the kitchen anyway," Jesse muttered, and

Nash laughed right out loud. The two of them sat down at their desks, with Jesse going to his computer, and Nash pulling his event book toward him.

During the last first and last ten minutes of breakfast, and again at the top of the eight o'clock hour, Nash would stand in front of the mic and tell guests what their morning activities were, if they could get a grab-and-go lunch that day, and where to meet for the afternoon outdoor activities.

In these late winter months—which was part of February and most of March—they didn't have a full lodge during the week. So their activity schedule wasn't as robust either.

"I have work to do," he said, turning away from Nash's knowing grin and Jesse's familiar frown.

"Wait," Nash said, and Blake breathed in deeply through his nose before he turned back to face his youngest brother. "I need you to sign off on the new riding boots for guests. Adam brought me an invoice..." He opened a drawer and then rifled through a stack of loose papers on his desk before finding it.

Their mother still ran the finances for the ranch and the lodge, and another brother, Adam, organized and oversaw all of their outdoor activities with animals. Specifically horses, as the man possessed the ability to speak to equines and had since birth. Nothing got through the accounting department of Sharon Stewart without Blake's signature on it, and he scratched it out with the pen Nash presented to him.

He finally left his brothers' office and returned to his

own. He considered closing his door, but he did so rarely, and he needed to be available to anyone coming to him this morning. The pull to go back into the kitchen to see how Gina was getting along had him checking the doorway every few minutes.

When his eight o'clock alarm sounded, he actually got to his feet as if he'd go get breakfast now. "You go get breakfast every morning at eight," he grumbled to himself, because he did. That was why he had the alarm set on his phone in the first place.

Today, he had an additional reason to get on down the hall and load his plate with bacon, eggs, and biscuits and gravy. He didn't usually concern himself with seeing how things were going in the kitchen or on the buffet. Starla ran a tight ship, and they hadn't had problems since she'd taken over a few years ago.

The food came out of the kitchen hot if it was supposed to be, and cold if not. She'd come up with the grab-and-go lunch program that guests paid a premium fee to get, and that had been really popular with families who didn't want to leave the ranch and drive to town for lunch. The guest cabins had kitchens too, but not everyone wanted to cook on vacation, even at a dude ranch.

His step slowed as he approached the main room, the chatter and laughter of happy guests meeting his ears. He liked that, and he paused as the large space that filled over half of the lodge opened up before him. The dining area buzzed with activity, but he had no problem spotting Gina.

The woman called to him in a way no one else ever had, and he didn't think he'd be able to stop himself from looking her way. She lifted an empty pan of scrambled eggs from the hot buffet and replaced it with a fresh one, her smile wide and bright as she set the spoon back in place.

She wiped down the counter, taking in the bar, and Blake didn't detect any unrest or stress in her. She'd worked in some premier kitchens, and running food from the kitchen to the breakfast bar wasn't going to be something she couldn't handle.

In fact, as he watched, she chatted with a mother and her son, cleaned up the spilled fruit in front of the platter, and then headed for the kitchen with her dirty pan. With her absence, Blake kicked himself into gear to go get his food.

He didn't particularly appreciate fruits and veggies, but he took a couple of obligatory pineapple chunks. Then he got the things he ate every day for breakfast— bacon, eggs, and two biscuits with plenty of sausage gravy.

"This hasn't changed," Gina said, and Blake looked up to find her standing across the buffet from him. She smiled at his plate and lifted those gorgeous eyes to meet his.

"I'm very routined," Blake admitted. He put the ladle back in the gravy and met Gina's eyes again. His brain went on vacation, which left his bodily functions to operate all on their own. "Are you seeing anyone?"

Gina's eyes rounded, and that was Blake's first clue that he'd said something stupid. His stomach growled, and his blood rushed through his ears in a stream of white noise. "Excuse me," he said gruffly. He took a couple of steps past her, seizing onto the fact that Kyle had just entered the dining area.

"Kyle," he very nearly barked. "How did things go with the bread delivery?"

"Great." His brother looked over Blake's shoulder. His eyebrows rose. "She...wants you."

Blake wanted to hurl his plate of hot food against the nearest wall and go back to his office hungry. Instead, he turned to face Gina again. She now held an empty container which had once been full of strawberries, and she blinked at him once, then twice. "Do friends eat lunch together around here?"

Blake did the blinking next. "Do you have time for lunch?"

"If we go out back for twenty minutes while the pecan tarts bake."

Blake didn't know how to say no to her, and he glanced toward the kitchen as if he could summon Starla and ask if they had grab-and-go lunches that day. If they did, could he possibly get a couple of extra for him and Gina?

Instead of being completely transparent with these resurfacing feelings racing through him, he looked at Gina and said, "If you can get Starla to get us two grab-and-go lunches, I think friends can eat them on the picnic table under the bald cypress."

She swallowed and looked toward the kitchen. She started in that direction, calling over her shoulder, "I'll text you."

Blake watched her go, forgetting that his gossipiest brother had just witnessed the whole exchange. Until Kyle said, "I thought you said there wasn't anything between you."

Blake glared at him and walked away. "There isn't," he tossed over his shoulder. Friends ate lunch together. Heck, his mother and sisters went to lunch in town at least once a week, meeting other ladies to socialize as they tried the new restaurants in Chestnut Springs.

This was no different, though every cell in Blake's body screamed otherwise.

CHAPTER
FIVE

Gina's feet remembered what it was like to support her body for hours on end. They hurt, but she didn't mind the pain. It meant she wasn't at her parents' house, wishing she had something better to do.

She didn't want to ask Starla about "grab-and-go lunches," and that was the biggest item on her to-do list all of a sudden.

She glanced at the other woman as she entered the kitchen, but Starla had her attention elsewhere. Three more pans of food waited for her, and Gina deposited her empty strawberry container in the huge sink in the corner and picked up two of the pans. One held sausage links, which had gotten low, and the other held perfectly circular four-inch Belgian waffles. The efficiency of this kitchen impressed her, and she shouldn't have expected anything less from Starla.

The woman's very presence demanded perfection, and Gina found herself wanting to provide it. That was the mark of a good leader, and Gina had worked for many diva-chefs. The good ones could bark orders and still laugh and drink coffee after a hectic service.

Back out in the busy dining hall, Gina couldn't even imagine what a full lodge would look like. The Texas Longhorn Ranch was much bigger than she remembered, with fourteen rooms right here in the main lodge, and an additional fourteen cabins out on the ranch. Nash had told her that, and he'd said to let him know if she needed anything.

She had no intentions of going to Nash Stewart if she needed something. She'd handle it like an adult, even if that meant she had to ask Starla about the grab-and-go lunches here at the lodge. After the breakfast service, that was.

Eventually, the people stopped eating, and the staff in the kitchen came out and started cleaning the tables. The two waitresses that had done so during the service refilled salt and pepper shakers, the artificial sweetener packets, and the ketchup bottles. Everyone had a job to do, and they moved from one to the next as easily as breathing.

Impressed, Gina did what the kitchen assistant, Dale, told her to, and before she knew it, the breakfast prep cooks were headed out the back door. Her work had just started, and she moved over to the oven station, which had been busy that morning with pans of cinnamon rolls and keeping waffles and pancakes warm.

She took a deep breath in the moment of silence in the

lodge kitchen, trying to decide what she could make in four and a half hours that would impress the mighty Starla. Her first thought was to make a jelly roll of some sort. She could flavor the cake with pumpkin, gingerbread spices, chocolate, or almond. Anything really.

The crème inside could also hold a variety of flavors, and she loved the autumnal ones the best. Cream cheese frosting with pumpkin. Mint crème with chocolate. Plenty of bark on the yule log.

She pulled herself out of the wrong season and said, "Spring." It was almost March, and perhaps she should go with something a little brighter in flavor and appearance. She made a terrific sugar cookie, and she hadn't met a human alive who didn't love a buttery, flaky, soft sugar cookie with plenty of delicious frosting.

She turned to start getting out the ingredients she needed. Eighty desserts, and half could be bright yellow and pink daisy sugar cookies. She could have them in the oven in half an hour, and she let her mind work while she put together the dough.

She rolled and cut and bent to put sixteen cookies in the oven. Once, then twice, then three times. With everything baking, and a few minutes until the first batch of cookies came out, she realized how close to lunchtime the time had drifted.

"Shoot." She stepped back to see Starla's office, but the door sat closed. The message got through loud and clear, and Gina licked her lips nervously. "Cake." Her only option was cake, if she wanted to have something in the oven before lunchtime, baking away while she snuck outside to enjoy lunch with Blake.

"Or a crispy treat," she mused, realizing she didn't have time for pecan tarts. She could put together a unique crispy treat, putting her flavorful twist on the marshmallows, adding in chips or candies, and then topping each square with a ganache.

"Spring, bright," she said, her mind moving through possibilities as she walked into the pantry. It was well-stocked, and Gina landed on butterscotch chips as well as peanut butter. This was a Texas dude ranch, and they didn't need fancy desserts. They should be beautiful and delicious, but she didn't need to make an eight-layer cake. She couldn't cut that into forty pieces anyway.

But she could whip up something more unique on the classic treat. Something that fit a ranch. Her eyes landed on a box of graham cracker crumbs, and a fully fledged dessert entered her mind.

She'd be rolling these crispy treats, and while she wasn't making cake or flavoring it with pumpkin, she still felt like she was making a yule log. She smiled to herself as she stirred the melted butter and marshmallows together, then poured in the cereal and graham cracker crumbs. After pressing it into a thin layer in three cookie sheets, she spread marshmallow crème over it all.

She melted chocolate and spread that over the marshmallow and got rolling. She'd just secured the last log in tight plastic wrap when the sound of footsteps drew her attention. Starla stood there, a huge bin in her arms.

"Can you help me put out the grab-and-go lunches?" she asked. "There's another bin in the walk-in."

Gina grinned at her and closed the fridge. "Of course." She only wanted to leave her crispy treats in the fridge for about five minutes, and then they could set fully on the counter, away from the ovens.

She went to grab the second bin of brown-bagged lunches. When she returned to the kitchen, Starla waited for her. "Do you do grab-and-go lunches every day?"

"In the summer, yes," Starla said, leading the way out into the dining area. Across from it, more cowboys and cowgirls had arrived at work, and about two-thirds of the desks were full today. What they all did, Gina had no idea. She set her bin on the table beside Starla's and watched as the woman turned and bent to get out a huge picnic basket full of plastic silverware. The lids had been removed, and the cutlery included a spork, knife, and napkin.

Starla sighed and looked at Gina. "That's it. Guests come get a lunch if they signed up. Lowry handles that list."

Gina didn't know who Lowry was, but it didn't matter. She didn't have to check off people as they took their lunches. Starla turned to go back into the kitchen, and Gina's pulse panicked. "Oh, uh, Starla?" She dashed after her boss. "Are there extra lunches?"

Starla paused with her palm pressed against the plastic door that led into the kitchen. "Usually," she said. "If you want one every day, you should talk to Lowry. He'll take a monthly payment."

"Okay," Gina said, her stomach still writhing from nerves. "Which one is Lowry?"

"You didn't meet him at the front desk yesterday?"

"There wasn't anyone at the front desk yesterday."

"I'm not surprised," Starla said with a roll of her eyes. She nodded toward the front of the lodge. "He's the one in the purple plaid. Can't miss 'im."

Gina turned, found the cowboy in question, and twisted back to tell Starla thanks. The woman had disappeared in the blink of an eye, and Gina took a steeling breath and headed for the front desk.

"Lowry?" she asked, and he looked up, his light green eyes somewhat startling. He did have sandy blond hair peeking out from underneath his cowboy hat, but still. His eyes looked made of ocean sea glass, and Gina had a sudden pang of missing for Corpus Christi, where she'd lived seaside for a few years.

"Are there a couple of extra grab-and-go lunches today?" she asked. "I can pay for them. I'll want one every day I work too." She pressed her fingertips together, her mind firing a reminder at her. "On the days we make them."

"Sure thing," Lowry said, his voice higher than she would've guessed it to be. Nothing about this cowboy made sense, and she wondered if he'd been pieced together by leftovers by the Good Lord. He opened a drawer and handed her a sheet of paper. "That's our schedule for this month. March is on the back. Cost for lunches is on the top."

Gina studied the sheet, noting that they made grab-

and-go lunches four or five days a week in this "off-season."

"Okay," she said. "So I want two À la carte ones today, and I want to sign up for the monthly plan."

"Just a sec," he said, tapping on a tablet in front of him. She had no idea what he was looking at, as he didn't seem too keen to explain himself to her. She stood at his desk awkwardly, blurting out, "My crispy treats," at the same time he said, "We have two extras for today."

She held up both palms and said, "I need a minute." Then she sprinted back into the kitchen and got her rolled crispy treats out of the fridge. With them safely resting on the counter near the door, she admired the cookies as well. They'd all come out perfectly golden brown while she'd contemplated what her second offering would be, and she couldn't wait to decorate them.

Later. Right now, she hurried back to Lowry as she set an alarm on her phone. She needed time to decorate those cookies, and time had a way of disappearing when she was with Blake. "Okay," she said, breathless. "I'm ready now."

"Great," Lowry said from his seated position. "How would you like to pay for today's lunches?" He looked at her expectantly.

"Uh, let me—"

"I've got it," a deep voice said, and all of Gina's cells vibrated at the familiarity in Blake's voice. He handed Lowry a ten-dollar bill and nodded at him. He did the same to Gina, minus the money, and then turned toward the dining area. "You're free for a few minutes?"

"Yes, sir," she said, her voice taking on a teasing quality all by itself. Embarrassment filled her, and she clomped after Blake in her tennis shoes. He took two lunches from one of the bins and went back toward the hallway that led into the office area. She simply followed him, hoping she could find her way back to the kitchen in time to make frosting and impress him and Starla with her cookie decorating skills.

Outside, sunshine assaulted her, and she took a deep breath of it. Her head cleared and her muscles relaxed, and she took the brown bag from Blake as he went down a wide set of steps. The huge bald cypress stood tall and proud about thirty yards away, and Blake didn't break stride as he went toward it.

He climbed right on top of the weathered picnic table there, as he'd done many times before. Gina grinned at him as she approached. "My legs aren't as long as yours."

He grinned at her. "How many times have I heard that?"

"Probably five hundred." She laughed as she joined him on the tabletop. "So, what's in these things?" She pulled against the staple keeping the top of her bag closed, and Blake did the same.

"Sandwiches, chips, fruit," he said.

"So we're back in grade school."

"I'll trade my carrots for your cookies." He offered her that sexy grin again, and the lopsidedness of it hadn't changed one single bit. Neither had the fact that it always elicited a return smile from her. It was like she couldn't stop herself.

She told herself to stop staring at him and focus on her lunch. "I still have to decorate my cookies," she said. "I don't have much time."

"I have an online meeting with the mayor," he said.

Gina lifted her head from peering into the contents of her bag. "Are you trying to one-up me?"

He chuckled and shook his head as he removed the ham and cheese croissant sandwich from its plastic bag. "No, ma'am. Just statin' facts."

"What do you and the mayor have to talk about?" She took out her apple and went straight in for a bite, realizing how hungry she was now that food had made an appearance.

"He wants me to sit on some...council thing," Blake said wearily. "Something about a Fourth of July event. He thinks we're the only ranch who can handle feeding large groups."

"You do a good job of it," she said. "There was hardly any waste at breakfast. I never waited longer than sixty seconds for new pans of what was out."

"That's Starla, not me," he said. "I don't have anything to do with the food here." He took a bite of his sandwich, gazing back in the direction of the lodge. He didn't focus his eyes, though, and she wondered what ran through his mind.

She'd been able to ask him in the past. Today, she ate her apple and then dug into her bag to start on her sandwich before she said, "What are you thinking about?"

He swung his attention toward her, and Gina held his gaze for as long as she could. Only five seconds later, she focused on unwrapping her sandwich. "You don't have to tell me."

"I was thinking I'm not quite ready for the weather to get hot."

Gina scoffed. "Really, Blake? The weather?" She took a bite of her sandwich and shook her head.

"What? You don't believe me?"

"No," she said around her ham and cheese and buttery bread. "I don't."

"You're talking with your mouth full." He grinned at her like he liked it, and Gina's heart boomed heavily in her chest. She continued chewing, swallowed, and then took another big bite, her eyebrows going up.

"Fine," he said with a sigh. "I was thinking about asking you if you still like hiking."

Gina wished she hadn't bitten off more than she could chew. She nodded emphatically, her jaw starting to hurt.

Blake nodded too and ducked his head. He wore his cowboy hat, a dark brown thing that had an extra-wide brim, and Gina had always had a soft spot for cowboys. *Not true*, she thought. *You have a soft spot for Blake Stewart.*

She finished her giant bite and looked at him. "What about you? Are there any new trails around here?"

"Not really," he said. "But you haven't been here for years." He looked at her, his expression open and unassuming. "Maybe we could go on some of our former favorites."

They'd hiked together in their young teens, before they'd started dating. Blake had kissed her for the first time out on a guided nighttime tour hike at The Discovery

Center. After that, hiking with him held new meaning and she'd been so excited to head out into the hills.

"Yeah," she said, her voice a bit pitched up. "I'd like that."

Blake nodded again and took out his single-serving bag of chips. Being with him felt easy and natural, and Gina didn't feel the need to stuff the country silence with words. After a couple of minutes, he wadded up his bag and cleared his throat.

"Things went okay this morning?"

"Yes," she said, hearing the trepidation in his voice. "Were you worried I'd quit?"

He chuckled as he slid from the top of the table. "I was, yeah."

Gina eyed him until he turned to meet her gaze. "I told you I needed this job."

"Yeah, I know."

"Why would I quit then?"

"I don't know."

She gave him a sly smile. "You're still not a good liar."

He tucked his hands into his pockets. "I just don't want you to be unhappy here."

Gina slid from the table too, wanting to reassure him but not knowing how. "Blake."

"Don't, Gina."

"Don't what?" She stood directly in front of him.

"Say my name like that." His dark eyes blazed at her, and she saw meteors falling through the black sky.

The alarm on her phone went off, and she fumbled to get it out of her back pocket. She only had ninety minutes left, and she had almost fifty sugar cookies to decorate. "I have to get back to the kitchen," she said, silencing the alarm and looking up at him. "I'm afraid I'll get lost on the way. Will you take me?"

Blake's expression softened as a beautiful curve donned his lips. "Yeah," he said. "Let's go."

Gina thought the most natural thing to do would be to slip her hand into his, the way she'd done many, many times in the past.

Later, her mind whispered. *Right now, make the cookies perfect.*

CHAPTER
SIX

Blake listened to his brother's fingers strum through the melody of a song they'd sung together countless times. He met Kyle's eyes, and the two of them smiled. Blake needed this right now. Having just finished lunch—and emailing Mayor Botswan that he couldn't talk today—he needed something to soothe his nerves.

Having Gina at the ranch and lodge was harder than he'd thought. For some reason, he'd thought he could wall off his heart to the woman. Todd had told him to do just that. Hadn't he been doing it for twenty years, since she left Chestnut Springs the first time?

He had, though he hadn't admitted it to Todd last night. They'd exchanged some words, sure, because Todd hadn't told him about the conversation with Gina in the parking lot at the grocery store. Deal or no deal, he could've sent a text.

Blake's fingers started to move over his guitar too, and the breeze added a little bit to the ambiance. They sat around the huge fire pit in front of the lodge, and several guests had gathered there after lunch.

Kyle could always be found where a gathering of their customers were. He ran all of the music and entertainment on the ranch. He played everyday for guests, he brought in bands and guest artists, and he put on the most amazing summer concert series for the Longhorn Ranch. Because of him, they booked out every first week of August a year in advance, as that was when Kyle organized a huge guitar festival.

Blake didn't play then, but Kyle did. He could've been a professional with any band, touring the country and making big money. Instead, he'd chosen to stay right there in the Texas Hill Country and work for their family ranch. Blake admired him on a lot of levels, only one of which was his rich, tenor voice as he started the song.

Blake's deeper bass would come in soon, and he bent his head and focused on the strings. He didn't want to think about the mountain of work on his desk. He didn't want to consider eating lunch with Gina every single day. He didn't want to obsess over which hike to take her on first.

He wasn't going to "take her" anyway. They'd meet at the trailhead like they'd done in the past, and they'd walk single-file to some destination in the hills. He wouldn't tell any of his siblings about it, and it wouldn't be a big deal.

As he started to sing, weaving his voice with his brother's, he knew anything he did with Gina—including sitting on top of a picnic table in the shade a stone's throw from the lodge—was a big deal. They hadn't said much, and Blake wasn't sure why that was. They had twenty full years of catching up to do. Shouldn't he have a few questions for her?

The truth was, he didn't. If she wanted to share the things she'd done in her life with him, she would. He knew her well enough still to know anything he asked might or might not get answered. She'd grown up. She'd changed, he was sure. She still looked like her, with shiny blonde hair and those pretty blue eyes. They held more wisdom than he remembered, and he supposed his did too.

He and Kyle finished their song, and the crowd who'd gathered started to clap. Kyle absorbed energy from other people, but Blake just wanted to go back to his office.

"One more?" Kyle asked, and Blake glanced at his phone on the bench beside him. He had another half-hour until the taste-test began. He could do another song, so he nodded.

Kyle grinned and reached to retrieve his pick. "This last one's going to be a real boot-stomper," he said. "So feel free to spread out, grab the person next to you, and get ready to swing 'er around."

He launched into a guitar riff that would've blown the roof off a barn had he been hooked up to an amp—or they'd been inside a barn. As it was, the wide open sky absorbed the sound and sent it heaven-ward.

"Yeehaw!" Kyle shouted. He stood and put one foot up on the bench where he'd been sitting. Blake laughed and got his fingers moving over the strings too. He could add a marching under-beat to Kyle's melody, and when his brother looked at him, they opened their mouths and sang together.

People clapped in time with the rhythm, and Blake's spirits lifted at the joy surrounding him. He loved this life here, and he couldn't imagine wanting to leave it. *You should probably find out if Gina wants to leave Chestnut Springs again,* his mind whispered at him. How the human brain could do so many things at once, he'd never know.

What he did know was that he was right. If he wanted to be her friend—and he did—he should probably find out if her time here in town was permanent or temporary. She'd told him she needed this job, but for how long?

"Up to heaven we'll go, marching like the saints," he sang with Kyle, and after they'd said it one more time, both of them at the upper limit of their singing register, Blake stilled his fingers and let Kyle finish the song with an epic guitar riff.

Whoops and hollers filled the air, and every face Blake saw as he got to his feet held a smile. His did too, because this music jam session had cleared his mind and lifted his mood. He set his guitar against the bench and clapped Kyle on the back, yelling, "Isn't he great? Kyle Stewart, folks!"

Kyle shook his head, his laughter getting swallowed by the applause. He'd take the guitars to the music room in the lodge, the only room on the second floor that wasn't for guests. He had a little desk in there where he planned out their events, and he'd probably spend the rest of the day there.

Once the clapping started to quiet, Kyle said, "We'll be back here tonight, about seven p.m., after dinner inside. My sisters are doing their duets tonight, and then we'll have the Boys From Boerne here at seven-thirty for their Longhorn Ranch debut. You won't want to miss it, as we'll have a hot chocolate bar as well."

The crowed started to disperse, and Blake took Kyle into a hug. "You're amazing, brother," he said. He stepped back grinning. "All right, I have to go oversee a taste-test. Wish me luck."

"With Gina's desserts?" Kyle scoffed, and Blake should've known that everyone at the lodge and on the whole ranch would know about this taste-test by now. News sure did travel fast, especially if it was the kind Blake wished wouldn't. "The only luck you'll need is to not overeat. Then we'll all have to listen to you bellyache about how sick you are." He gave Blake a knowing smile and bent to start gathering his things.

"Sure, yeah," Blake said in a deadpan, but he couldn't really argue with Kyle. So he liked sweets. What red-blooded cowboy didn't?

Inside, he nodded to Lowry at the front desk and scanned the area where the desks sat. Besides the Stewarts, the lodge employed about a dozen people to work in hospitality and grounds. Then they had the kitchen staff, which easily topped a dozen as well. They brought in outside entertainers and guests, as well as professionals who did demos with horses, on animal care, horseshoeing, and even rodeo roping shows.

If there was a way to give someone an authentic western experience, it happened here at the Texas Longhorn Ranch. A swell of pride for what his father had built moved through Blake. He wanted to maintain their family traditions and take the lodge into the future with as steady of a hand as Daddy had. He'd been learning and growing and working toward that for as long as he could remember, and now, all he could do was pray he could make his father proud.

The dining room sat in stillness, the lunch bins already cleaned up. Dinner service started at five and ran until seven, and the tables and chairs he walked by right now would be dressed in cream cloths by then. All the condiments would return, and the buffet bar would be set and ready ten minutes early.

He pushed through the swinging plastic door into the kitchen, the lodge remodel they'd done five years ago making so much sense to him. Before, the kitchen had been back in the administration wing, which was a long walk for the food runners, waitresses, and bussers. Now, it sat on the other side of that wall, an easy few steps in and out.

Just inside the door, he paused. The scent of sugar hung in the air, but it was creamier than that. Frosting. Wow, Blake loved frosting.

Gina looked up, a piping bag with bright yellow icing in her hands. "You're early."

"I just came inside," he said. "You don't have to start right now."

"Time's up," Starla said, emerging from her office.

Gina threw her a look too, but with her face turned away from Blake, he couldn't see it. "I have three more minutes."

"Do you?"

Gina bent over her cookies on the counter. "Look at the clock. Three minutes."

Blake found the nearest clock, and the analog minute hand wasn't straight up. The digital clocks on the row of microwaves straight in front of him all read one-fifty-seven. As he watched, the seven flipped to an eight.

"We'll find a spot at a table in the dining area," Starla said, holding her chin high. She didn't like being argued with, but Blake could see how Gina thought she had more time, even if it was only two minutes. She couldn't be expected to synchronize her clock with Starla's.

He stepped back and opened the plastic door for Starla to go through, which she did. He followed her when it became obvious Gina wasn't going to give him a single second of her decorating time. She moved with surety, her hands making quick movements as she piped on decorations.

Out in the dining hall, Blake sighed as he sat next to Starla. "How's she doin'?"

"Honest opinion or what you want to hear?"

"Start with honest," he said. "Then tell me what I want to hear." He grinned at her, and Starla finally broke. She smiled back and rolled her eyes.

"They're actually the same," she said. "She's good,

Blake. The moment you told me you'd hired her, I knew she'd be good."

Blake ran his hand down the side of his face, his beard getting a little long. His mother hated all the extra hair he allowed to grow, but he loved it. He liked how it curled out from underneath his cowboy hat, and he liked the gray that had started to appear in his beard. "Do you think she'll fit in here?"

"You know what?" Starla asked as her phone chimed the top of the hour at her. She quickly silenced it. "I do."

In the very next moment, the door opened again, and Gina came out of the kitchen carrying a silver platter. A legit silver platter that Blake had only seen used at Christmastime. She smiled like she'd won a terrifically amazing contest as she approached, and she slid the tray between him and Starla.

"Okay," she said. "I'm having Nash bring out the rest." She turned to see if he was coming, and Blake followed her gaze. His brother did emerge from the kitchen with another tray, and then Holly and Jesse did too. Blake could only blink, because Gina had charmed them all already.

Himself included.

He looked up at her, wonder pouring through him like water over a tall cliff. With Nash, Holly, and Jesse's trays on the table, it filled right up with pink, purple, and blue daisies. The yellow icing had gone in the white centers as little pollen drops, and Blake had never seen anything so beautiful and so mouth-watering.

His eyes traveled back to Gina. Except maybe her.

He banished the thought as Starla reached for a treat,

bypassing the cookies and going for what looked like a pinwheel. "Gina, explain to us what we have here." She looked at the treat in awe, and Blake was just glad he wasn't the only one.

Gina took a deep breath. "Okay, so that's a s'mores pinwheel. It's a rustic, ranch-inspired take on a rice crispy treat. But I added graham cracker crumbs to the cereal, a layer of marshmallow fluff and then chocolate. That got rolled and chilled just to set the chocolate. Then, I cut them into rounds. Pinwheels."

She exhaled, and Blake knew the sound of that. She was actually nervous. Did her eyes not work properly? Could she not see how perfect these desserts were? She hadn't gone uppity, like he'd feared. She'd gone in a sophisticated direction, but one that still fit with Longhorn Ranch. How she'd done that when she hadn't been here in forever, he'd never know.

"Go ahead," she said. "They're not poisonous."

Blake reached out and picked up a pinwheel. He could see the layer of chocolate and marshmallow as they wrapped around themselves, and he smiled at the treat. Their guests would love these. He met Starla's eyes, and he knew she was thinking the same thing.

They both lifted their crispy treat pinwheels to each other in a silent toast and then each took a bite.

CHAPTER
SEVEN

Gina's muscles quivered while Starla chewed. A moan came from Blake's mouth, but she was expecting that. The man had enjoyed everything she'd ever made—and she'd seen all those biscuits and gravy on his plate this morning. His taste buds clearly liked anything.

Starla, on the other hand... Gina watched her chew, Starla's face one blank slate. She went in for a second bite, which had to be a good sign. Still, Gina couldn't relax.

"This is *amazing*," Blake said. He shoved the rest of the pinwheel into his mouth, and Gina offered him a thankful smile.

Starla finished her treat, really drawing out the agony for Gina. She dusted her hands together and said, "It's delicious, Gina."

She sagged into the table, catching herself with both palms flat against the top of it. "Thank you."

"How many different kinds of rice crispy treats can you make?" Starla reached for a second pinwheel, a hint of a blush in her cheeks. Blake consumed another treat too, while Gina tried to make sense of the question.

"I don't know," she said. "Lots."

Starla looked from her to Blake. "Could be a signature dessert. Monday is campfire night. Tuesday is sandwich night. That kind of thing."

"I can make a PB-and-J crispy treat," Gina said. "I had a boss once in New Orleans who did that." She tried not to let the hope infuse her voice, but she failed. If they liked her treats, she wouldn't feel like she was walking on thin ice.

"Friday is fried chicken," Blake said as if she hadn't spoken. "What crispy treat would go with that?"

Starla shrugged one shoulder and finished her second pinwheel. "Gina?"

"Snickers bar," Gina said without thinking too hard. "You put a little peanuts on the top. Pour caramel over it. Dunk in chocolate. Snickers bar crispy treat."

Blake's smile lit the whole lodge, and probably could've done so for the whole world had he been outside. "I do love a Snickers bar."

Something else that hasn't changed, she thought—and precisely why Gina had mentioned it.

"Okay." She took a breath in through her nose. "The second item is a sugar cookie. It's basic, but it's not. They're delicious, and everyone loves a sugar cookie they don't have to make. We can do any shape, for any event and any season."

LOVING HER COWBOY BEST FRIEND **69**

"What's going on over here?"

Gina turned toward the familiar voice, and sure enough, an older version of Rebecca Stewart came toward her. She was fairer than Gina, her hair blonde and her eyes blue, but a shade or two lighter.

She laughed as she crashed into Gina. "It's Gina Barlow."

Gina giggled as she hugged Becks too. "I didn't know you worked here."

"I do all the website stuff. Online blah blah. It's boring." She stepped back and beamed at Gina. "What are you doing here?"

Gina indicated the table in front of her, which housed over eighty desserts. "I made desserts for dinner. My bosses are tasting them to see if I can keep my job."

"No, we're not," Blake said at the same time Becks said, "You said she couldn't keep the job?" and as Starla said, "She can keep her job," around a mouthful of cookie and frosting. She'd selected a pink daisy, and that didn't surprise Gina at all.

Gina blanked for a moment, and then she burst out laughing. Becks did too, and she reached for a cookie. "Can I?"

"Go ahead," Blake said, pushing the last petal on his blue daisy into his mouth. "They're fantastic."

"You have to do my wedding," Becks said, sending surprise right through Gina.

"What? You're getting married? When? To whom?"

Becks gave her a sly smile and took a bite of her cookie. She nodded to Blake, who said, "Luke Miller."

"No." Gina covered her mouth with both hands, her eyes wide. "Luke Miller? Becks."

She chewed and swallowed and said, "It's this horribly romantic story I'll have to tell you another time." She flashed a grin at Blake and Starla. "Our caterer just canceled. That's why I left the admin dungeon."

"It's not a dungeon," Blake said, rolling his eyes. He went in for a second cookie, and Gina wondered if there'd be any left for guests that evening. The man possessed a serious sweet tooth, and he always had.

"The light bulb in my office has been out for a week."

"You're on the back wall and have a window," Blake shot back. He also shot a few crumbs from his mouth. He covered it quickly, and everyone at the table started laughing. Gina finally relaxed, glad her culinary creations had gone over well. She wasn't sure what she was so nervous about. Maybe that rice crispy treats and sugar cookies would be too basic.

She once again reminded herself she wasn't at a luxury, all-inclusive resort. Desserts like what she'd made strengthened the down-home feeling of Longhorn Ranch. People probably wouldn't even like her crème brûlées, even if she made one raspberry and one butternut squash.

"You hit this out of the park," Starla said. "I think we best be getting these back into the kitchen, though. Or there won't be any left come dinnertime."

Blake swiped another cookie from the tray as Starla picked it up, earning himself a dirty look from her. Gina could only smile as the kitchen manager went back toward the kitchen. She met Blake's eyes and said, "She liked them."

"Yes, she did." He stood up and bit off a petal. "They're great, Gina. Really."

Becks hadn't gone anywhere, but Gina could hardly see her when she looked at Blake. Or rather, when he looked at her. She cleared her throat, and that got Gina to blink and look at her long-ago friend. "So, my wedding? Could you maybe do the desserts?"

Gina had no idea how she'd fit that in. "When is it?"

"The end of March," she said. "We have plenty of time."

"She works here," Blake said.

"Yes, and you promised me the ranch would take care of everything," Becks said, rounding on her cousin. "The facility, the food."

"You're the one who hired an outside cake expert," he said, throwing the last two words at her. "Starla will have an amazing feast."

"And now, Gina can provide an amazing cake and dessert display," Becks said, her voice taking on the tone of the high and mighty. "She works here now, right? So the lodge can handle the wedding."

Blake looked like he'd swallowed a frosting-covered frog instead of a cookie, and he looked at Gina with pleading in his eyes.

"If the lodge is doing everything else for her wedding..." Gina shrugged and reached for a cookie too. She tasted her food as she made it, of course, but she never dined or experienced it until after everyone else. "Then I'd get paid to do the wedding."

Becks squealed and grabbed onto her, causing her to drop the precious daisy.

"No!" Blake yelled, immediately crouching to retrieve it. Becks and Gina stood side-by-side and watched him scoop it right off the floor. "Two-second rule." He held it out to Gina, who really didn't need to eat a cookie that had been on the floor.

She started to giggle and couldn't stop. "There's a bunch more, Blake," she said between her laughter. She'd get one that hadn't been on the floor, even if the frosting side hadn't touched the tile.

"It's still perfect," he said, licking his thumb. "Except where I put my finger in the frosting."

"Then you eat it," Gina said.

"I will," he fired back. He looked at Becks. "She's earning more than twenty bucks an hour to do the cake and desserts at your wedding. Catering fee for her too."

Becks lifted her chin. "Not a problem." She turned toward Gina and added, "When you're done here, come see me in my *dungeonous* office." She tossed a look at Blake that was really looking past him and turned to leave.

"You can change your own light bulb," he called after her, but Becks didn't look back or break stride.

Gina couldn't stop smiling as she faced Blake. "Wow, Becks Stewart and Luke Miller." They'd dated in high school too, and she couldn't help wondering if her and Blake's story would end the same as Becks and Luke's.

In marriage.

She swallowed, because friends didn't get married. Did they?

He shrugged and took a bite of his fourth cookie. "They seem to love each other." He took a step past her and paused. "Do you need help carrying these back?"

"Are these for eating?" another man asked, and Gina turned to see him leading a pack of ravenous cowboys.

Blake stepped in front of her. "No, fellas. Not for eating."

They started to complain, and Gina picked up one of the trays and hurried it into the kitchen. "Starla, the cowboys caught the scent of the sugar."

"Over my dead body!" Starla shoved the last of yet another pinwheel into her mouth and charged toward Gina. They laughed together as they swiped the last two trays off the table while Blake held back his men by shouting and threatening to fire anyone who so much as inhaled the scent of that frosting.

———

"HERE SHE IS," BECKS SAID, EXPLODING TO A STANDING position from behind her desk. Gina paused in the doorway, unsure of what she'd just walked into. She'd walked past this office once already, but no one needed to know that. Baby John had given her a single cocked eyebrow as he poured himself a cup of coffee from the pot along the counter on the wall that butted up against the kitchen wall. A couple of tables filled the small space, clearly a staff eating and break area, though no one sat there a moment ago.

A man rose from the single chair in front of Becks's desk, and Gina recognized him too. She started to laugh again, and she threw herself at the tall, sandy-haired cowboy. Luke Miller laughed too, caught her around the waist, and squeezed her tight.

"Look at you," he said, setting her back on her feet and releasing her. "Working at Longhorn Ranch."

"How long have you been here?" Gina asked. "You had your own family farm, didn't you?"

"Dalton took it over," he said. "I worked at Chestnut for a while, and Becks and I have been here...what?" He glanced at her. "A year?"

"A little over a year, yeah," she said.

Luke gestured toward her. "We're gettin' married."

Gina chuckled and shook her head. "I heard, Luke. Why do you think I'm here, when I could be going home for a nap?" She pulled his chair away from him. "I'm sitting down. I've been here since six a.m., and I'm tired."

Luke laughed too and said, "I'll go get another chair."

"I promise this won't take long," Becks said. "Starla's handling all the food. I just need you to do the wedding cake and the individual desserts."

"You're not going to serve the wedding cake?" Gina asked as Luke left the office.

"Here's the thing," Becks said, and Gina wouldn't like anything her friend said next. Especially with the way Becks suddenly had to check something on her giant desktop computer screen.

"Becks," Gina said. "You want what? A sixteen-tier cake? What's the big deal?"

"I want white wedding cake," Becks said. "White frosting. Silver decorations. No color."

Gina waited, but Becks didn't say anything. She did meet Gina's eyes. "Okay," Gina said. "And the desserts? They have to be separate."

"Did you show her the folder?" Luke asked, re-arriving in the office with a chair and a grin.

"Not yet," Becks said through nearly clenched teeth. "I didn't want to scare her away in the first ten seconds."

"Oh, come on, love," Luke said. "Your insane demands weren't what drove the other caterer away." He plunked the chair down on the corner of the desk and sat. Gina could only look at him, and since she felt no weight on the side of her face, Becks had to be doing the same. "What?" he asked.

"Did your other caterer call your...demands insane?" Gina asked, swinging her attention toward Becks.

"I maybe changed the menu a time or two."

"Or six," Luke said cheerfully, and Gina wondered if he wanted to get married or not. He sure wasn't acting like it.

"Anyway," Becks said, every syllable laced with venom. "I don't think they're that hard to accommodate, especially now that I have the menu all decided."

Gina nodded and strained to see what Becks had called up on her computer. "So can I see it?"

"You're exactly who I needed," Becks said. "I'm so glad you're here." She beamed at Gina, her eyes warm and full of friendship. It streamed through her, and Gina hadn't felt that in a while. Her whole life in Dallas had been built around the time she could clock in and start creating. She'd go out for drinks with friends, but she didn't date there, and she rarely talked about anything other than baking.

She didn't want her life to be like that again. Here, in Chestnut Springs, she wanted to live again. She wanted to rebuild her life, and she wondered if Blake was still handy with a hammer. Maybe he wouldn't mind helping her to rebuild things.

"...Gina?"

"Yes," she said, her mind sharpening again. It had gone soft for a few moments, and she blinked her vision back to sharp as she looked at the folder Becks had opened in front of her. The wedding cake stood about six tiers tall—not that uncommon for a wedding—and it was decorated with silver balls and roses, as well as what looked like bark.

"Do you want the bark to be edible?" she asked, the concoction well within her ability.

"I want it to be rustic," Becks said. "Yes. Bark and such. That's why we need other desserts."

Gina shook her head. "No, you don't. I can make that look like real bark and have it be edible. Chocolate, pretzels, fondant, all kinds of things can be made to look like bark."

"Maybe the Lord did send her here," Luke said.

Gina swung her attention toward him again, and he still wore that bright smile. She definitely thought the events of her life had led her around and around, and yes, she was back in Chestnut Springs.

"How long will you be here?" Becks asked. "Through the wedding?"

"Yes," Gina said. "I hope long past the wedding."

"Really?" Becks asked, glancing behind her. Gina twisted to look too, expecting to see Blake loitering there. No one stood in the doorway, and she twisted back to Becks. "How long?"

"Did someone ask you to ask me this?" she asked.

"He just wants to know if you'll be here for a month or a year," Luke said.

"No," Becks practically yelled over him. She gave him a dirty look and added, "You're ruining it."

Gina looked back and forth between them. "You can report back to your master that I'm planning to stay." She closed the folder and tucked it under her arm. "I'll take this with me and study it after I eat and am tucked in bed."

"It's three-thirty," Becks said as Gina stepped through the doorway.

She knew what time it was. Every inch of her body knew. She glanced further down the hall, catching sight of Blake's open door. He was probably in there, maybe hovering just out of sight as he eavesdropped on the conversation.

No, Gina decided as Becks and Luke started to bicker behind her. Blake was a lot of things, but an eavesdropper wasn't one of them. She did wish he'd just asked her himself if she was planning to stay at the lodge and Chestnut Springs.

With the fresh image of Luke and Becks in her mind, all Gina could think about on the way back to her parents' house was that maybe she and Blake could have their second chance turn into happily-ever-after too. Blake had even said he wanted her to be happy at the lodge.

It wasn't until the full twenty minutes had passed that she realized her face hurt from all the smiling she'd been doing.

CHAPTER
EIGHT

"So this is where I live," Blake said as his cabin came into view. The Stewart family had a private lane with their own cabins, away from the guest cabins, and away from the other cowboys who got housing as part of their wage.

His stomach lurched, mostly from hunger, but also because today was the seventh day in a row that he and Gina had met for lunch. They'd walked down the road once, talking and eating until her timer went off. They'd sat on the picnic table. He'd taken her over to Becks's cabin, and they'd eaten with Luke and Becks.

Today, he'd brought her to his personal space. The one refuge he had from everyone and everything else. If things weren't going well on the ranch or in the lodge, Blake could always come home. Todd was his very best friend and his closest brother in age, and Todd would always come over after a long, terrible day.

They'd sip coffee and eat frozen pizza instead of dining at the lodge. All staff and family members could eat breakfast and lunch in the dining hall at the lodge, but they were on their own for lunch. Sometimes Blake got a grab-and-go lunch, and Gina had paid for the monthly plan.

Rather, Blake had paid for Gina's lunches for a month, a fact she hadn't discovered yet. She'd never been terribly great at math and budgets, though she could measure things and do complicated fractions in her head. She said it didn't make sense, and it sure didn't to Blake.

"I'll make coffee," he said, letting her pass in front of him to enter the cabin first.

"Can I have tea?" Gina glanced at him, her smile reaching all the way up into her eyes.

"Don't reckon I have tea," he said, frowning.

"That shocks me," she said, clearly teasing him.

"Why would I have tea?"

"For the women you bring home," she said.

Blake's face heated as he went inside and closed the door behind him. "Haven't brought anyone here in a while," he said. "Heck, I can't even remember the last time I went to town."

"You don't buy your own groceries?"

"No," he said. "Todd goes to town and gets what I need."

"Ah, yes, I did run into Todd in the grocery store parking lot." She walked all the way to the back of the house, where the kitchen and dining room took up the space. She looked out the window in the back door and then faced him. "It's nice, Blake."

"It does the job," he said. "When it's cold outside, it's warm in here. When it's hot outside, it's cool in here." He smiled at her and started making coffee. "I really don't have tea."

"All right," she said, taking a seat at the bar. "What are you going to make me for lunch? We left our grab-and-go's at the lodge."

"Grilled cheese sandwiches?" he offered, his pulse rattling against his ribs. He could admit he had feelings for Gina, at least late at night when he woke up in midnight darkness. He hadn't asked her out, and they hadn't gone hiking. They ate lunch together, because they worked in the same building.

They were friends again.

"I love a good, toasty grilled cheese sandwich," she said. "Do you have apples? I can cut some up."

"Your mother always cut up apples for us after school," Blake said, throwing her a smile. She didn't catch it though, and instead he watched something negative flicker across her face. He paused with the coffee pot under the running water. "Gina? How's your mom?"

"Oh, she's…fine." The last word came out as a whisper, and she busied herself with digging through his fruit bowl. "Blake, these aren't good."

"Throw 'em away then," he said. "I tell Todd I don't eat fruit unless forced."

"Of course," she said with a giggle. "So grilled cheese sandwiches and…"

"Tomato soup?" he guessed. "That's a fruit, right?"

"Are we ten?"

"I like grilled cheese sandwiches with tomato soup."

"I suppose all you have is the canned kind." Gina put her hands on her hips and studied him.

"Do you see any tomatoes on the counter?"

She couldn't, because he didn't have any.

"Oh, you know what?" He stepped past her, maybe a little closer than he needed to, and opened his fridge. "Todd brought me some of that fire-roasted organic stuff." He spotted the box of tomato soup in the fridge and grabbed it. He'd had it a while, and he searched for an expiration date as he closed the fridge.

"This might work," he said, giving up on finding the date. "It might be expired though."

Gina took the carton from him and turned it around. "No, it's good," she said. "Especially if you haven't opened it yet."

"I haven't opened it yet," he said. He finished getting the coffee on while Gina pulled out a pan and emptied the tomato soup into it. The gas line clicked and flared to life, and Blake tried really hard not to think of this as his real life. Him and her, in a house, making lunch together in a perfect dance.

It wasn't real.

They were just friends.

His imagination kept conjuring up ways he could press her against the countertop and kiss her, but he wouldn't allow himself to do it.

"I looked up our first hike," she said, pulling something from her pocket. She proceeded to unfold a printout and lay it flat on his counter.

"You did, huh?" He stepped next to her. "When are we doing this?"

She leaned on her elbows beside the paper and then looked up at him. "I was thinking Saturday morning."

"Saturday morning," he repeated. He'd like to say he didn't work weekends, but that would be a lie. The weekends were some of the busiest times at the lodge, as they booked out weeks in advance.

"They serve breakfast an hour later," she said. "I know the routine now. If we get up just a titch before the sun, we can get to the top of the rock and back before anyone needs us."

"Define a 'titch' before the sun." Blake gave her a dry look, his tone matching it. "I already get up before the sun."

"Meet at the trailhead at six?"

He groaned and swung around to get a loaf of bread out of the drawer. "Thick slices or thin?" he asked, holding up the loaf.

"Did your mother make that?"

"Yes."

Gina blinked and dropped her eyes to look through a drawer.

"What?" Blake asked, but he suspected he already knew what.

"I'm just wondering if you do anything for yourself," she said, her voice light and airy.

"I do things," he said.

"I can't find a wooden spoon." She looked at him. "A whisk?"

"Who uses a whisk?" Blake stepped over to the drawer too and started rifling around. "I don't know. The house-keepers—" He cut off, because he'd just played into Gina's hand.

She giggled, and his annoyance soared at the same time his hormones fired at him. He told himself he just hadn't dated anyone in a while, but he knew that wasn't it. He didn't care about dating. He didn't go to town for a reason. He didn't want to meet someone else.

He wanted Gina Barlow. He always had.

He stopped looking for some stupid kitchen utensil and looked at her. Her eyes danced with delight, and that only ticked up his attraction to her. "Is the hiking a date?" He didn't mean to bark the question, but he totally did.

"What?" Gina asked.

"I just need to know," he said without breaking eye contact.

"Do you want it to be a date?"

"Yes." He saw no reason to be dishonest about it. In the next moment, he realized what kind of can he'd just opened. He fell back a step, trying to get his mind to quiet. "I need to turn back time."

"I don't think we can do that anymore," she said.

"Why not?" he asked. "We used to."

"Twenty years ago," she said, turning away from him. She held a wooden spoon in her hand, and how she'd found it, he didn't know. "We were younger, when there was all the time in the world."

"There still is."

Gina shook her head, and Blake hated that he'd intro-duced awkwardness into their friendship.

He took a big breath and tried to find a way out of this mess he'd made with just a few words. "I want to turn back time," he said. "Thirty seconds."

"Then do it." She stirred the soup and cast him a side-ways glance that didn't hold that flirty quality he wanted.

"Okay," he said. "Yes, I have housekeepers. They work for the lodge, and we as family members can pay a fee and have them come clean our cabins once a week."

"Mm hm."

"My mother doesn't know what to do with herself now that she's not as active at the lodge," he said. "She still does the accounting, but she wants to be home with Daddy too, and when she's home, she bakes. Who am I to tell Sharon Stewart that I don't want her bread?"

"You wouldn't dare."

He wanted her to stop stirring that blasted soup. The spoon made a scratching sound on the bottom of the pot that was slowly driving him toward madness.

"I just want to know where we stand. The hiking, the eating lunch together, the talking about our lives, and the past, and all of it."

She looked at him, her eyes wide and unassuming. The fire gathered, and Blake held up his hand. "I'm not done."

Gina frowned, but she did snap her mouth shut. She also flipped off the gas, and the flame beneath the pot extinguished. Blake sure hoped this second, budding rela-tionship with her wasn't about to go as cold.

"I have feelings for you," he said quietly. "I can't help

it. You're here, and you're so much the same while being a completely new person too. I want to get to know you." He took a breath and kept on going, having committed himself to the lion's den now. At least he wasn't barking his sentences anymore.

"I know I belong here, on this ranch and at the lodge. I guess I want to know if you think you can belong here too."

She looked at him, her eyes wide.

"My family is huge and loud, but they love you the same way they did when we were younger."

"You realize Nash was eight when we dated before. *Of course* he loved me. I brought him cookies and those giant cinnamon rolls from town."

Blake grinned at her and dared to take one small step closer to her. "Yeah, so we could sneak out to the moon-trees and kiss." He lifted his hand like he'd slide it along her waist. Something told him not to touch her, and he let his arm fall back to his side.

"You're the one who said we could be friends."

"We can be," he said.

"But not *just* friends."

"If you put me in the friend-zone, I'll stay there," he said. He would too. He was older now, and he could handle it. He really wasn't a good liar, but when it came to his own thoughts, he could pretend like they were true for a little while.

"I don't know, Blake."

He nodded and started buttering bread. If the soup was done, he better get the sandwiches grilled. He buttered bread as she set a pan over another burner. "What are your plans?" he asked. "Moving forward."

"I want my own place," she said.

He nodded as he put the bottom slice of bread in the pan. The butter hissed, and he layered cheese over the bread, then topped it with another slice. That done, he returned to the drawer to find a spatula.

Gina held it up for him, and their eyes met again. "I think having this lodge on my résumé will be great," she said. "Plus, Becks's wedding."

Ice stabbed him, the shards going right through his heart. "This is just a stop on your way somewhere else." He hated the words, but he should've known better. Gina had never been happy in Chestnut Springs.

Becks hadn't been either, and he couldn't help comparing the two of them. She'd come home, and she was here to stay. She was marrying her high school sweetheart, and Blake would've never thought he'd have the same chance.

Gina stood in front of him now, though, right there in his house. Making soup and sandwiches. Talking about the future.

"I don't think so," she said, her voice quiet again. "My mom is getting...worse, and I think if I can find somewhere here in the area where I can be happy, I'll stay."

He whipped his attention to her, his next question surging through his throat. He caught it at the last moment before it left his mouth. He wouldn't ask her if she was happy here. It had been one week since she'd started.

Eight days since she'd walked back into his life and practically demanded a job.

He wouldn't ask her if she could possibly belong here at the Texas Longhorn Ranch. He'd always felt so welcome here, but he knew some of his siblings and cousins had struggled to feel as seen and as accepted.

"You look like I hit you with a snowball," she said, finally smiling. It barely snowed in the Texas Hill Country, but once, decades ago, a horrible winter freeze had come through Texas and dropped enough snow to make balls and men and forts. For a couple of days at least. He and Gina had had a snowball fight with their friends at the town park, and of course, she'd whacked him right in the face.

He'd run at her at full speed, tackled her, and they'd rolled around in the snow, laughing. There was definitely some kissing in there, and in-all, that was one of Blake's happiest memories.

"I'm sorry about your momma," he said, his nose telling him that his sandwiches were about to be burnt. He quickly flipped them over, the butter sizzling in the hot pan. "If there's something I can do to help you, or her, or your daddy, you'll tell me, won't you?"

"Yes," she said quietly.

He nodded and pointed to the cupboard next to her. "Bowls are up there, sweetheart. These are almost done."

She didn't trip up over his use of an endearment, and Blake told himself he'd have called anyone that. Another lie, but he didn't have to answer for it right now. He just wanted to eat lunch with the gorgeous and fun Gina

Barlow, and he didn't need all of the answers straight away.

She wasn't just here for a moment. She was looking for happiness—true happiness—and belonging, and Blake had achieved both of those with her once. All he could do now was pray he could again.

He slid a sandwich onto one of the plates she'd gotten down. She ladled soup into bowls. Together, they rounded the counter and sat at the bar. He looked at her, and she looked at him.

"So...Saturday?" She looked so hopeful, and Blake knew he wouldn't be saying no to her. She had to know it too. "We meet at the trailhead at six?"

"It's out past the ranch," he said, grinning at her. "Why don't you stop by here and pick me up? No sense in both of us driving out there when you're goin' right by here."

She smiled too, her eyes telling him that if he managed to keep eating lunch with her, he might be able to kiss her again. His lips tingled just thinking about it. "All right, Blake. I'll pick you up."

"Great." He picked up his grilled cheese sandwich. Before he took a bite, he asked, "Does that mean it's a date?"

CHAPTER
NINE

Gina slid the wrapped egg-and-sausage muffins into a semi-rigid container and secured the lid. She'd made them last night, then warmed them in the oven this morning, wrapped them, and placed them beside a long tube she'd also heated in the microwave. It held water, and it should keep their breakfast warm until they reached the pinnacle of their hike.

She smiled as she put the container in her square-bottom backpack. She hadn't been hiking in a while. "Haven't been on a date in a while either," she murmured to herself. A flash of fear stole through her, but she turned to grab the single-serving bottles of orange juice she'd bought at the convenience store last night.

Blake had volunteered to bring the coffee, and Gina grabbed her plastic baggie of coffee-doctoring supplies, which included packets of real sugar-in-the-raw, as well as tiny tubs of creamer. She had a shaker of cinnamon and one of hazelnut syrup too, because her parents liked their coffee black as tar, and she couldn't drink it like that.

With everything packed, she closed the top of her backpack and headed for the back door. Even her mother wasn't awake yet, and Gina let her mind turn somber while she went around the back of the garage to her car.

Mama wasn't dying any time soon. She'd just gotten older while Gina had been away, and she'd started losing some of her mental capacity. Ella had called last year and said she'd been diagnosed with the early stages of dementia, but she still had so many lucid moments. A great many. When Mama was tired or stressed, she forgot things, and a sense of sadness pulled through Gina.

It was hard watching her parents get older and realizing she'd missed a lot while she'd been away. In the car, she settled her pack in the backseat and then swiped to open her phone. She'd applied to a couple of apartments this week, and she wondered if anyone would ever get back to her. She had no new emails pertaining to the matter, and the text notification at the top of her screen only showed her that Blake was up and getting ready for their Saturday morning date.

She smiled again, laughed at the picture of his coffee pot filling and the caption of, *I can't believe it, but I'm up. This better be the most amazing hike in the world.*

"It will be," she said, sudden giddiness prancing through her. The Wolf Mountain trail was a loop, and they wouldn't do the whole thing. It was something like six or seven miles, and she hadn't been out in the wilderness much at all in the past decade.

She noted the change in herself as she got moving toward the Texas Longhorn Ranch, and she let her mind wander through the conversation they'd had at Blake's house for lunch leading up to this morning.

Yes, she'd finally bitten at him after he'd asked for the second time if this hike would be classified as a date. *It's a date.*

He'd grinned and grinned, clinked his grilled cheese sandwich against hers, and eaten. She couldn't dislike him for wanting to know where he stood with her. He'd admitted things that were hard to say, especially for someone like him. The only person she knew who couldn't express how they felt as bad as him was...her.

She had feelings for Blake. Real feelings, and she hadn't told him. She probably should, and maybe today, on the wider parts of the trail, she'd slip her fingers into his and tell him without words. Admitting today's hike was a date had probably clued him in too.

"Maybe," she said, making the turn onto the ranch. Blake liked knowing specifics, and he needed a plan for most things. She understood why now that he ran the majority of the ranch by himself. He didn't really, as he had a slew of siblings and some cousins living and working there too. But he had to oversee it all, and Longhorn wasn't just a regular ranch. They were that, plus a tourist attraction, a hotel, a restaurant, and an entertainment venue. He had a right to want to know plans and definitions for things.

She pulled up to his house, her headlights cutting through the darkness and illuminating the front porch. His front door opened a moment later, and he exited wearing a pair of gym shorts, a T-shirt that had to belong to one of his younger brothers, and a backpack. He settled a ball cap on his head instead of his trademark cowboy hat, and Gina could only stare as he came springing down the steps.

"Hey," he said as he opened the back passenger door. He put his backpack there and then got in the front seat. Or tried. He couldn't fold his tall body into the seat as close as it was to the dashboard, and he groaned as he bent his back weird and straightened again. "This is so close to the front."

"Sorry," Gina said. "No one ever rides over there. Well, except for my niece and nephews, and they're little."

He moved it back, then got in the car. He looked at her, and asked, "Ella's kids?"

"Yeah," Gina said, struck by his handsomeness in these close quarters. She had half a mind to lean over and kiss him but stopped herself at the last moment. She squeezed the steering wheel too hard, but it didn't budge. "Ready?"

"So ready," he said, twisting to reach behind him. He pulled out a thermos of coffee and put it in her cupholder. "This is yours."

"Thanks," she said, putting the car in gear. Her brain buzzed at her, and her heartbeat trembled. "Listen, I wanted to tell you something today."

"Before we even get there?" He chuckled and reached to buckle his seatbelt. "You didn't say this was going to be a serious hike."

"Did I sound serious?"

"Yeah," he said. "You sounded like you might tell me my dog died while you were babysitting him."

She looked at him, his smile so charming and so wide. "You have a dog?"

He laughed then and nodded. "What cowboy doesn't own a dog?"

"I'm sure there are plenty," Gina said.

"Yeah, well, Luke came from Chestnut, and Seth Johnson—you remember him?"

Gina nodded, because she remembered Seth. The Johnson family had been pillars in the Chestnut Springs area for years. They ran a ranch to the west of town, and her daddy had told her about Conrad's accident. "I heard their daddy got hurt."

"Yeah," Blake said, his voice sobering. "Anyway, Seth runs a dog rescue operation at his ranch. Becks can't keep herself away from animals, but Luke said she can't have a billion dogs. So I took one a few months ago."

Of course he did. His heart was big enough for a bunch of brothers and sisters, his parents, the guests, his employees, and animals.

And you, she thought, and she didn't immediately try to drive the thought away. "Let me guess," she said, deciding to take things a bit lighter before she told him about her past. "It's a cattle dog, and it's yours, but it lives with Todd."

Blake let out a scoff, his gaze heavy on the side of her face. "How did you know that? Did you ask Todd already? Did he say something to you about it?"

Gina laughed then, fueled by the distaste in his tone.

"No," she said, still giggling. "I just didn't see a dog—nor any evidence of a dog—at your place the other day. So if you have one, it must live with Todd."

"He's the foreman," Blake said, looking out his passenger window at the darkness streaking by. "It made more sense for him to keep Azure. The dog wasn't happy laying on my feet in my office. He's meant to be herding cattle."

"So he *is* a cattle dog."

"He's a blue heeler."

"Mm." Gina couldn't believe she was right, though the fact that she'd guessed correctly only told her how well she knew Blake. He could handle the harder thing she wanted to tell him this morning. "I just wanted you to know that I was engaged a few years ago." She cleared her throat. "I don't know why, but it felt like something I should tell you."

She looked at him as he swung his attention across the windshield and back to her. "Interesting. What was his name?"

"Brock Palmer," she said. "He obviously wasn't from here."

"Was he a chef too?"

"No," she said. "He owned a skateboard shop in the resort where I worked." She focused on the road again, her heart tearing a little bit. "I loved him, and he loved me, and we were engaged for about five months."

Blake reached over and took her stiff right hand from the wheel. "What happened?"

She breathed in deeply and then let it all out. "His ex-girlfriend came back into town and wanted to get back together. It was like he didn't even remember that he'd met me." She gave a light laugh, though she'd been in one of her lowest lows of her life after Brock had left. He'd closed his shop and just…left.

"I'm so sorry," Blake said.

Gina took another big breath. "What about you? You're a good-looking man. Who have you been out with?"

"I'm a good-looking man?" he repeated, a chuckle following.

"Come on," she said, squeezing his hand. "You know you are."

"Do I?"

Gina looked at him, her foot easing off the accelerator. "Blake, I think you're super good-looking." Her throat turned to dust, and she tried to swallow past it. She needed to lighten this, and fast. "That cologne? Mm, yeah, that smells nice too."

He blinked at her in the dim light, and Gina offered him a smile. She increased the pressure on his hand again, and he returned the squeeze this time. "Thank you," he whispered. "I think you're beautiful, of course."

"Thank you," she said simply, the moment between them tender and sweet.

He looked away, and she realized she was going ten under the speed limit. She jammed her foot on the gas, which sent both of them back into the head rests. "Whoa," Blake said, laughing.

"Sorry," she said.

He cleared his throat. "I was datin' Mari Lucas for a

while there," he said. "A year or so. I thought we were real serious."

"Mari Lucas, huh?" Gina asked. Of course she knew Mari. The Lucases had lived in the Chestnut Springs area for decades too. "She's a couple years younger than us."

"Yeah," Blake said. "She didn't think we were real serious. We went to dinner one night, and I was going to ask her about us maybe getting married, and she broke up with me instead."

"Oh, no."

"I didn't read it right at all," he said. "I'd rather just use words now rather than try to figure out what someone else is thinking. But—" He hit the T really hard. "Most women around here don't like that."

"They don't?" She glanced at him just as her phone started to tell her of her upcoming turn.

"Not that I've noticed," he said. "Even you had to be strong-armed into admitting this was a date."

She removed her hand from his to make the turn, and only a few hundred yards later, she parked the car in a spot in the trailhead parking lot. She looked at him, the words she wanted to say filling her throat. "Maybe the women around here just need more time getting used to the idea of saying personal things out loud."

Gina reached for her thermos and got out of the car, Blake scrambling to do the same beside her. "We used to tell each other everything," he said over the top of the car. "Even when I finally got up the nerve to tell you I didn't want to be just friends."

She met his eye, that same current moving between

them. "Got up the nerve? That suggests that you didn't just *tell me everything*." She opened the door, the hinges squealing, and pulled her pack from the car. "I have breakfast."

He shouldered his pack and came around the back of the car, his eyes trained on hers. "I don't want to be just friends." He reached up and adjusted his ball cap. "In fact, I don't even know how to be just friends with you, Gina."

Her heart thundered through her chest, hanging there and rumbling around her ribs the way it did in the Texas skies during a summer storm. She searched his face, disliking how unsettled he looked.

"Say something," he said, the frustration right there in his voice.

She wanted to ask him what he wanted her to say, but she already knew what. She wasn't sixteen years old anymore, and she didn't need to play games. "I brought your favorite sausage and egg English muffins," she said. "With that dill mayo? Because I really want you to be happy, and I want this to be an amazing date, because." She swallowed. "I don't want to be just friends either."

There. She'd said it. Bounced that ball right back into his court, and if the smile spreading across his face meant anything, he'd caught the ball and was ready to play.

CHAPTER
TEN

Rebecca Stewart turned toward her front door as it opened. Holly entered with a huge box in her hands, talking to someone over her shoulder. That would be her sister, Sierra, and sure enough, the youngest of the Stewarts entered carrying Becks's wedding dress.

"…on his way to get Aunt Thea, and you need to go get Mama." Holly faced Becks, who lifted her coffee mug to her lips. She'd eaten breakfast at the lodge with all of the guests currently staying at Longhorn Ranch, the way she usually did. Luke had been there too, as neither of them believed in any of the traditions of not seeing the bride before the wedding on the wedding day.

Her heart did a nosedive toward her toes, because she was getting married today.

"Good morning," she said, wishing she had more lazy days like this one. She usually showed up at the lodge in her professional clothes, ready for work. She ate her breakfast—fruit and scrambled eggs—and went down the hall to the administrative wing of the lodge. Since the lodge didn't serve lunch, she usually met Luke at one of the tables down the second hall from her office, or they met at one of their cabins.

They ate dinner together at the lodge most nights, except for when he took her to town for something at one of her favorite restaurants or to visit her parents and choke down some of her mom's overcooked meat.

Holly beamed at her, her naturally wavy hair already perfectly styled into an elegant up-do. Her makeup hadn't been done yet, and she wore the same thing Becks usually saw her in around the ranch—jeans and a tank top. "Morning," she said, her personality strong and gentle at the same time.

She ran the lodge in the evenings, and she could charm guests, horses, dogs, and snakes alike. In fact, all of Becks's dogs—all five of them—perked up at the sound of Holly's voice. The younger two—the puppies—went scrambling toward her from their mass bed, where all five of them crammed in to sleep.

"Oh, look at you," Holly cooed just as she set the box on the kitchen counter. She bent down to scrub the puppies, one named Chestnut and the other named Arrow. Becks's other three dogs were all older, adult rescues, but they loved Holly too.

"Go on, you old geezer," Becks said to Harold, the oldest of the rescues she hadn't been able to leave at Chestnut Ranch. Luke had forbidden her to go see Seth's

Canine Encounters again, as he was going to be moving into her more secluded family cabin come tomorrow.

After the wedding, at least. He hadn't brought by a single box yet, but he'd also moved here in a single day, with a single load in the back of his truck, when he'd shown up from Chestnut Ranch a year ago.

A year, she thought. She couldn't believe it had been a year since he'd shown up to tell her that he'd left his best friend behind, talked to Becks's cousin, and gotten a job here. He loved her, and he wanted to be with her, wherever she was.

Even now, warmth filled her as Sierra folded the garment bag over the back of the couch. "Thanks for the help with the dresses." She shot Holly a glare and shook out her arms. "Those things are *heavy*." She switched her gaze to Becks, and everything about Sierra softened. "Happy Wedding Day."

"Thank you," Becks said, giggling. Sierra had been putting a heavy red in her hair for years, and her coppery curls looked like metallic ringlets. She shone like a lucky penny when she was around family and familiar people and friends, but she wasn't the most people-y of people otherwise. All of those genes had gone to her only sister, Holly, and that had landed Sierra on the ranch side of the family business.

It suited her, and she loved working with Todd and the other cowboys and cowgirls who labored outside with animals, the land, or with anything agricultural. Becks swore, if a meteor hit the earth and obliterated all of the foliage on the earth, it would be Sierra who could cultivate everything back to life. Her green thumb was incredible, and she was the only reason Becks's plants hadn't died yet.

"I'm going to get Mama," she said as she rounded the counter and engulfed Becks in a hug. "But we'll be right back, and then we're going to get everyone all dolled up and perfect for this wedding."

"I just got a text from Nash," Holly said. "He said Starla is on track for the one-thirty meal-time."

"Great," Becks said. She hadn't doubted Starla Masters for a moment. Gina had texted her pictures of the cake over the past couple of days, because apparently it took more than a few hours to make a wedding cake.

Gina had mixed up the batter on Friday night after work, and she'd baked all of the tiers. Then she'd frozen them over night, crumb-coated them in the morning, and put them back in a huge freezer in her parents' garage.

A squeeze of gratitude moved through her for all of the people working to make her wedding so perfect. Gina herself was under a lot of stress, as she'd found an apartment and would be moving in a week or so. When she'd told Becks, they'd celebrated together, and then Becks's guilt had descended upon her like a load of bricks.

"We'll be on our honeymoon," she said. "Luke and I won't be able to help."

Gina had simply grinned like she'd been presented with the largest plate of bacon and cheese French fries. "Yeah," she'd said dryly. "Because there's not enough muscle around here to get me out of my parents' house."

They'd laughed then, but Becks still felt a thread of guilt move through her. Baking at her mom's house was hard for Gina, and even living there had been wearing on her.

"Okay, be back in a minute," Sierra said, and she headed for the door, leaving Holly and Becks.

"Makeup," Holly said. "Let me get the kit from the truck, and we'll get you going."

"You haven't done yours yet," Becks said, following her cousin out onto the porch, as did all of the dogs, even the elderly ones. Harold wouldn't go down the steps without Becks carrying him, and she'd asked Luke to build a ramp off the back door for him. He had too, which proved to Becks how very much Luke loved her.

"There's so much time," Holly said.

"It's almost ten-thirty," Becks said from the porch while Holly bounded down the steps. She had so much energy all of the time, and Becks couldn't even imagine how she functioned so late at night.

Life around the ranch would go on after this wedding, and by tonight, when Holly had to be back at the lodge to check-in with guests during dinnertime, Becks and Luke would be married and almost boarding their flight to Florida.

They'd stay there for a few days, then board a ship for their first cruise. Neither of them had ever been on a big ship before, and a touch of anxiety accompanied Becks's thoughts. She didn't like the idea of being trapped on the ship, even if it was huge, and she told herself once again there would be opportunities to get off at the three ports where the ship would be stopping.

"It's fine," Holly called over her shoulder. She drove a

rickety pick-up truck when she could afford better, and she went to the lowered tailgate and retrieved her mega-massive makeup kit. Despite her not working out on the ranch lifting hay bales, Holly possessed some muscles, and she brought the huge tote toward Becks without a hitch in her step.

"Promise me you won't let your mother do a beehive," Becks said. "One more time."

Holly grinned up at her from the bottom of the steps. "I promise. She'll yield to me, I know it."

"She hasn't listened to much of what I've said." Becks sighed as she turned to enter the house. Her dad and Uncle Max were brothers, and it had taken Aunt Sharon several years to accept Becks and her mother after the divorce from her first sister-in-law. Apparently, her dad's first wife and Aunt Sharon were still friends, but Becks didn't talk to her about that.

Friendships and relationships could be so complicated sometimes, and Becks didn't want to interfere with that. However, as a result, the relationship between Becks and Aunt Sharon wasn't super-strong, and with Becks's mother almost invisible to her, Aunt Sharon had taken on much of the wedding.

Becks hadn't asked her to, but her personality could be described as an ox, which only worked in some situations.

"I have the certification in aesthetics," Holly said. "She'll listen to me."

"Okay," Becks said, because if she had to put her faith in someone, Holly was a very good choice. "You want me at the kitchen table?"

"Yep," Holly said, grunting as she took the first step up toward the porch. Becks went back inside, calling her dogs to go with her so they'd be out of the way when Holly arrived. That sort of worked, as the puppies never really followed directions.

Holly made it inside despite the canine obstacles, and within ten minutes, she had Becks's face completely one color as more people filled the cabin. She got up to embrace her mom, thanked Todd for bringing her, and watched him smile and then fade back into himself. There was something going on there, but she wasn't sure what, and with all the women around, she wouldn't ask him.

She loved him as her cousin, and they'd grown closer over the past year. She raised her eyebrows, but he just shook his head, refilled his thermos, and said, "Good luck, Becks. See you over there," before skedaddling out of the cabin quickly.

"Mom," Holly said in a very firm voice. "No. It's not nineteen-sixty-two. Becks is *not* wearing a beehive for her wedding."

Becks turned back to the table, where Aunt Sharon had started to get out the hair supplies. She stayed out of the way as they bickered, shooting her own mother a knowing look. The two of them smiled, and then Sierra said, "Mama, I'm doing her hair, and it's going to be so amazing."

She turned toward Becks and gestured her closer. "Come on now. We don't have much time."

Becks went back to her seat, grateful for Holly and Sierra for keeping Aunt Sharon at bay, her own excitement for her upcoming nuptials really starting to bubble and boil in her stomach.

————

WITH ONLY A MINUTE UNTIL ONE O'CLOCK, BECKS AND HER father arrived at the end of the long aisle leading toward the altar. Up ahead of her, Luke stood with Blake and Seth, the three of them talking about something that caused them all to smile and laugh.

She had a moment to look around at all the guests who'd come to the Texas Longhorn Ranch this fine afternoon to see her and Luke get married. His parents and siblings and their families. Her parents. One of her half-brothers, Adam, had made the trip from Austin, and she mourned the loss of Jacob. He'd passed away a few years ago, and Becks thanked the Lord that Adam had forgiven her and her mother enough to come to the wedding.

She hadn't seen him yet, but their eyes caught on one another's, and he lowered his head in a silent greeting. She pressed her hand to her heart, her way of saying, *I'm sorry. Thank you for coming,* all at the same time.

Again, life could be so complicated, and she wished the human emotions weren't so frail or so tangled.

At the same time, when her wedding music began to play, everyone turned toward the aisle where she'd been standing for almost sixty seconds. The crowd got to their feet, and all the noise could've been made from the sudden way her heart started leaping against her breastbone.

Seth Johnson and Blake sat down, leaving only Luke at

the altar. Becks locked her eyes on him, shutting out the rest of the world. He'd wanted to marry her such a long time ago, and she was the luckiest woman in the world today to be marrying someone she loved so much.

Each row only held four chairs on each side, which created a long aisle to the altar. Because both her family and Luke's were from Chestnut Springs, it felt like the whole town had stayed in their Sunday clothes after their Sabbath services and simply driven out to the Texas Long-horn Ranch for this wedding.

She arrived at the spot where she had to say good-bye to her step-father, and he leaned over and kissed her cheek. Her biological father hadn't been in her life for three and a half decades, and she had no idea where he was.

"You're beautiful," her step-father said, and then he faded to Mama's side on the front row.

Luke took her hand and brought her to his side, also leaning over to press a kiss to the corner of her eye. "I'm so lucky," he whispered so only she could hear, and she could've said the same thing to him.

"I love you," she whispered back, because she did, and she wanted him to know.

"Welcome," the pastor said on the other side of the altar. Another cousin, also named Adam, had carved it from one of the fallen trees on the ranch, and it bore intri-cate flowers and horses and clouds across the top. "It's a beautiful thing to see two people so in love, and I see it so clearly in Rebecca Stewart and Lucas Miller."

"Uh, it's just Luke," he muttered, and the pastor's face turned bright red in less time than it took to breathe.

"I apologize," he said smoothly. "In Becks and Luke, who are about to be bound in holy matrimony."

She looked at Luke, and Luke looked at her. His hand in hers tightened, and she responded to that. Then they faced the pastor together, Becks beyond ready to start this new chapter of her life—as Rebecca Miller.

CHAPTER
ELEVEN

Todd Stewart whistled through his teeth as Luke bent Becks back and kissed her, the two of them now man and wife. Joy streamed through him, with a chaser of jealousy. They looked so dang happy together, and Todd wanted that for himself too.

He looked over to Blake, who wore an even wider smile than the one Todd felt stretching his face. They both wore their darkest black suits, with the bright blue bow ties Becks had ordered for everyone in the family. Matching flowers had been pinned to their lapels by their sisters, who now swarmed the altar to hug Becks and Luke.

Todd joined the fray, his mind already moving past the wedding to what the rest of his day held. They'd serve lunch to everyone, and that would take a while. Becks and Luke didn't want a dance or a reception, as their flight to Florida left that evening.

The lodge was hosting live music that evening in their honor, and all the guests they'd invited to the wedding had been told about that. The guests here at the lodge would benefit too, and Todd did love the familial atmosphere his siblings worked hard to provide here at the Texas Longhorn Ranch.

He didn't have much to do with the commercial side of things. He spent his days dealing with the real ranch on which they all lived and which people came to experience. He and the rest of the cowboys doing the real work behind the scenes knew that the experiences the guests had were a "cleaner" version of real ranch life, but that was okay with him.

After the luncheon, he'd retreat to the office he shared with Sierra, his second-in-command out on the ranch, in the new barn they'd built a couple of years ago. It stood only a stone's throw from the lodge, and the closer proximity had helped both him and Blake as they worked to coordinate things between the ranch with real cattle who needed tending and the guest operations of the lodge, which usually provided activities like doing milking demonstrations and letting the guests participate.

They weren't even a dairy operation, but they had a few dairy cows for that. Todd needed to go over the applications for a new veterinarian, as theirs had decided it was time for him to retire.

He'd miss Kenneth, and Todd had been trying to find a new vet for at least a month now. There had been some good applications, but Longhorn wanted a full-time vet. Someone who came out to the ranch every single day and worked only with them. Most had practices or traveled between several ranches.

With all the things they had going on here, Todd and Sierra had decided to keep their daddy's idea of having someone dedicated fully to them.

So while vets applied, they didn't really want to give up the other aspects of their business in order to be the full-time animal caretaker at only this ranch. Todd understood, or at least he tried to. He'd also been very clear in his job listing, and he didn't understand why people applied if they didn't really want the job.

His email had dinged at him that morning, and he had a couple of new applications to look at.

"It's time for the cake-cutting," Holly announced into the microphone. She wore a dazzling, sparkly dress in the same bright blue as Todd's bow tie, and he could never look at his oldest sister and not smile. She always smiled, and the only time she ever slipped and let anyone know she wasn't one-hundred percent happy to see them was behind the closed door of her cabin.

Right now, she lived with Sierra, and they got along great. Todd shared his house with Kyle, his next youngest brother and who organized all of their events here at the lodge. Todd enjoyed it, because the evenings were never dull with Kyle around. He had a great sense of humor, and he could play just about any instrument someone put in his hands. Todd wasn't new to the guitar, and the two of them could sit on their front steps and play tunes for an hour, which soothed him after a long day of dealing with tiring ranch chores.

He hugged Luke and then Becks while the guests started to move down the aisle and back to the lodge. Todd went with them, striding to catch up to Kyle and Adam right now. The two of them talked about their night of singing and sleighing coming up, and Todd was content to just listen.

Inside the lodge, the whole front space had been transformed into wedding central. All of the desks that usually took up the left side had been pushed against the wall or removed. The guest dining area that spanned the right side now bore the same circular tables, but with pale yellow cloths and towering centerpieces of wheat, pine boughs, and white roses.

"Wow," Kyle said. "This is beautiful."

"I'll say," Todd said, pressing in beside him. The buffet sat along the kitchen wall, where Starla attended to it with a couple of other chefs. The head table spread in front of the windows to the right, and Todd backed up as Daddy said, "Boys, you can't stop in the doorway."

"Have you learned nothing?" Mama added, slipping by them too. She gave Todd, Kyle, and Adam a quick shake of her head, not really chastising them. She had been preaching at them for years to not stop in doorways, so she had a point.

Still, Todd simply wanted to enjoy the beauty of the lodge. Its raw-wood walls added charm to the country wedding, and he recognized the look on Holly's face as she pressed in beside him. "We should be doing more weddings here," she said.

"We'd need an entirely new hall for that," Blake said,

LOVING HER COWBOY BEST FRIEND   115

smashing into the group now. "Don't get any ideas, Hols." Blake turned back to the tables and moved away, clearly going to find his seat.

"Why not?" his sister asked as she went after Blake. "We have the land right over by—" The rest of her sentence got cut off as the Johnson brothers crowded into the room too. They were tall and broad and wore cowboy hats, just like every one of the Stewarts, and Todd grinned at Travis Johnson, who was the same age as him.

"Howdy, Trav."

"This place is incredible," Travis said.

"Let's go find a table," Seth said. "Then Russ and I will go help Daddy in." They all went off to do that, and Todd figured if he wanted to sit by his siblings, they better get choosing their seats too.

Kyle led the way, and Todd and Adam went with him. They landed at a table near the front, and there was enough room for the three of them, plus Sierra, Holly, Nash, and Jesse. Blake stood over by the enormous wedding cake with Gina.

Another round of jealousy nipped through Todd. Blake and Gina had dated in high school, and he hadn't been jealous of them then. Todd dated a lot—more than any of his siblings—and he always had.

He'd just never found that one right person for him. He hadn't even come close. He wasn't sure what he was doing wrong, but watching Blake simply stand close to Gina while she worked, saying nothing and doing nothing, and he could tell how very right Gina was for his brother. Blake had never really stopped loving her, and Todd wouldn't be all that surprised if Blake and Gina had a wedding very much like this before too much longer.

"Do you think they're dating?" Nash asked, nodding toward Blake and Gina. Todd kept his mouth shut, because he knew they were dating. It was new, within the past few weeks, and Blake had told him privately. As the rest of the siblings started to gossip about Blake and Gina, Todd pulled out his phone and opened his email.

"They have to be," Jesse finally said.

"How do you know?" Holly asked. "He could just be asking her something."

"One, he hasn't said a word," Jesse said, and Todd felt the weight of the world land on his face. He looked up from the third application he'd gotten during the wedding.

"What?" he asked, looking around at his siblings. "I'm reviewing a vet application."

"You haven't said anything about this," Jesse said, grinning. "So it has to be true."

"Or else it's not, and he knows that too," Sierra said, peering at Todd. He didn't hide much from her, and he couldn't really hide this either.

He cleared his throat, and that only made Jesse's smile wider. "You guys, this is not your business."

"And...that's confirmation," Jesse said, looking back over to Blake. Their oldest brother turned toward the family table, and Todd realized there was only one seat.

He jumped to his feet and said, "I'm getting another chair for Gina." He quickly found one at a nearby table and returned to all of his siblings about the same time Blake and Gina arrived. "Here's a chair for you, Gina." He looked around at everyone. "Come on, guys, move around. Make room."

He opened the folding chair and put it next to the empty one where Blake would sit, noting that Blake held Gina's hand in his. Todd supposed he wasn't hiding anything anymore, and he didn't have to feel bad for revealing something to the siblings he shouldn't have.

Everyone settled in silence as Blake and Gina sat down, and then Blake finally said, "Jeez, you guys. What's the deal? I'm not allowed to have a girlfriend?"

"Of course you are," Holly said quickly, and they all chorused the same. Todd said nothing, because he'd already assured Blake that he could and should start a relationship with Gina if he wanted to.

Her face held a hint of red, and thankfully, Starla said, "All right, folks. The bride and groom are here!"

Applause broke out and every eye turned toward the door as Becks and Luke entered hand-in-hand. Before it had quieted fully, Starla added, "They want to cut the cake first, so you can have it for dessert. Then Max, Becks's uncle, is going to say grace. Then, we'll have you come back to the buffet to get your lunch."

She smiled at the couple, then the cake. Todd looked at it too, his breath whooshing right out of his body. "Gina," he said, as he sat only one place from her. "That is an amazing cake."

"Thank you," she said, keeping her voice low as Starla outlined what was on the menu, and what foods people with allergies might need to be aware of. The wedding cake stood six tiers high, done in all white, with bark poking up along intervals. It looked like an exact rendition of an aspen tree, with some silver flowers stuck in some seams, and a pretty, sparkling B and L sitting on the top.

Becks positioned the knife, and Luke put his hand on top of hers. The photographer they'd hired moved around, clicking and clicking as they sliced through the middle tier. The crowd went wild again, and Todd joined in clapping this time.

The veterinary applications could wait for a minute. He just wanted to enjoy lunch—complete with cake—and his family.

———

A WEEK LATER, TODD ARRIVED BACK ON THE RANCH WITH only moments to spare before his next veterinarian interview. He rolled his shoulder as he leapt from his truck, noting that he shouldn't have tried to carry so many boxes. Gina had plenty of help, and it didn't matter if he took in two or three at a time.

He'd left before her moving truck was completely empty, but he didn't feel bad about it. Almost every Stewart was over at her new apartment, helping her move in today. Blake would be gone all day and well into the evening, and Todd needed to interview this vet.

He needed someone.

"Doesn't mean you're going to take just anyone," he told himself sternly as he opened the barn door and stepped inside. It was a real, functioning barn, and they did use it for real ranch things. But it was also far cleaner than most barns, as they used the area immediately inside the door for guest demos.

His office sat down the hall a little bit, right before the tack room, feed room, and then the storage room. The stables ran along the back, and the loft was usually filled with hay.

The outer room of the barn sometimes got decorated during the holidays for the guests, but today, it just looked like a regular barn.

Except for the gorgeous woman turning toward him. Todd's feet stilled, and his heartbeat crashed like cymbals through his whole body.

The woman wore jeans that curved around her hips and hugged her legs to her ankle. She wore work boots with thick soles on her feet, and dang if that wasn't one of the hotter things Todd had ever seen a woman wear.

Her shirt came in purple and white plaid, and it went really well with her shoulder-length hair, which shone with a bit of violet as well. She'd clipped back the front, and as she approached, a smile spread across her face and drew Todd's attention to her mouth.

Looking there was a huge mistake, and Todd's mind went blank. That mouth moved, but his ears didn't register the sound.

The beauty in front of him tilted her head, her eyebrows bunching together, and that made Todd snap back to himself.

"I'm sorry," he said. "Can I help you?"

"Yes," the woman said again, her voice pleasant and musical in his ears. He wondered if this was how Luke felt around Becks, or Blake around Gina. Like they'd just met the woman of their dreams and God Himself had pressed pause on life for a moment to make sure they paid attention.

"I'm Laura Woodcross," she said. "I have an interview for the veterinary position today."

Todd shivered at the sound of her name, wishing it was because of the wind and cold that had come on this April day. *It is uncharacteristically chilly in the Hill Country right now*, he reasoned. He also knew that wasn't why the thrill had run down his spine.

"Right," he said, his voice hardly sounding like his own. "I'm Todd Stewart, and I'm who you're looking for." He nearly kicked himself in the teeth with those words, but Laura didn't think anything of them. He cleared his throat and indicated the hall behind her. "My office is this way. Do you want anything to drink? I've got water or coffee."

He also already had this woman's phone number, and as she said, "Water would be great," and followed him down the hall to his office, he hoped he could kill two birds with one stone today: Hire a vet and get a date.

CHAPTER
TWELVE

L aura Woodcross had been looking up to people for her entire life. Because she only stood at five-foot-two-inches tall, it was inevitable. She followed the tall, broad-shouldered cowboy into an office near the mouth of the hallway, and she liked that it hadn't been intricately done into a room she might find inside a house.

The wood walls could've been those of a stable, but this room held two desks...and a Christmas tree. Laura did a double-take and then looked at Todd Stewart. "You have a Christmas tree in here."

He settled at his desk and flicked his eyes over to it. If cowboy looks could set fake pines on fire, his would've. "Yes," he said. "My sister shares this office with me, and she loves to set things up. Taking them down? Not her strong suit." He indicated the only other chair in the room, and Laura took it.

She perched right on the edge of the seat, her back straight so she could appear taller than she really was. She was used to having to hold her own and not let others walk all over her. She'd been through almost a decade of veterinary school, where her classmates all stood a foot taller than her and often tried to shoulder her out of the way when dealing with some of the bigger farm animals.

"Where'd you go to school?" Todd asked, and Laura blinked to keep herself right here in the present.

She didn't believe for a single second that Todd hadn't looked at her application yet. She'd put it in three days ago, and he'd called within a half-hour. "Texas A&M," she said.

Todd maintained eye contact with her, and she appreciated that. "What drew you to veterinary medicine?"

Laura smiled, her soul lighting up. "I've always wanted to be a vet. Always." She blew her breath out, a small giggle going with it. "I grew up on a farm out in the Frio area. Corn. Lots and lots of corn. Corn for miles." She gave another chuckle and tucked her hands under her thighs. "We had a small stable with horses, a couple of cows, goats, chickens. I...really liked taking care of them."

She wasn't going to tell him her desire to take care of the animals stemmed from how easily she could connect to them. She didn't want this particular man to think she wouldn't be able to carry on a conversation at dinner. Something zinged through her, and she prayed she could make it through this interview without saying something that would reveal how badly she could misread people.

He leaned forward, his eyebrows furrowing. "Laura?"

"Yes." She cleared her throat. "Sorry, I was...I didn't hear what you said." She couldn't tell him that she'd been imagining the two of them at dinner together. She should only be thinking of him as her possible boss.

"I asked why you chose large animal care."

"Oh, well—"

"Hey," a woman said as she entered the office, drawing Laura's and Todd's attention. The woman who'd entered wore jeans and a plaid shirt too, and Laura grinned at her. She'd rolled her sleeves up to her elbows, and when she saw Laura, her step hitched. "Sorry, I didn't realize you were doing an interview. I just need to change my boots."

"I thought you were helping with the move."

"Sammy Boy called and said we had a ewe go into labor."

Laura perked up, her eyebrows following suit. She looked from the woman to Todd, and she was clearly his sister. Neither of them offered to have her go out and take a look at the ewe. Sheep weren't exactly large animals, but Laura had expertise with all ranch animals.

The woman switched out her boots, making plenty of noise in the process, and Todd said, "Call me if you need me."

"Yep," the woman said as she left the two of them alone again.

"That's Sierra," Todd said with a sigh. "She picks up all the slack around here, so I can't complain." He flashed the briefest of smiles, and Laura wondered what kind of light would radiate from his face when he unleashed a full grin.

She told herself to keep her composure, and she put the brakes on her crazy-train thoughts. "She seems nice."

"She's great, yeah," he said. "Okay, so where were we?"

Laura put up both hands. "I have no idea." She chuckled again, glad when Todd did too. He seemed to relax too, and she allowed her back to curve into the chair behind her.

"Experience," he blurted out. "I didn't see much of that on your application."

"I just finished school a year ago," she said. "I've been trying to find a place where I want to stay for a while." She told herself not to fidget or clear her throat.

"You don't want to open a practice?"

"No, sir," she said, deciding she didn't need to elaborate unless he asked specific questions.

"Do you—?" He cut off as his phone rang. His attention diverted to it, and he said, "This is Sierra. Sorry, I need to answer it."

"It's fine," she said, though he didn't need her permission to talk to his sister and take care of his ranch.

"What's goin' on?" he asked instead of hello. In the next moment, he got to his feet. "I'm on my way." He shoved his phone in his back pocket and headed for the door. "We've got a sheep in trouble."

Laura jumped to her feet too and followed behind him quickly. "What kind of trouble?"

"Too much blood, Sierra said." Todd glanced at her as they gained the bigger room.

"Is the lamb out?"

"I didn't get that information." Todd burst out of the barn, and they walked quickly around it to the pens behind it. "Our lambing shed is just over here." He started to jog, and Laura kept up with him. She hadn't done much running in her life, and her lungs felt it. She managed to follow him into the lambing shed, the scent of blood heavy in the air.

She paused, her adrenaline firing on all cylinders. Sierra waved her hand above her head, clear panic on her face. Laura felt none of it moving through her, and she didn't wait for Todd to move.

She went, and she went quickly, going right over the waist-high fence and into the pen where the sheep lay. The lamb wasn't all the way out yet, and the mother looked at Laura with blank eyes.

"We're going to lose them both," she said, pressing on the shoulder of a man kneeling near the sheep. "I need gloves and lubricant." She looked at the man there. "Now."

She put her hands on the ewe's face and leaned closer. "Hey, there, mama. You're okay, okay?" She looked at another nearby cowboy. "How long has she been trying to deliver?"

"About forty-five minutes."

"And nothing?"

"We've seen hooves," he said. "The lamb is breech, we think."

Laura swallowed and nodded. "A breech lamb is still a normal birth," she said, taking the gloves as the first cowboy returned with them. She slid her hands into them, noting how big they were, then held her palms open for the lubricant. With that coating her gloves, she inched closer to the ewe.

She bleated, and Laura shushed her with a soft, continuous noise. "Help her hold up the hind-quarters," she said, and the two cowboys did what she said. Then she slipped her hand inside the ewe, committing to helping with this birth. She indeed met front legs—and not just two. She said nothing about that but looked at one of the cowboys. "I need a couple of lambing ropes."

They appeared at her side, and she slid one into her hand already in the lamb. She hooked it around one hoof, then repeated that with a second rope. "Okay," she said. "Let's see what we've got."

She tugged gently, and the little lamb came slipping out. She grinned at it while another cowboy started to wipe it down.

"That seemed easy," Todd said.

"There's another one," Laura said, retrieving the lambing ropes. "My guess is she couldn't get them out because they're both crowded into the birth canal." She went back in for the second lamb, and now that there was room, he came out easily too.

The mother sheep bleated and got to her feet. She went to her lambs and started caring for them, and Laura watched them with immense love pouring through her. When she realized she might be acting a little creepy, she cleared her throat and got to her feet. She removed the gloves and tossed them into the nearby garbage can, suddenly embarrassed that all eyes seemed to be stuck on her.

She looked at the cowboys now cleaning up the birth and then Todd. He grinned at her, those dark eyes sparkling with what Laura could only categorize as a combination of mischief and delight.

The heat inside her doubled, and her face flamed. She ducked her head and took a couple of steps away from the pen. "Should we go finish the interview?"

"No, ma'am," Todd drawled at her. "The job is yours if you want it."

Laura blinked, surprise flooding her. "Really?"

"The salary was published on the listing, and if you need a cabin, we can provide one here on the ranch. You're welcome to live in town too." He opened the door to the lambing shed and gestured for her to go first. "You're okay being exclusive to the Texas Longhorn Ranch?"

"Yes," Laura said, finally getting the word out. "Yes, I want the job."

"Great," Todd said. "Let's go get some paperwork done."

———

"I'M NOT KIDDING, MOM," LAURA SAID LATER THAT DAY. SHE did a pirouette in her hotel room. "I got the job at Texas Longhorn Ranch, and I'm going to live out there. I saw the cabin and everything."

Her mom whooped, and that made Laura laugh. "Oh, honey, I'm so happy for you."

Laura sighed as she sank onto the loveseat, pure happiness streaming through her. "Thank you, Mom. How's Daddy doing?"

"Really great," she said, pulling the phone away from her mouth, probably to check on him. "Every day, he's moving better and feeling better."

"I'm glad." Laura paused, some of her joy fading. "Chestnut Springs is quite far from Hidden Hollow."

"Don't you worry about that at all," her mom said. "We're fine here, and Eddie's here with his family. It's what? An hour? You can come any time you want."

"Maybe I should—"

"No maybe's," her mom said, and Laura appreciated that. "You've been looking for a job like this. We've all been praying for it for months. This is the answer we've been waiting for. Don't worry about us. This is your next step, Laura."

She nodded, tears coming to her eyes. She didn't want to speak through such a narrow throat. She rarely cried, but her mom would hear the emotion if she tried to say something.

"And a cabin," her mom said. "That's amazing, Laura. Oh, honey, you've done it." Her voice broke, and that caused Laura's own emotions to surge too.

"I love you, Mom," she said, not caring if her mom heard the strain and the pinch in her voice now.

"I love you so much, sweetie," she said. "When do you move in?"

"Todd—he's my new boss—said the cabin is ready any time I am." She took a deep breath and exhaled it out. "I'm going to come home and get my stuff tomorrow. Then make the drive back here on the weekend. So I'll be home for a few days before I come back here."

"Sounds wonderful," her mom said. "I'll make those onion-smothered pork chops you love."

Laura grinned, the weight of this huge change in her life pressing on her suddenly. "Mom, you don't have to do that."

"I know, but I will. Call me when you leave in the morning."

"All right."

"All right. I love you, dear."

"Love you too, Mom. Tell Daddy I love him."

Her mom said she would, and the call ended. Laura leaned back into the couch, her smile filling her whole face. She laughed and jumped to her feet. "Thank you, Lord," she said right out loud. She'd been working so hard for so long for an opportunity like this, and she let her euphoria fade into gratitude for this second chance she'd been given to make something of her life.

CHAPTER
THIRTEEN

Blake let out a sigh through his nose, taking care not to make any noise whatsoever. His mama had a way of hearing even the most minute of sounds, and he didn't want her or Daddy to know he'd reached the end of his patience.

He turned from the coffee maker and took a breath. "Here you go, Daddy."

"Thanks, son." His father looked up from the counter, his spoon already in his hand. He pulled the sugar bowl closer and started shoveling in the sweet stuff. "How are things in the kitchen?"

"I already asked that," Mama said, and Blake swept his hand toward her. She sat next to her husband at the bar, and Blake stood on the other side of it. They'd "stopped by" for a quick chat, and he usually didn't mind. He hadn't dated anyone for a while, and he was either home or in his office.

Frankly, in the past, when his parents stopped by after work, he didn't have to spend the evening alone. Todd came over often, as did most of Blake's siblings, actually. Since he'd started seeing Gina again and he'd held her hand at Becks's wedding, she'd been driving back out to the ranch to see him in the evenings, or he'd gone into town.

She got off work at two o'clock, and until she moved out of her parents' house, she'd been either staying at the ranch until he got off or driving back out.

Tonight, though, he had a dinner date at her new apartment. She'd moved in a week ago, but tonight would be the first time they'd dined there. She'd been working on unpacking, getting settled, and decorating, and she'd promised him several small plates, both savory and sweet tonight.

He couldn't wait to see her, because while he could've kissed her behind the bald cypress tree just beyond the lodge, he wanted their relationship to exist somewhere besides the ranch. He hadn't kissed her yet at all, but it wasn't for the lack of thinking about doing it.

In front of him, Daddy and Mama squabbled over what Mama had asked and how Blake had answered. The more they talked, the less he had to, and perhaps they'd get the hint that he had somewhere else he'd rather be.

Finally, Daddy looked at him with both palms up. "Fine, I guess Mama already asked you about Gina."

"Gina's great," Blake said. "I'm going to dinner with her tonight." He lifted his wrist and checked his watch,

LOVING HER COWBOY BEST FRIEND   133

though he knew exactly what time it was. "In about a half-hour."

Neither of his parents moved, and Blake drew in another silent breath, held it, and started to release it through his nose.

"Adam says he's going to get a couple more horses at the auction this weekend." Daddy lifted his mug to his lips and sipped, obviously not worried about leaving any time soon.

"Yeah, he told me," Blake said. "Did you get the invoices from Becks, Mama?" He turned and got a washrag out of the sink. "She left them for me to give to you, and I don't want to get in trouble for not doing it."

"I got them," Mama said. "They looked good."

"When are they getting back?" Daddy asked. He used to know every single thing happening around Longhorn Ranch, but since he'd stopped coming into the lodge every day, he only heard things through the grapevine.

Blake was the one who took care of all the details of the ranch and the lodge, and he did update his father about things almost every day. He supposed it had been a few days, and he changed tactics.

"Kyle's almost got the summer concert series finalized, so that's good," Blake said. "Todd and Sierra both like the new vet, and I think we all know how hard it is to impress Sierra." He chuckled, and his mother shook her head, her lips pursing for a moment before she smiled.

"That girl," she said, reaching up to pat her hair. Her reddish-brown hair had been recently cut, and when she went to church on Sundays, she hair sprayed it into a helmet shape. Today, it flowed a little looser, and Blake smiled at her too. "She's never going to find someone with her attitude."

"I don't think she cares that much to find someone, Mama," Blake said. "Not everyone does."

His mother raised her eyes from her eyes to Blake's, wearing some surprise in her expression. "They've just been waiting for you," she said.

"Come on, Mama," he said, rolling his eyes.

"Don't put that pressure on him, Sharon," Daddy said.

"Besides it's not true," Blake said at the same time Mama said, "The others all look to him."

"Jesse and Adam have both been married," Blake pointed out. Granted, neither had lasted long, but they certainly hadn't been waiting for Blake to find someone to settle down with.

"I think Todd likes that new vet a little too much," Daddy said, and that whipped Mama's attention to him.

"Really?"

Blake started wiping the kitchen counter, his head tipped down so the brim of his cowboy hat hid his face. Daddy knew how to get Mama talking about something else, that was for sure, and Blake would be sure to thank him later. If she'd gotten started on Jesse and Adam's first marriages, Blake might've been late to work in the morning.

He tossed the washrag back into the sink and turned to face his parents. "I hate to kick you out, so stay as long as you want, but I'm gonna be late to Gina's." He opened the drawer in the island and extracted his keys.

Barstools scraped as each of his parents stood, both of them suddenly clamoring about how they needed to get home and start dinner. He hugged them both, thanked them for coming, and followed them to the front door.

They'd just stepped outside when Todd pulled up to the cabin. The blue heeler in the back bed of the truck barked, and Blake grinned. He stopped at the top of the steps as his parents shuffled down. Todd got out of the truck, and a brand new conversation started.

Blake whistled through his teeth, and Azure leapt down from truck. He bent down, chuckling. "Hey, buddy. How are you, huh?"

The dog arrived, and Blake reached to pat him. The dog licked his hand, and then Blake's met some dried mud. "Oh, you've been out in the fields, I see."

"Checking the wheeled sprinklers," Todd said, his footsteps coming up the steps. "You're headed out?"

"Yep." Blake straightened and hugged Todd. "You can leave him inside."

"He's dirtier than the bottom of my boots." Todd shook his head. "I'll hose 'im down at my place."

"Thanks, Todd." Blake didn't know how to properly thank him. "You should just call him your dog." He met his brother's eyes, and Todd blinked back.

"Who says I don't?"

"Well, you bring him over to see me all the time, like I'm the divorced father and get to see him on weekends." Blake grinned at Todd, and the two of them laughed together.

"He's just the ranch dog," Todd said, but when Azure

licked his hand, he bent down and stroked his head. "Come on, bud. You need a bath, and your daddy's got a date." He turned to go back down the steps.

Blake followed his brother, pressure building in his chest. "Listen, Todd."

"Hm?" He clapped his palm against the truck, and Azure went around to jump in the back. Todd lowered the tailgate, and the dog jumped up as Todd met Blake's eyes. "What's makin' you look like you're about to throw up?"

"Daddy said something about you and Laura."

Todd turned into a statue. "He did?" His mouth barely moved, and Blake didn't like how the whole world had gone quiet. "What did he say?"

"He said he thought you liked her a little too much, and then Mama...well, you know what Mama's like."

His phone rang, and Todd dug it out of his pocket. He looked at it and then held it up toward Blake. Mama's name and picture sat there, and he cocked his head and his hip. "So I suppose I shouldn't answer this."

"She probably just wants to know if you're going to get married before me," Blake said dryly.

"I don't like Laura," he said, swiping the call to voice-mail. "I mean, she's a great vet and a nice woman, but that's all."

"Of course," Blake said, noting how even Todd remained. They usually didn't keep secrets from one another, and Blake reasoned that if Todd did like Laura as more than a vet, he maybe just wasn't ready to say anything yet.

Which was well within his right.

"Next time she calls, just tell her what you just told me. It's usually easier to nip this in the bud with her."

"Yeah," Todd said as his phone rang again. He sighed like he carried all the oxygen in the world in his lungs and slid on the call. "Mama, I don't like the vet." He opened the door and got in his truck, saying, "I don't want to hear about this again."

Blake chuckled to himself and hurried to get in his own truck before someone else stopped by and delayed him from getting to Chestnut Springs and Gina.

———

He pulled up to the duplex where Gina lived, killed the engine, and jumped out of the truck. He grunted as he remembered the bread he'd stopped to get. Gina hadn't asked him to stop, but the Texan in him didn't know how to show up at someone's house for dinner without something to eat.

The bakery had zucchini-lemon bread with crystallized sugar on top, and if Gina didn't want it, he could make it into some amazing French toast for lunch tomorrow.

He jogged to the end unit and knocked. The sound punctuated the silence in the neighborhood like gunshots, and he winced as he stepped back. He told himself to calm down, that he and Gina were already dating. He didn't need to try so hard.

She opened the door, a cute, flowered apron tied around her waist. She smiled at him as her fingers curled around the edge of the door. "Howdy, cowboy."

"Boy, are you a sight for sore eyes," he said, grinning at her. "I'm so sorry I'm late. I couldn't get my parents out of the house."

She nodded to the bread in his palm. "And you stopped for bread." Her eyes came back to his. "When I told you I was making small plates of dinner and dessert."

"Breeding," he said, handing her the loaf and then taking her straight into his arms. She giggled and turned in his arms. He pressed a kiss to the back of her neck, and they walked into her apartment together.

"Wow," Blake said, taking in the space again. He'd been here last weekend to help her move in. All of his brothers had come to help, as had Gina's brother-in-law and her father. They'd gotten everything in over the course of a few hours, and Blake had ordered food and helped her unpack until evening.

He hadn't been back since, and the clean, crisp, cactus-y scent hadn't been here then. A couple of candles burned on the credenza she'd positioned along the back of the couch. There wasn't a loveseat to go with it, because the apartment wasn't quite big enough for it.

"The new recliner looks great," Blake said, his eyes landing on the floral print. Blues, greens, and grays swirled around, and they matched the denim couch.

"Look at the rug." Gina went around the couch and indicated it. The front feet of the recliner sat on the cream-colored rug with long plies, and a television stand had been pressed against the wall. The TV sat dark, and Blake sure did like the aesthetic of the room.

"It's great," he said. "Things really look different with

curtains and furniture, don't they?" He grinned at Gina, who turned toward the kitchen.

"I painted my table and chairs," she said. "So they match." She ran her hand along the now-blue items in the tiny dining room, which she'd already set with placemats, utensils, and a vase of live flowers that spoke to her level of detail.

"They look great," he said, following her. "It smells great in here too." He got sugar, spices, and her sweet perfume. All of it made his head spin, and Blake caught Gina's hand as she walked into the kitchen. She turned back to him and put her free hand against his chest. "I've missed you this week," he murmured.

"This might not be as good as the food at the lodge," she said as he brought her closer to him.

"Are you kidding?" He looked at the spread on the countertop in her kitchen. Small plates of food already sat there, and his mouth watered at the sight of the chicken wings, brisket and potatoes, and asparagus spears. The next three plates held desserts, each one featuring chocolate. "This looks absolutely amazing."

He focused on her again. "Thank you for doing this. Thanks for inviting me. I love you place, and I...I'm starving." His gaze dropped to her mouth, which curved up into a smile.

"There's only one plate with veggies," she teased, releasing his hand so he could plant it on her lower back and hold her close.

"Mm." He dipped closer to her, his heart pounding down into his stomach and up into his ears. "Do you kiss your friends, Gina?" He touched his lips to her lower jaw, the desire to taste her lips beyond anything he'd felt before.

She cradled his face in her hands, her touch light and delicate. If they'd been dating for several months, he'd categorize it as loving and kind. He moved his eyes back to hers, where they locked. The question he'd asked streamed between them, and Gina nodded.

Blake smiled and slid one hand up her back and into her hair. He let his eyes drift closed as he inched toward her, praying he still knew how to kiss a woman. His lips touched hers, and instant heat exploded down his throat.

He hung on, trying to experience the touch, the taste, and the thrill of kissing her in that very moment. Then the next. She kissed him back, her fingers sliding behind his ears and into his hair, and Blake knew he'd never kiss another woman and feel the way he did about Gina Barlow.

Never, ever, ever.

CHAPTER
FOURTEEN

Gina had always felt adored and cherished when Blake kissed her as a teenager. He'd grown and changed over the years, and his kiss echoed that maturity. He didn't rush, and he knew exactly where and how to move his mouth against hers.

She breathed in, trying to get even nearer to him when she already stood as close as she possibly could. Her cells burned as if someone had lit them on fire, and she'd never be able to walk into her kitchen without reliving this kiss.

He pulled away, and they breathed in together. The first time he'd kissed her, he'd been shy and nervous. He'd chuckled and actually asked her if she was okay. Tonight, their eyes met, and there was no nerves in his expression at all. No chuckles and no questions.

Blake reached up and brushed her hair back out of her face, his eyes traveling the arc his hand made. He hadn't backed up a single centimeter, and neither had she. Her head still spun slightly from the beauty in that kiss, and she didn't want to move quite yet.

His gaze dropped to her mouth, and Gina had enough time to breathe in before he kissed her again.

She'd been hungry before, but everything else fell away under this man's touch, and Gina could've kissed him for a good long while. Unfortunately, he pulled away again, took a big breath, and let his stomach tell her why.

It roared at the two of them, and that brought the chuckles and giggles to the kitchen. She clung to him while she laughed, and once she'd found her strength she stepped back and looked at the food.

"All right," she said. "I think most of this is still edible." She turned to the cream puffs. "Wait. I was going to put cream on those." She opened the fridge, where the door almost hit the island behind her, and got out the bowl of whipped cream. Lucky for her, she'd put it in the fridge before all the kissing started. It would probably be melted if she hadn't.

She dolloped cream on each of the six puffs already filled, dipped, and sugared, and admired them. "There."

"You're a genius," Blake said, sliding his big hand along her waist again. She sure did like that he could touch her now without nerves or apprehension—she didn't want any of those between them—and she leaned into him.

She looked up at him, his eyes dark under the brim of his cowboy hat. "Are you feeling adventurous?" she asked, and he met her gaze.

"Adventurous? Is this like you leading us down the wrong side of the trail?"

"No," she said, laughing, though she had done that on their hike a few weeks ago. "This is us eating dessert first." She picked up the three dessert plates and took them to the table.

Blake joined her there, saying, "I always want dessert first. That's why I kissed you before we sat down to eat." His deep voice chuckled, and the warmth inside Gina kicked up another notch.

"Okay," she said. "In a restaurant, the chef goes over the specials for the night for the front-of-house staff." She adjusted the plate with the chocolate-dipped caramels. "Will you indulge me?"

"Go for it," Blake said with a smile.

Gina returned it and looked at her creations again. "Okay, so this is a vanilla sea-salt caramel with a dark chocolate coating. It should be smooth and salty, with that bitter chocolate at the end." Blake had once adored dark chocolate, and she hoped his taste buds hadn't changed too much.

"Then we have a cream puff, with a pistachio pastry cream inside, a white chocolate ganache on top, and that whipped cream I just put on. They should be crisp and light on the tongue, which is why I went with the white chocolate over dark."

"Hm," he hummed, standing almost directly beside her as he gazed at the desserts too.

"The last item is a molten chocolate brownie, with crispy edges, a liquid middle, and a cone of mint-chocolate frosting."

"I want that one first," he said, already reaching for it.

Gina beat him to the plate and served him a brownie, pausing as she turned back to the island. "Do you want whipped cream?"

"Does the sun rise each morning?" He kicked another grin at her and went with her to the island—the two steps it took—and picked up the dessert spoons. When they'd both returned to the table and had their brownies with whipped cream, she lifted her utensil to him in a toast.

He clinked his against it, and they each dove into their desserts. Blake moaned the moment his chocolate concoction touched his tongue, and Gina realized he'd made that same sound a few minutes ago while kissing her. She hadn't heard it then, but her ears had an excellent memory.

She giggled and put her own bite in her mouth. Her eyes rolled back in her head at the decadence and richness of the chocolate, the smooth frosting, and the crispy edges of the brownie. "I nailed this," she said around her mouthful of dessert, and Blake nodded emphatically.

As he took another bite, she swallowed her first. "All right, cowboy," she said. "Tell me something about you that I think I know but that is different now." They'd started this game on their hike, and she'd liked it enough to continue it every few days.

He finished his second bite and said, "Remember how it was Todd who used to annoy me the most as a kid?"

"Yes," Gina said.

"It's not him anymore," Blake said, already scooping into the middle of his molten brownie. "Guess who it is."

Gina had sat with his family at the wedding last week, but that didn't mean she knew them. Holly and Sierra had been extremely nice, and they'd engaged her in conversation the most, besides Blake and Todd. Jesse, Adam, and Nash had bent their heads together to talk about something, but Gina had been clear across the table.

The last Stewart sibling had moved from conversation to conversation, and he'd been friendly enough. She guessed, "Kyle?" anyway, and Blake shook his head.

"It's Adam," he said with a smile. "He runs all of our horsey activities, and he treats them like they're royalty."

"Horsey activities?" Gina said just before she burst out laughing. "I don't know why, but that sounded so funny."

"He's too serious about non-serious things," Blake said.

Gina finished laughing and scooped up another bite of brownie, this time with less frosting. She needed to dial down the cone of that next time. "Maybe he has a reason."

"He does," Blake said with a sigh. "I just get tired of giving him a pass because he was married for six months and it didn't work out."

Gina's eyebrows went up. "Wow, he was married?"

"Yeah, Jesse too," Blake said.

"Anyone else?"

"Nope."

She nodded, not quite sure why she expected life at the Texas Longhorn Ranch to stall just because she'd left. It hadn't. Days went by and became months, and hair grew grayer and bodies got older. People changed, as she'd seen so keenly in her mother—and herself.

"What else do I need to know about your family?" Gina asked. "When is your mama going to come into the kitchen and insist I come over for dinner?"

"Oh, you mean she hasn't yet?" Blake asked, clearly teasing.

She cocked her head at him. "Seriously."

"I don't know," he said, finishing his brownie. "I'd probably expect that any day if I were you."

"Great," she muttered, deciding she couldn't spend all of her dessert calories on just the brownie. "I'm going in for a cream puff. Do you want one?"

"Is the sky blue?"

———

GINA LEFT THE KITCHEN, BUT IT WASN'T ANY COOLER OUTSIDE than in. The door slammed closed behind her, shutting out the chatter, the hissing steam, the arguing, and the banging of pots and pans.

She exhaled, wiped her bangs out of her face, looked up into the far-too-bright sky, and screamed.

Only a breath of time later, the door opened and another person crowded onto the small landing outside the kitchen entrance to the lodge. "Oh," Starla said. "You're right here."

"I haven't had a chance to run yet," Gina said, her throat still a bit raw from that primal yell.

"Was that you screaming?"

"Yes, ma'am," Gina said, and she wasn't going to apologize for it. She went down the steps to the gravel lot where the chefs parked, but she wasn't headed for her car. Her feet crunched over the rocks, but she still heard Starla call her name.

"Wait," she said. "Don't go."

"I'm not leaving," Gina called over her shoulder. "I just need five minutes." She'd yelled that inside too, but she doubted highly that anyone had heard her. With the mess going on in there, she'd be surprised if the guests hadn't been evacuated by Nash.

Starla's footsteps ran through the gravel to catch her, and they walked side-by-side to the shade of the bald cypress. Gina climbed up on the table and sighed. "If I drank, I'd need something stiff right now."

"Same," Starla said.

Gina looked at her, noting the lines around her eyes and the exhaustion weighing down her shoulders. "Aren't you supposed to be the boss? Shouldn't you be in there breaking up that squabble?"

Starla leveled her gaze at Gina, and she almost cowered. "They're grown adults. I gave them their directions. If they choose not to follow them, that's on them."

Gina looked back to the lodge. It sure didn't seem like pandemonium had broken out over that night's menu from her perch on the picnic table. Things could be deceiving sometimes, she supposed.

"I think you leaving was the smartest course of action," Starla said. "So I followed you." She nodded toward the back door, which hadn't opened again. "Give them another five minutes. Then Mindie will come out, and she'll have a truce ready."

"She will?"

"They'll elect her to come speak to me, because they think I like her the best."

Gina looked at Starla, and she didn't seem concerned that her chefs thought she didn't like them. "Do you?"

"I like all of them the same," Gina said, blinking her gaze away from the door and back to Gina. "Except for you. You're the sanest of them all."

Gina scoffed, sure that wasn't true. "I've only been here for a couple of months. They'll hate me if they think we're such great friends now."

"You're never late," Starla said. "Who else can you name who's never been late in the two months you've been here?"

Gina could only stare at her. The heat in her face started to rise again, but not from frustration that she'd been baking all the wrong desserts for two hours.

"You listen to me and do what I say," Starla said.

"They all do that," Gina said. They did; she'd seen them.

"They grumble. You don't, at least not that I've ever heard or seen."

"I make pies and cakes," Gina said. "It doesn't matter what I do."

"Yes, it does," Starla said, putting her hand on Gina's knee. "That's what I'm trying to show them, Gina. Just because your course comes last doesn't mean we consider the dessert menu last."

Gina nodded and looked at Starla's hand on her leg. It slipped away, but not before she saw the short nails and long fingers—the hands of someone who knew food and how to prepare it. She looked up at Starla, and said, "I didn't mean to complain that I'd spent time making bread pudding when it would be too heavy to go with the bread bowls and soup bar."

"You didn't," Starla said. "You had the right menu. Everyone else had the wrong one. It was my fault, and I owned it. They marched me down the gangplank and pushed me off, using you as a shield."

The door banged against the lodge, and Starla and Gina looked in that direction. Mindie spotted them, lifted her hand, and came down the steps. "See?" Starla said almost under her breath. "I'm prepared to take the fall for you, Gina. So tell me before she gets here: Can you set the bread pudding and black forest pudding aside until tomorrow, or not?"

"I can," Gina said. "I said that in there about fifteen times." No one would listen to her, and she didn't entirely blame them. It would be much harder for them to start over on an entire dinner buffet than it was for her to start a ginger cake and a pretzel-peanut butter bar batter.

"All right," Starla said as she slid from the picnic table. "They're going to owe you one—and I am too." She turned back and smiled at Gina, offered her hand, and Gina put hers in Starla's, though she didn't really need help getting down.

Something cemented between them, and they faced Mindie together. She pressed the tips of her fingers together and stopped a pace or two away. "We're sorry, Starla. You're right in that we messed up today's menu, despite being given the wrong cards. Gina's desserts were correct." She looked at Gina. "We're wondering if you could switch to tomorrow's desserts, Gina? Dylan and Rosie said they'd help you with anything you need."

She looked at Starla, who lifted her eyebrows. "It's fine," Gina said. "I can switch."

"All right," Starla said, taking the first step. "Let's go get everyone on the same page again." She led the way back inside, and Gina stayed out of her way. She didn't need to get hit by Hurricane Starla, and once everyone was all on the same menu for that night's dinner at the lodge, Gina went back to her station and looked at the prefect bread pudding she'd already taken out of the oven. "Into the walk-in for you," she said to it. Inside, she once again met Starla, who took the wrapped dessert from her.

"I'll take it to Blake's for you," she said with a smile. "He loves this stuff, and I know you go to his cabin for lunch sometimes."

Gina smiled back at her, not sure if she should hug her or simply nod professionally. She did a half-hug, with the bread pudding between them, and said, "Thank you, Starla. He'll love that."

Then she put on her game face and returned to the kitchen to get her desserts done for the day so she could spend the afternoon eating bread pudding with her boyfriend.

CHAPTER
FIFTEEN

Blake hid his smile as Gina concentrated on the cornhole board across from her. He stood by it, and he wanted to call encouragement to her like he'd done in the past. She said it didn't help, so he kept his mouth shut. Her determination to improve her cornhole skills made him chuckle every time he thought about it, and she didn't like that either.

They destroyed us, she'd said last week after the first week of the tournament at the lodge. The summer activities had started, though school had a few more weeks, and she sure didn't like being in the last spot on the family leaderboard.

The Stewarts liked showing guests that they did the same activities they planned for the lodge, so they always started their friendly cornhole tournament a few weeks before peak season.

Blake was just thrilled he wasn't partnered with Jesse

again this year. Gina, however, had a competitive streak he'd forgotten about until they'd landed in last and she'd come to him and said, "That absolutely can't happen again, Blake. We have to practice every night after work."

He wasn't going to say no to spending more time with her, even if it was with her face scrunched up in concentration as she swung her arm like a smooth pendulum and released the corn bag. It flew in a nice arc, and he said, "Good one, Gina," as it hit the board and slid up toward the hole.

It didn't quite fall through, but it was a vast improvement over last weekend's disaster. They'd played three rounds and lost every one in less than fifteen minutes.

Gina grinned at him, already bending to get another bag. "Your turn," she called. Blake wasn't sure if he should flub the throw or not, and in the end, he decided he didn't have to hide his skills from Gina. He'd been playing cornhole for years—this wasn't a new summer tradition at the Texas Longhorn Ranch—and he wanted her to know she had a good partner out there in the cornhole arena.

He tossed his bag, unsurprised to see it sail directly for the target and drop through the hole. She stared at it, then lifted her eyes to his. "I have no idea how you do that."

"Practice," he said as he walked toward her. His cowboy boots sank into the gravel and made crunching noises, and she waited until he arrived at her side before she took aim with her last bag. "We can go to dinner after this, right?" he asked.

"You're distracting me."

"Maybe you'd like to partner up with someone less distracting," he murmured.

"Maybe I would." She swung her arm back and forth, really trying to find the right movement. She didn't pretend, and she really wanted to improve. She released the bag, but it sailed right slightly, missing the board completely.

She harrumphed and turned toward him. "You have to stay on your side until I'm done."

He could only laugh at her and take her into his arms. "Really? My very presence is that distracting?" He wasn't sure if she was complimenting him or disgusted by him. Honestly, he'd take both, because he just liked being with her so dang much.

Everything in his life had brightened since Gina's return to Chestnut Springs. No, she wasn't precisely where Blake wanted her—on the ranch with him full-time—but she was close. She was back. She showed up to work every day, did phenomenal work, and kissed him like she once had. Like she meant it. Like she maybe could fall in love with him again, and then his dreams of having her on the ranch with him full-time would be a reality, the way they were for Becks and Luke.

"It's the cologne," Gina said, relaxing into his arms and taking a deep breath of his chest. "Very sexy."

"Mm," he hummed through his throat. "Watching you throw that corn bag is sexy." He leaned down and kissed her, not caring who happened by the cornhole arena. It was open all the time for family and guests, and it sat out in front of the lodge only several paces from the fire pit.

Someone cleared their throat, and Blake broke the connection between him and his girlfriend. Jesse himself stood there, and Blake dropped his hand to Gina's and turned toward his brother at the same time. "We were just talking about you."

"Were you?" Dark, stormy Jesse looked from Blake to Gina. "I can't imagine why."

"Gina thinks she needs a new partner for the cornhole tournament," Blake said. "I told her you were the best player in the family."

Jesse's tumultuous look turned even more sour, but Blake only continued to smile at him. "That's ridiculous," he said. "We'd be starting a week behind everyone." He frowned at Gina. "Besides, Blake's the best, and he knows it."

"You two did win last year," Gina said.

"I'm not playing this year," Jesse said.

"You should," Blake said. "Everyone always plays."

"Yes, well, I don't have a partner."

"Starla said she'd play," Gina said, her voice pitching toward innocence. "I was talking to her about it this week, and she said she'd love to play." She looked from Jesse to Blake. "No one ever asks her to team up with them, she says."

"Starla?" Jesse asked as if he didn't know who Starla was.

"Yes," Gina said. "She says she's pretty good too."

Jesse looked back to the lodge like the head chef and kitchen manager would be standing there. "I guess I could ask her." He sounded really doubtful about it, though.

"I'll text her," Gina said, her hand slipping away from Blake's. Her fingers moved like lightning over her phone while Jesse swung his head back to her.

"No, you don't—"

"Done," Gina said, smiling up at him. "She's really great, you guys." She looked between Jesse and Blake again. "Why don't any of you like her?"

"I like her fine," Blake said. "She *is* great." He blinked at her, somewhat surprised by her question. "I didn't think *you* liked her."

"Well, we've had some moments together in the kitchen," Gina said with some measure of aloofness in her tone. "She's... I don't want to betray her confidence, but I know she'd love to be more involved with family things around the ranch here. Everyone else seems to be. Nash asked Ashley to be his partner, and I think that hurt Starla's feelings."

"Nash has a crush on Ashley," Jesse said without any emotion at all.

"Jess," Blake said. "I don't think that's common knowledge." He shot a look at Gina. Ashley worked in the kitchen here too, and with Nash the morning manager he saw her often.

"Sure it is," Jesse said. "Didn't you see them at the cornhole tournament last weekend?" He glared at Blake and Gina. "They're almost as bad as you two."

"Hey," Gina said in defense. "We weren't bad. In fact, by the end, I was mad and would barely speak to Blake."

"It was still cute enough to make me puke," Jesse said, folding his arms.

Blake shook his head, his smile determined to stick around today it seemed. "What did you need? You totally interrupted us, you know."

"Heaven forbid," Jesse said, rolling his eyes. "Todd was looking for you. Something about Azure. I said I'd seen you out here practicing, and I came to get you."

Blake pulled his phone from his pocket, a dash of alarm ringing through him. "He didn't text me." Not that he'd heard or seen anyway. Sure enough, his phone didn't hold a single notification. That was kind of odd actually, and Blake pressed and held the power button to restart his phone.

"He said he did," Jesse said. "I texted you too, but you just kept grinning at your girl."

Blake looked up at Jesse. "Sorry," he said. "I'm restarting now." He took a step toward the lodge and away from the cornhole arena. Six stations stayed set up year-round, and someone on their grounds crew raked the gravel every day. "What's with Azure?"

"He hurt his paw or something," Jesse said, stepping with Blake. He stayed right at his side and added in a murmur, "Starla and me? Really? Do you think that would work?"

Blake took in the worry and doubt on his brother's face. "You don't have to date her to play cornhole for the summer," Blake said. "Stop worrying so much, Jess."

"I'm not worried about falling in love with her," Jesse said with a scoff.

"What *are* you worried about then?" Gina asked, and she wasn't embarrassed she'd been eavesdropping. She was right there in the conversation, and she moved to Blake's other side and caught his hand in hers. He loved that she touched him as freely as he did her, and that she seemed to want to hold his hand as much as he wanted to hold hers.

He seated his fingers in hers and squeezed while Jesse walked without speaking. Just when he reached the bottom of the steps that led up to the wide, wrap-around porch on the lodge, he paused. He put one hand on the railing and looked up. "I don't know what I'm worried about. That I'll do something stupid and hurt her feelings." He looked at Blake and Gina, who'd paused with him. "I do that sometimes, and Starla is great and doesn't deserve that."

"It's *cornhole*," Blake said. "It's not serious. Just be nice."

"I agree with part of that," Gina said. "Be nice, but the cornhole? *That's* serious." She went up the steps and into the lodge while the brothers stood at the bottom of the steps and watched her.

Jesse finally chuckled and clapped his hand on Blake's shoulder. "She's somethin' else, Blake." He started up the steps too.

"What does that mean?" Blake asked, hurrying after him. "She fits with us, don't you think?"

"You know what?" Jesse paused again. "Yeah, I think she does. It doesn't mean anything."

"It means something, or you wouldn't have said it." Jesse didn't just talk to hear his own voice.

"It means I think she's perfect for you," Jesse said.

"She's passionate about some things, and so are you, and you guys are like, perfectly balanced." He actually grinned and opened the door to go inside the lodge. "Now, come on. Todd's probably hyperventilating right now."

As Blake followed Jesse inside, his phone started chiming and wouldn't stop. Notification after notification shrilled out at him, and he hurried to silence his phone as text after text, missed calls, and voicemail messages streamed in. "My word," he muttered to himself. At the same time, he thought he could benefit from turning off his phone for an hour every morning, because the last one with silence and Gina and cornhole had been spectacular.

He stood near the door and read through the messages, only looking up when he heard Starla asked, "Can I really partner with you for cornhole, Jesse?"

Jesse nodded, most of his storminess subsiding. "Sure, Starla," he said. "Maybe we can practice together some-time tomorrow before the tournament."

Blake smiled to himself and went back to the messages about Azure and his hurt paw. He tapped to call Todd and lifted his phone to his ear. Gina had gotten an apple and stood with Jesse and Starla, and Blake turned away from them when Todd said, "There you are."

"Sorry," he said. "My phone went dark, and I had to restart it. Where are you?"

"Out in the barn," he said. "I'm having Laura look at him."

"She's still here?"

"Yes," Todd said, something odd in his voice in that single word. "Come out when you get a chance."

"I'm on my way," Blake said, moving through the lodge. He nodded to Gina, indicating the back of the lodge, and she nodded that she got what he was saying. "Is it bad?"

"Laura thinks he might have to go into an office," Todd said. "He's got some ticks under his skin we can't get out."

Worry needled Blake, and he increased his pace. He arrived in the barn where Todd's office was housed, finding him and Laura and Sierra all in the lobby of sorts, Azure on a blanket in the middle of their trio.

"Hey, bud," Blake said, crouching down next to his dog too. He did love the canine, even if Todd took care of him most of the time. "What did you get into?"

"He's got three lone star ticks," Laura said, looking from Azure to Blake. "And two American dog ticks." She indicated a small medical bin next to her. "I got those two out already, and I'm sure I can get out one of them, but the other two are deep and moving fast."

Concern exploded through Blake. "Okay," he said. "Let's move faster."

CHAPTER
SIXTEEN

Gina stroked Azure's back while Blake did the same to his head. The dog lay across both of their laps, clearly exhausted. Blake looked the same, and Gina wasn't even sure she'd be able to drive herself home.

Darkness had fallen a while ago, but Blake had needed her. She wanted to be his support, the way he was to her. After another couple of minutes, though, she said, "I should go, Blake," in a whisper.

"Yeah, of course." He sighed as he nudged Azure off his lap and stood. "I'll be right back, bud." He extended his hand to Gina, and she gladly put her fingers in his.

"You'll be okay now?"

"Yeah," Blake said, giving her a weary smile. "Sorry you're not going to get your beauty rest."

She batted her eyelashes at him. "I don't really need it,

though, right?" She giggled, relieved with he chuckled too. Blake usually operated on two emotions—happy and busy. He was either at work, accomplishing things, or he was laughing and kissing her. She liked that his emotions didn't swing from one side to the other very quickly or very hard, because hers did, and she needed a sense of stability in her life.

"You definitely don't," he said. "Sorry I kept you so late, though. You could've left anytime."

"I know." She turned back to him at the front door of his cabin. "You seemed like you needed a friend, though."

"A friend, huh?" He took her into his arms and swayed with her. "I thought we agreed we were way past friends."

"We did," she said. "But that doesn't mean we can't also be friends." She gazed up at him, suddenly very serious. "I want to be best friends with the man I—" She swallowed, not quite sure what she was saying.

Blake's eyebrows went up and his mouth stayed closed. He wasn't going to save her from herself this time.

"I should go," she said.

"No, finish what you were going to say." He held her tighter, and Gina pressed her palms against his shirt. She looked at her fingers there, the white lines of them against his black and white plaid.

"I...I want to be best friends with the man I love," she said, the words choking in the back of her throat. "The man I marry *should* be my best friend." She dared to look up into those dark, dreamy eyes Blake possessed. He had no idea what they did to her, and one day, she'd tell him.

Today was not that day, not with all the word vomit she'd already spewed. "Don't you think? Don't you think two people should be the absolute best of friends before they try to build their life together? Raise children? All of that?"

"Yes," he murmured.

"So it's not bad if I acted as a best friend tonight and kept you company. That's what friends do."

He nodded and closed his eyes. He leaned closer to her, but he didn't dip his head to kiss her. He pressed his cheek against hers and whispered, "Do you see yourself getting married, Gina?"

She thought of Becks and Luke. Becks had more of a free spirit than Gina did, and she seemed so, so happy now. "Yes," she whispered back. Maybe she couldn't have done it fifteen years ago, but now? Gina felt like she could get married now.

"Children?" Blake asked next. "You see yourself with those?"

"Yes," she whispered. "I mean, one or two. I don't want to be outnumbered or anything."

Blake chuckled, but he didn't pull away so she could see his face. That was probably for the best, as she wasn't sure what she'd find there, and she couldn't know for certain if she'd like it.

"You want kids, right, Blake?"

"Sure," he said.

"How many?"

"I don't know," he said. "One or two, I guess."

Gina did move then, putting space between them so

she could see his face. "Are you just saying that because I did?"

"Yes," he admitted, but his playful, teasing smile didn't make its appearance. "I'm very serious about us, Gina. I'm falling in love with you more and more every day."

Fear reached right inside her chest and grabbed hold of her heart. She fought against it, because she wasn't afraid of Blake. She wasn't afraid of being his girlfriend—or his wife. She wasn't.

Not anymore.

So many things had changed inside her over the years, and while the idea of living out her life in small-town Chestnut Springs had terrified her at age eighteen, she no longer felt that way. The intense emotion faded, and she allowed herself to smile.

"I'm serious about us too, Blake," she said, reaching up to slide her hand down the side of his face. His soft beard tickled her fingers, and she adored the way he leaned into her touch.

"Good," he said. "Kiss me good-night and get on home so I don't have to feel guilty for keeping you so late."

"Don't feel guilty," Gina said just before she touched her mouth to Blake's. He kissed her in such a familiar way while also keeping things exciting and new between them. He didn't say *I love you*, but Gina certainly felt loved by him as he pulled away.

"See you in the morning, sweetheart," he said, opening the door behind her.

Gina slipped out into the evening air, the darkness enveloping her the very moment she stepped into it. The cabin next door—where Todd and Kyle lived—shone with light, and her movement caused Blake's bulb to flare to life too.

He followed her to the top of the steps, and while she continued down, he called, "Text me when you get home so I know you made it."

"Yes, sir," she said over her shoulder. She made the drive and went into her apartment. A sigh pulled through her whole body as she did, but it contained only happiness. She loved this small space that belonged to her, and she threw her bag over the back of the couch as she went past.

"Thank you, Lord," she said to her empty kitchen. She opened the fridge and took out her favorite peach soda. "Bless Blake and Azure tonight, and help us all to...make it." She wasn't sure exactly what she meant by that, but she did want to "make it" work with Blake this time.

She couldn't help thinking of Becks and Luke, as well as her mom and dad, who'd weathered many storms of life together. Gina didn't want to continue rocking back and forth on her solo sailing vessel. She wanted a co-captain— and he came in a tall, cowboy body, with a dark beard and dazzling midnight-sky eyes, and a quick smile, a loud laugh, and a family ranch to run.

————

"THEY LIKED THE CINNAMON ROLLS," STARLA SAID A COUPLE of mornings later. "They're gone."

Gina looked up from icing her banana cake. "They are? I made four dozen."

"The lodge is full this weekend," Starla said, setting the last cinnamon roll pan on the dishwashing station. The man who stood there, Abraham, looked at it with distaste and then started spraying it with hot water. "They don't get sweet stuff every day."

"Yes, they do," Gina argued. "I make raspberry muffins and chocolate chip pancakes every single day."

Starla gave her a grin and picked up the tiered trays of English muffins, bagels, and breads they'd decided to put out should all the cinnamon rolls get eaten. "Different guests."

"I can make more tomorrow."

"Don't worry about it," Starla said over her shoulder. "If the word gets out about the amazing cinnamon rolls that are gone in the first forty-five minutes, they'll come down to breakfast earlier."

"The dining room is packed," Nash said from his spot at the back of the kitchen. "We don't need a rush right when we begin."

Starla ignored him, and Gina flicked him a glance before she went back to her maple frosting. Her duties for breakfast had finished once service started, as she wasn't dealing with waffles or pancakes today. She'd moved on to the lunch box desserts a couple of hours ago, and she needed to finish icing her cakes, cut them, and put them in the plastic containers before she moved on to dinner.

Well, that wasn't entirely true. She already had the

chocolate mousse cake in the oven, with the custard cooling in the walk-in fridge. The life of a pastry chef moved in layers, as she had downtimes during baking she filled with making frostings and fillings. Then, during cooling time, she had to work on putting together more batters and toppings.

Gina could move around the kitchen with ease now, as she'd been here for almost three months. She wasn't the newest employee in the kitchen anymore, and she threw a look over to Olivia, who currently fried more sausage links while also manning a grill full of bacon.

"Biscuits," someone called. "Dill butter and honey butter."

"I've got the butters," Gina called, bending to the small fridge below her station. Sometimes she needed to chill something instantly the moment she finished making it, and she pulled out a big tub of both the dill butter and the honey butter.

She took them over to Jill, who acted as one of the runners that morning. "Here you go. How are the bacon corn muffins holding up?"

"Great," she said. "We have about a third left."

Gina nodded, proud of her savory muffins. She'd stuffed the batter with bacon, sweet corn kernels, and shredded cheese. Some people put herbs in the batter, but she liked to infuse it into butters instead, and they'd put out three types that morning: Dill, parsley and lemon, and honey butter.

"Biscuits," Ashley said, setting down the pan of biscuits that went with the sausage gravy they served on the bar. She smiled at Gina, who'd actually taught Ashley how to make the biscuits, and went back to her station.

"Gina," Mindie called. "Your timer is going off."

Gina turned and hurried back to her oven. There had been a slight scuffle when someone had turned off her timer once without telling her. Another when another chef had turned it off and then taken out her cake. Since those disasters, Starla had told everyone to keep their hands off Gina's timers and ovens and to simply *communicate* with her, so they didn't have blackened black forest cakes or raw honey bars.

She bent to open her oven and check on the pineapple upside down cakes. Today's lunch dessert menu included fruity cakes, and she'd chosen to do a trio of choices for guests who'd ordered a grab-and-go lunch. Banana with maple frosting, the pineapple upside down cake with a cinnamon-flavored powdered sugar, which gave it something special, and a white-chocolate raspberry swirl cake which looked as elegant as it sounded.

Gina sometimes hated to put it in a "lunch box," but the comment cards about the lunches had been the best they'd been in months, so she wasn't complaining. No one else was either, and that made a sliver of happiness move through her. Her skills were admired and valued here, and she'd never thought that would happen in Chestnut Springs.

She continued to work through the morning breakfast service, and she managed to get her fruit cakes all cut, boxed, and delivered to the tables for the grab-and-goers on time. As the food disappeared faster than she could even believe, she blew out her breath and tightened her ponytail.

"It's amazing how fast they go," she said to Starla, who stood next to her, checking off meals as people went through the line.

"Right?" Starla didn't even look up from her clipboard. "We work for hours, and the food is gone in minutes." She flashed a smile at a guest, nodded at his bright blue wristband that told her he got a lunch, and made another mark on her list.

Once everyone had gone through, several lunches remained, one of which belonged to Gina. The cowboys and cowgirls who worked at the lodge and the ranch often ordered lunch here, and she'd been doing that since she started.

Blake had paid for her first month, and when she'd found out, she'd tried to pay him back. He wouldn't have it, though, and she'd given up trying.

"You ready for this?" she asked, picking up her lunch and then taking the white-chocolate raspberry cake.

Starla clipped the pencil to the top of the board. "I'm so ready."

"How did your practice with Jesse go?" Gina glanced at Starla, then continued to look as the other woman ducked her head, a flush creeping its way into her face right before Gina's eyes. "Starla?"

"Great," Starla said, her voice almost a whole octave higher.

"Why doesn't that sound great?" Gina grinned at her.

"What happened? Was he rude to you? I swear, I will give him a piece of—"

"He wasn't rude," Starla said, throwing her a glare. "You don't need to say anything." She walked away from Gina, her head held high, but that blush still staining her cheeks.

Gina couldn't help giggling, and her smile only widened when she caught sight of Blake coming out of the administration hallway with Adam and Jesse himself. "Hey," he drawled as he approached. "Are you on lunch?" His hand slid along her waist as his brothers picked up their food.

"I'm holding my food, aren't I?" She looked past him to Jesse. "Hey, Jesse, are you playing with Starla today?"

Jesse looked up, his dark eyebrows bunching together. "Yes."

Gina grinned at him. "I told you Starla was a good player."

Jesse went back to his cake choices, but Gina saw the redness in his face too. She linked her arm through Blake's and said, "I can't *wait* for this afternoon's tournament."

He looked at her with a questioning glint in his eye. "Is that right?"

"Yeah," she said, leading him away now that he'd gotten his lunch too. "Maybe we won't be last after today."

"You will be," Jesse called after them. "Starla and I are practicing during lunch, not kissing on the picnic table."

Blake chuckled, and Gina couldn't contain her smile either. Once they'd left his earshot she whispered in a loud voice, "But kissing is more fun."

"I thought you wanted to win," Blake said between his chuckles.

"No," Gina said. "I don't want to be in last place." She danced ahead of him. "Are you seriously suggesting we go practice cornhole instead of hiding behind the bald cypress and kissing?"

"Absolutely not," Blake said, and Gina laughed along with him.

CHAPTER
SEVENTEEN

Blake clapped his hands together, whooping for his sister as Holly's corn bag landed on the board and slid up, up, up...and dropped through the hole. The crowd gathered around the family tournament roared, and Holly gave a double-high-five to her partner, Sierra.

He grinned at his sisters, who had just taken the top spot on the Stewart family leaderboard with their win over Adam and Lowry. The man who sat at the front desk, Lowry, jogged over and congratulated them, giving Holly and Sierra hugs while Adam bent to pick up all the bags. He wouldn't be happy, but he'd be gracious.

"Our last tournament today," Todd yelled above the quieting chatter and applause. "Is Blake and Gina, who currently sit in last place, against Mama and Daddy, just one rung above them."

"Game time," Gina said, and a mask slid into place over her features. Blake shook his head and prayed for a miracle. He wasn't sure what the next week would hold if they couldn't beat his elderly parents. "Do you want your mom or dad?"

"Better give me Mama," he said. "She can talk some trash and make it sound pretty."

Gina looked at him with wide eyes. "Really?"

"Have you met my brothers? Did you just see Sierra taunting Kyle? Where do you think they get that?" He shook his head, chuckling. "It ain't from Daddy."

Gina glanced over to Mama, who actually had her hands up above her head, stretching. "You take your mom then."

"Yep." Blake took the blue bags from Adam and offered them to Gina. "Do you want to go first?"

"Yes," she said. "Then the whole game won't be dependent on me." She juggled the loose bags in her arms and started toward the other cornhole platform, the one Blake would be tossing toward. Daddy already stood there, bagless, and Blake joined Mama and all of her red bags.

The cornhole platforms bore red, white, and blue paint, with a giant Texas star at the bottom. Nash and Little Nick had made them several years ago, and someone on the ranch repainted them every spring so they always looked like a million bucks.

"At this station, we'll have Jesse and Starla playing Nash and Ashley," Todd bellowed. "The last one down here." He took a few steps and looked at his clipboard.

"Will be Sammy Boy and Baby John against me and Kyle." Todd handed his clipboard off to Adam, who'd already finished his game, and Nash stepped to the station next to Blake and Daddy. He grinned across the space to Ashley, who shook Jesse's hand like they were super good sports.

Starla, who stood next to Nash with square shoulders and the straightest back Blake had ever seen on a person, looked like she might throw up at any moment. He smiled at her, but she didn't seem to see it.

"All right," Todd called from his position down on the end. "Let's play."

Red started, and that meant Mama selected one of her bags, lined up her throw, and tossed it. The thunk of the corn against wood met his ears, and the bag slid to the left. "Nice one, Mama," he said, though she was a good two feet from the hole.

"Oh, you," she said, swatting at his bicep.

"What?" He flinched away from her and put an extra step between them. "I said it was nice."

"You're teasing me."

"I am not," he said. "The game is young." He quieted to watch Gina throw, sending her all the good vibes he currently possessed. "It wouldn't kill you to let me and Gina do well, I have to say." He barely moved his mouth as he spoke, and Gina let her blue bag fly.

It also hit the wooden platform and slid up toward the hole. Friction stopped it short of dropping in, but only by a couple of inches. Holly and Sierra cheered for her, and she gave both of them a high-five.

The game continued, and Gina scored two points for their team by getting two of her bags to stay on the board while Mama scored three by getting a bag in the hole. She clearly wasn't going to give Gina and Blake a pass at all, and Blake scowled at her behind the brim of his cowboy hat as he bent to gather the blue bags Gina had tossed his way.

He didn't really care about the family cornhole tournament. Sometimes he and Jesse won, and sometimes they lost. It was all fun, and usually for the guests so they'd sign up and play cornhole during their time here at the lodge.

Now, though, he wanted to destroy the competition just to make Gina happy. When it was his turn to throw, he blocked everything out except the Texas star across from him. His throws were flawless, and he downed all four of his bags, one after the other.

The crowd around him and Gina, Mama and Daddy, grew as his team suddenly went from three to two, up to fourteen to six.

Gina wore sunshine and moonbeams on her face as she bent to gather the bags, but Blake didn't even break a smile.

"What is going on with you?" Mama asked.

"My girlfriend would like to win," Blake said, once again barely moving his mouth. "It wouldn't kill you to help me out so I don't have to get quite so in the zone."

"You must really be liking Gina."

"Mama, I'm not talking about this right now."

She didn't seem to mind talking and throwing at the

same time, but Blake noticed that Daddy and Gina weren't engaging in small talk. She scored another four points—one for each bag she left on the board—and she grinned at him across the pitch.

She hadn't even been able to do that last week, and all Blake had to do was land one bag in the hole and they'd win. Mama scored two cornholes, bringing their score up to twelve.

Blake gathered the blue bags and held them while Daddy made his throw. The bag didn't even land on the board. Blake caught his eye and knew that mistake hadn't been a mistake at all.

He grinned and held two bags in each hand and lifted them up.

"Blake and Gina could win with this throw," Adam yelled, drawing everyone's attention. "Let's have a drum-roll." Hands got clapped on thighs in a fast rhythm, and Blake grinned and grinned around at everyone.

"They're in last place right now," Todd said, having come down the row from his game. "But a win this fast, by that many points would definitely lift them up the leaderboard."

"Come on, Blake!" Gina called, clapping her hands together and jumping up and down on the other side of their game board. Daddy grinned, a resigned look on his face. He didn't mind being last at all. Actually, Blake thought his dad would gladly be last so none of his children ever had to be.

Mama, on the other hand, gave Blake a friendly smile

that really held iron teeth. "Are you going to ask her to marry you?"

"That's not going to work, Mama," he said, letting his arm swing back and forth, his attention on the platform across from him. He'd thrown plenty of cornholes; *one more, please*, he prayed just before he released the bag.

It sailed through the air. The crowd held its breath, the drumroll silent.

The bag landed, slid, and dropped right through the hole.

Blake threw his arms up into the air, a primal yell coming from his chest and throat. Starla shrieked, and Nash next to her whistled through his teeth. Everyone cheered and clapped, and Blake turned just as Gina ran into his arms.

He lifted her right up off her feet, the two of them laughing and laughing.

"That's gonna put them in…" Todd paused while he did some math, checked times, and did whatever Todd did to calculate the family placements. He looked up, his eyes smiling. "We need to finish the other two games first. Then I'll figure it out."

"What does that mean?" Gina asked as Blake set her on her feet. She met his eye, concern in hers.

"Don't worry, sweetheart," he said. "We'll definitely not be in last place, and that was your requirement, remember?" He bent and picked up the single red bag his father had thrown. "Let's see how Starla's doing."

His adrenaline continued to pump through his veins as he watched Jesse and Starla toss their cornhole bags, and he found himself watching his brother more than the game. He wasn't sure he'd ever seen Jesse this calm during the family cornhole tournament, and Blake had for sure never seen him smile so much when bags slid off the platform.

For Starla, though, Jesse only seemed to have smiles. He leaned down as shoes and boots crunched over gravel to gather bags, and whispered to Gina, "I think Jesse might have a crush on Starla."

Gina leaned in to hear him, and then she shook her head. "Nope," she said.

"How do you know?"

"Wrong brother," she said. "That's how I know."

Blake immediately started looking around at the siblings and other cowboys and employees gathered to watch the last two games. None of his brothers even looked at Jesse and Starla as they played Nash and Ashley. Each team kept bouncing back and forth into the lead position until Jesse and Starla only needed one more point to win.

"Drumroll," Blake called as Starla held one bag in her hand and studied the cornhole platform across from her. Nash, who'd been playing the whole time on the same side as Starla, chuckled and grinned at her, but he didn't join in the drumroll.

Blake's smile widened, because he'd just spotted the brother who had a crush on Starla. His mind riddled with confusion, because Nash also had eyes for Ashley. Pieces clicked into place a moment later when Starla launched her corn bag, because Nash had always been indecisive.

He probably liked Starla for her mad skills in the kitchen, but he was physically attracted to Ashley because she was younger with a lot of blonde hair.

The crowd roared again, and Blake tore his eyes from his brother to the other end of the cornhole pitch. He couldn't see what had happened, because Jesse was already running toward them, and he did the same thing Blake had done to Gina: He picked Starla up and swung her around, the two of them laughing.

Nash stood on his side of the board, applauding while Ashley joined him at a slower clip than Jesse had. "Congratulations," he said good-naturedly, and he hugged both Starla and Jesse.

Starla turned to Gina, and the two of them squealed. "You were right," Starla said, and Blake patted her awkwardly on the shoulder too.

"Congrats, Starla."

"Thanks."

"What was I right about?" Gina asked, linking her arm through Starla's. To think she'd been nervous to work for the woman only a few months ago.

"Cornhole is fun," Starla said with a glint in her eye that said more than that. Unfortunately, Blake didn't speak Female super well, and especially Non-Verbal Cue Female.

"It is," Gina agreed, grinning far too much for what Starla had said.

"Okay," Todd said, coming through the crowd. "I've got the new leaderboard." He waved everyone out of the way to the pole that held the leaderboard, which stood about ten feet high. "In first place, we've got Holly and Sierra."

Everyone clapped, and both Holly and Sierra did some ballerina move though neither of them had taken a dance lesson in their life.

"Then Adam and Lowry," Todd said to more applause. From there, it was Monday Mack and Little Nick, Nash and Ashley, and then Todd and Kyle.

"In sixth place, we have making a big comeback from last week, Blake and Gina."

Gina curtseyed for everyone, which drew some laughter, and Blake simply welcomed her back to his side and pressed his lips to her temple. Such a feeling of contentment and adoration filled him, and he wondered if that was what love felt like.

He'd thought he'd been in love with Mari Lucas, but he'd been dead wrong about that. He knew what familial love felt like, and he knew how fond he was of his horses and Azure. But Gina?

He honestly didn't know.

Sammy Boy and Baby John took seventh place, and Todd said, "Jesse and Starla are in eighth."

"Yes!" Jesse high-fived Starla, and the two of them could've lit the whole lodge by themselves that evening.

"Which leaves Mama and Daddy in last place," Todd said, finally looking up from his clipboard. Along with everyone else, Blake looked at his parents. Daddy grinned like he'd won the lottery, and Mama patted her hair in a nonchalant way that made Blake shake his head and smile.

"Don't be expectin' any favors in the next round,"

Mama said loudly, to which most people laughed. The crowd started to disperse, and Blake moved with them, Gina right as his side.

They separated themselves from the others slightly, and she leaned into him. "Am I a bad person for being glad we beat your parents?"

"Totally," he joked. "I mean, my daddy is what? Sixty-eight? You're lording your victory over an old man."

Gina giggled and stepped in front of him. "Thank you, Blake. Really."

He gazed down at her, wondering what about him had caught her attention. "For what?" he asked, taking her easily into his arms. The rest of the family and guests kept moving, leaving the two of them alone in front of the lodge.

"For practicing with me this week," she said.

"Do we still need to do that?"

"I think so, cowboy." She grinned at him and reached up to tap the underside of his hat. "Sixth is good, but I think we can do better."

"Monday Mack and Little Nick should be our next target," Blake said, watching the two cowboys enter the lodge. "Or Todd and Kyle. I think we can crack them."

"So..." Gina fiddled with the buttons on his shirt near his throat, sending a thrill through Blake he couldn't contain before it shivered out of him. "Tonight? We can practice at my place."

Blake looked down at her, his pulse blipping out a bit of surprise. "You have a cornhole set at your place?"

She dug her toe into the gravel, making a grinding sound. "I maybe bought one to practice with."

Blake blinked and then he burst out laughing. "Gina, you're...amazing." He leaned down and kissed her, meaning every syllable of that word. She was amazing, and he found it amazing that she let him kiss her.

She broke the kiss too soon, her giggles getting in the way. Blake didn't mind, because things were going so well with Gina right now. He let his mind look forward, and all he could see was her and him and the family they could build together. He'd longed for that family, and he didn't want it with anyone but her.

Maybe he did love her, but he wasn't going to say it until he was sure.

————

A WEEK PASSED, THEN TWO. THREE, FOUR, AND BEFORE BLAKE knew it, the Fourth of July sat right around the corner. The Texas Longhorn Ranch went all out for the patriotic holiday, and they held a huge Texas-state celebration at the same time.

Local vendors, food trucks, and celebrities traveled to the ranch for a four-day celebration that usually sold out the lodge, the cabins, and the nearby hotels in town. Everyone at the ranch had been working extra hours for a week, including Blake and Gina.

He needed a break. He kept telling himself he'd get it as soon as July fifth came, and he could hold on until then. They had a parade to get through, a dog show, the chuckwagon dinner, two talent contests, four nights of concerts, and then of course, the fireworks show that drew the whole town of Chestnut Springs out to the ranch.

Blake sat at his desk one afternoon, reaching for handful after handful of sour candy to keep himself awake and working, when his phone rang. A number sat there he hadn't attached to a name, but Blake didn't hesitate. It wouldn't be ranch business, and his number got passed around town sometimes.

"Hul-lo," he said after answering and tapping on the speaker button. He then went back to the schedule in front of him, wondering why Todd needed him to double-check this. Sierra should be doing this kind of thing, as Blake barely knew all of the things they needed to do on the ranch to be ready for Independence Day.

"Is this Blake?" a woman asked.

"Yes," he said.

"Blake Stewart?"

He looked up, cocking his head as he tried to place the tone of voice. She sounded familiar, but he didn't talk to her every day, he knew that. "Yes," he said again.

"This is Ella Tillon."

Ella Tillon, he thought. *Ella Tillon?*

"I'm Gina's sister," she said. "Ella Barlow."

"Oh," he practically yelled. "Sure, of course. How are you, Ella?"

She exhaled in a very long hiss, clearly telling him she wasn't well. Adrenaline spiked through him, but not the good kind where he'd just sunk a cornhole. He and Gina were in third place now, and they wouldn't be budging

Adam and Lowry or Sierra and Holly. The two of those teams had gone back and forth from first to second, and Blake had told Gina that third was their number one.

"I hate to do this," Ella said, and she sounded sincere. "I'm wondering if you can…come into town for the holiday?" Now she sounded unsure, maybe even a little hesitant.

"What?" Blake asked. "For the Fourth of July?"

"Yes," Ella said. "I know Gina works out there, and that takes a lot of her time, but she moved back here to help me with our parents, and well, she hasn't. She's always out there. She does everything with your family, and…my parents feel neglected. Like they're not good enough." She took a breath, as she'd been speaking very fast. "They would probably come out there, but Gina hasn't invited them, and well, I don't know what to do. So I'm calling you."

Blake leaned back in his chair, the wheels squeaking as he did. "I…" He had no idea what to say. He supposed Gina did spend a large percentage of her time out here at the ranch with him.

No, he thought. *All of it.* She spent *all* of her time out here with him, and he hadn't even considered her family in Chestnut Springs. Guilt gutted him, and he turned away from the open doorway like he could escape it that way.

"Y'all are absolutely welcome out here," he said, his voice gruff. He tried to clear away the emotion. "I know it wasn't Gina's intent to exclude you. Any of you. Mine either."

"I know," Ella said, her voice half made of relief and

half of defensive dignity. "Are there enough tickets for us? I have three kids, my husband, and my parents."

Blake swung around in his chair and started making tally marks as she kept talking. "Then there's Brody and Kit. They're coming from San Antonio, and you know, my brother never leaves the city. They have three kids too. So that's ten people."

He'd noted the same number. "I'm sure it's fine," he said. "Which events do you want to come to? All of them? Some? It's a four-day extravaganza."

"My folks won't stay up for the fireworks," she said. "But Brody and I would love to bring our families."

"Sure," Blake said. Fireworks were easy, because they didn't have assigned seats. There were no tickets; anyone could come and spread out on the ranch and watch the night sky light up in red, white, and blue.

"The chuckwagon dinner?" Ella asked, and Blake swallowed hard. "My parents would love that, and they want to see you. Meet you again."

"I've met them," Blake said, now on the defensive. "Loads of times."

"But not for a while," Ella insisted. "It's like Gina's hiding you from us. Or she's withdrawing from us all over again, just like she did before she left town after high school." She continued to talk, and Blake agreed with whatever she said.

Part of him had gone cold. Had he really prevented Gina from spending time with her family? Was she preparing to quit her job here and leave Chestnut Springs again?

He hated all these doubts inside him, but he didn't know how to answer them adequately enough to get them to quiet.

The call with Ella finally ended, and Blake looked at his chicken scratched notes. He suddenly had six more problems to solve before bedtime, and the biggest one was where to seat ten more people at the Friday night chuckwagon dinner when they'd been sold out for months.

CHAPTER
EIGHTEEN

Gina put the last two blueberries into the blue rectangle she'd reserved for the top left corner of the American flag. Her back ached, as did her head, and she wasn't going to be able to feel her fingers for a good, long while.

She'd ice them once she cleaned up her station, and she'd eat something real instead of fruit and cake—all she'd eaten in the past twenty-four hours—and she'd take a healthy amount of painkillers before she collapsed onto the couch in Blake's office.

"Done," she breathed as she stepped back from the cake. She only had one more insane day to prepare desserts for, but tonight's chuckwagon dinner had definitely stretched the kitchen to the maximum.

Starla had been barking for a week, and everyone kept their heads down and their hands busy. Which was why no one congratulated her on the biggest flag cake she'd ever made. It was just another task that needed to be done.

Later tonight, it would be cut into four hundred individual squares and fed to the ticket-holding people at dinner. The red, white, and blue frosting hid a delectable chocolate cake, and Starla and Nash had assigned no less than ten cowboys to scoop ice cream from huge barrels that had arrived earlier that day.

Gallon upon gallon of root beer had been purchased as well, and anyone could have a root beer float after dinner. Kyle had arranged for Chip and Threat Gunnison to perform that night, and Gina couldn't wait to see the country duo sensation on stage. She'd heard their show was spectacular, and the way Blake had talked about how picky they were being about their special effects, she believed the rumors.

"That's beautiful," Ashley said, coming up beside Gina. "Great job, Gina."

"Thank you," she said, sighing. "Where are we? Who needs help with what? I'm done with my last thing for today." She looked around the kitchen, which still bubbled and boiled with activity though breakfast had ended long ago. The room was usually cleaned and cleared by now, with the dinner crew coming in about three to finish the prep work the breakfast crew had started that morning.

Now, it seemed like the kitchen here at the Longhorn Ranch ran around the clock, and Gina knew they all needed a break.

As she looked around, she caught sight of Nash exiting Starla's office, his neck flushed red. The color moved up into his face, and he looked into the kitchen before ducking out the back door. He *stomped* his way outside, and Starla filled the doorway, watching the direction he'd gone in.

She faced the kitchen, and Gina saw the discontent before Starla wiped it away. Their eyes met, and Gina raised her eyebrows. The black plastic door opened, drawing her and Starla's attention there.

Jesse entered, and he made a beeline for Starla and her office. The two of them disappeared inside, and Starla actually closed the door behind her.

"Wow," Ashley said, twisting to look at Gina. "What's going on with them?"

"Nothing," Gina said, turning back to her messy station. "Help me move this cake, would you?"

Ashley didn't answer, but she did move to help Gina pick up the huge board on which she'd layered the cake. Only two layers, but the cake along with the board weighed too much for the two of them. "Martin," she said. "Can we get some help getting this into the walk-in? I already have a spot cleared."

The cook nodded and wiped his hands. He said something to the cook next to him and then joined Ashley and Gina. The three of them stutter-stepped the cake into the fridge and around the corner to the rack she'd prepared, and Gina admired it one more time while the others left.

The door opened again, and Starla said, "Jesse, I'm not telling him that."

"You need to," Jesse said, and Gina pulled in a slow breath and held it. "Starla, he has to know already." The level of tenderness with which he spoke made Gina want to disappear into a puff of smoke.

"Then why do I need to tell him?" Starla sounded small and wounded, and Gina had never seen her like that. Jesse didn't answer, and Gina ducked her head. She expected to see the two of them caught in a glaring contest, but instead, she found Starla in Jesse's arms as he kissed her.

She gasped, immediately pressing her palm over her mouth. She had to get out of this fridge right now. She pressed her eyes closed and pretended to be feline, thinking that if if she couldn't see Jesse and Starla, they wouldn't be able to see her.

The door opened, and someone said, "...pudding in here. Just a sec." Footsteps sounded, and then Ashley said, "Starla, don't we have more banana pudding?"

"Yes," Starla said, her voice far lower than normal. Scuffling and movement echoed through the fridge, and then to Gina's great relief, everyone exited the walk-in. She breathed out, her breath hanging in the air in front of her, and sagged against the wall behind her.

Her phone rang, and she fumbled to get it out of her apron pocket. If that had happened while Starla and Jesse were kissing... She didn't even want to think about having to face the two of them. That would be like staring straight into a category five tornado and expecting to live.

Ella's name sat on the screen, and Gina swiped on the call. "Hey, El."

"Gina," her sister chirped. "Brody just got into town, and we're wondering if you want to meet us at the downtown park to go around with the kids as they do their carnival activities."

"Uh." Gina looked toward the door, her internal body temperature starting to chill. "I'm still at work, and the chuckwagon dinner is tonight."

Ella stayed silent, and Gina waited for her sister's displeasure. "I'm sorry," she said. "I am planning on seeing you guys at 'the breakfast tomorrow morning. You're still coming out here for that, right?"

"No," Ella said, the word more like a shout. "We're coming to the chuckwagon dinner tonight. Momma then wanted to go to the fireman's breakfast, which we've done for decades. It's family tradition, and you're part of *our* family, Gina."

She blinked, unsure of why Ella sounded so venomous. "I...well, I have to work tomorrow morning, Ella."

"Ask for it off."

"There is no way I can do that." Gina left the walk-in fridge, glad she'd given the others some time to vacate the area. She didn't need Jesse or Starla seeing her coming out of the fridge mere moments after they'd been kissing inside.

She went through the kitchen and out of the black plastic door, saying, "You guys are coming to the chuckwagon dinner? Since when?"

"Since I called your boyfriend and told him we needed tickets." Ella spoke in her high-and-mighty voice, and Gina came to a complete stop.

"You didn't," she said. Her chest hollowed, and her blood turned icy. "Ella, tell me you didn't do that."

"I did," Ella said. "I've been telling you for weeks that you need to spend more time with Momma and Daddy. They miss you. I miss you. My kids miss you. You moved back here to help, to spend time with us, and we see you less now than we did before."

"I—that is *not* true." Gina's chest heaved, because she couldn't quite remember the last time she'd gone to her parents' house for longer than a half-hour. She'd taken her dad a carton of eggs and a gallon of milk earlier this week, but she'd been on her way to work, and her mother hadn't been out of bed yet.

Helplessness filled her, and she turned in a full circle, trying to find the right answer. Ella kept yapping in her ear, lecturing her about her neglect, and that she might as well go back to Houston to make her fancy-pants desserts.

"Dallas," Gina whispered, but that didn't stop Ella. Her restaurant had been in Dallas, not Houston. She also couldn't stand to continue to be yelled at by her sister. "Enough," she said, snapping her eyes open. "Okay? I hear you. Okay?"

Ella panted on the other end of the line, and Gina's shoulders straightened and then slumped. "When will you be at the park?"

"We're leaving in fifteen minutes," Ella said, her dignified voice back in place.

"I'll find you," Gina said, and then she ended the call. She glanced around the dining room, expecting everyone in the vicinity to be looking at her, sorrowful looks on their faces for the way she'd been utterly humiliated and dressed down by her sister.

No one looked her way at all, and that only made her tears burn hotter. She spun toward the administration hall and marched that way. Blake knew her family was coming for the chuckwagon dinner and he hadn't told her? Why not?

He stood in the employee break room, talking to Adam and Kyle, all three of them sipping coffee and eating the extras from breakfast. He looked over to her upon her entrance, his smile disappearing in less than a breath.

"What's wrong?"

"My family is coming to the chuckwagon dinner?" She copied Nash and did the stomping as she approached him. She folded her arms and stopped in front of him. "When did that happen?"

Blake slid a look to Kyle and Adam and put his hand on her elbow. "Let's talk outside."

"Yes." She pulled her elbow away from his touch. "Let's." She ignored Adam and Kyle as she went by them, and Blake came with her. Outside, Gina breathed a little easier, but her step didn't slow as she practically ran toward the picnic table.

Nash sat there, and he turned as Gina and Blake approached. He didn't look happy either, and Gina had enough room inside her heart to feel bad for him. He clearly liked Starla, and yet Starla and Jesse had been kissing in the walk-in. Life and relationships could be so complicated sometimes.

"More than sometimes," she muttered to herself.

"Thanks, Nash," Blake said, and they'd clearly had a

conversation she'd missed. Nash left, and Blake faced Gina.

"Okay, look," he said. "Ella called me a few days ago, saying that...she wanted tickets to the chuckwagon dinner."

"You tell me everything." Gina whipped the words at him, and Blake reached up and rubbed the back of his neck. Instant regret lashed at her, and she sighed. "I'm sorry, Blake. Please tell me what she said."

"She's worried that you came home to help, but you're not helping," he said, blurting out the sentence. "She says you never visit your mom and dad. You don't invite them to anything, and they wanted to come out here for the dinner. I gave them tickets. I invited them to everything. I thought she'd tell you."

Gina searched his face, which held anxiety and compassion at the same time. "I..." She threw up her hands, spun, and went around the picnic table. She stood on the other side of it, next to the bald cypress, and looked out over the ranch. "I don't know what to do."

"She thinks you'd rather be part of my family than yours." His footsteps came closer, and Gina craved his presence in her life.

"I would," she whispered, looking at him as he joined her at her side. She put her fingers in his and held on as tightly as she could. "The truth is, Blake, I like being here. I love your siblings. I love this job. I love this ranch." She looked up at him. She didn't—couldn't—say *I love you*, but the more time she spent with him, the more she fell in love with him.

"My family is…boring," she said. "Ella is bossy, and Brody is like a stranger. I do love their kids, but again, it's like I barely know them."

"Yeah," Blake said, and then he let a few seconds pass. "You barely knew me or my siblings when you got here. You *get* to know them."

Gina sniffled, the things she needed to acknowledge foaming inside her. "My mom is sick," she whispered. "I don't know how to be around her anymore. It's like…all I can see is everything I've missed by leaving years ago, and I don't want to see them."

Blake put his hand around Gina's waist and pulled her into his body. "I know, sweetheart." He didn't tell her it would be okay. He didn't say she'd find a way to make things right. He didn't try to give her advice about what to do.

He simply held her while the sun shone brightly over the Texas Hill Country. While life went on, and the earth continued spinning on its axis, and while her heart throbbed out painful beat after painful beat.

When she started to cry, she turned into his chest, and he hushed her and stroked her hair. He let her cry as long as she wanted, and then he pushed her hair back and asked, "How can I help you?"

"They're going to the park this afternoon," she said, wiping her face. Crying made everything in her head hot, and she certainly didn't need more heat during a Texas July. "They want me to come. I'm going to go."

"Okay," he said.

"I guess we'll be back for the chuckwagon dinner," she said. "I'm going to sit by them."

Blake gave her a soft smile. "Okay."

"Will you come sit by us?"

"Yes," he said. "As much as I can. Sometimes there are minor emergencies I can help with."

"If you can," she said, tipping up to touch her mouth to his. "Thank you, Blake."

"Of course, sweetheart," he murmured. Then Gina turned and walked away from him while he still stood under the bald cypress. Layer upon layer of guilt stacked on top of one another as she drove from the ranch to the downtown park to meet her family.

She knew how to make cake layers stable, how to cement them together so the masterpiece she'd spent hours on wouldn't collapse, and as she parked her car and looked out the windshield at the activities and children in the park, she had a feeling that she'd never be able to knock down the walls of guilt forming inside her.

"What do I do?" she prayed to know. How did people balance their relationships with their family obligations? Gina had never been very good at balancing, and the truth was, she *would* rather be with Blake's family.

She had things in common with Holly and Sierra, and she liked listening to Kyle talk about the band members he knew. Todd had a way with animals, and he had a kind heart that Gina had seen several times.

The stormier brothers—Adam and Jesse—smiled when she entered a room, and Nash told her every single day that the ranch was better because she'd come to work there.

In her family, all she saw was ruin and missed opportunities. No one ever asked her about her job or expressed gratitude for the desserts she brought to family dinners. Her mom barely remembered that Gina was back in town, and Ella had been lecturing and making Gina feel insignificant and not good enough since she was twelve years old.

"You can still apologize," she said out loud, and then she cut the engine and got out of the car to go do exactly that. She did love the Stewarts, because she felt like she belonged with them. They'd accepted her and taken her right into their midst, but that didn't mean that Gina couldn't try to get along with her siblings and spend more time with her parents.

She could. She would. Starting today.

CHAPTER
NINETEEN

Todd whistled for Azure to leave the cows where they were, and the dog came trotting toward him. "Good boy," he said, bending down to pat the blue heeler. "Let's go see what Kyle has for dinner."

If Todd was lucky, there would be food in the cabin. He and Kyle—and everyone on the ranch—had been working long hours this summer. Kyle's summer concerts had begun, and that meant he worked late nights, every single night.

There definitely wouldn't be food at the cabin, and Todd pulled out his phone and tapped to call his brother.

"Yeah, go," Blake said instead of hello.

Todd's hunger almost had him barking back. "Dinner tonight? What are you doing?"

"It's pizza night at the lodge," Blake said. "I meant to send a text about that, and I've been up to my eyeballs in guest requests. I haven't been in my office for hours."

Todd wouldn't go to the lodge right now then. "Wow, I'm sorry," he said.

"Where are you?"

"Heading in from the pastures," he said. "Azure and I got the fences fixed, all the pastures rotated, and the sprinkler programmed." He'd rather work out on the farm, even if the jobs never ended, than deal with people and their demands.

He swung into the saddle on Bronco, the horse he'd ridden out to the fields and pastures that day. "Do you need me at the lodge?"

"No," Blake said. "Just one moment, ma'am." A couple of seconds passed, and then Blake said, "Actually, maybe. There's something going on with Nash and Jesse, and Adam just broke up what was a near-fight."

Shock coursed through Todd. "Really? Nash and Jesse?" He got Bronco moving, but he didn't spur him to go very fast. "Cornhole?" His brothers also shared an office, and sometimes they grated on one another's nerves.

"I don't see how," Blake said, his voice dropping in volume. "Jesse and Starla are no threat in cornhole. The girls are going to win anyway."

Todd didn't mind doing the family tournament, but he didn't take it as seriously as some of his other siblings. "Besides, it's Adam who's the most intense about cornhole. He broke up the fight?"

"Near-fight, but yes." Blake let out a sigh. "Something's going on there, but I've asked both of them about it, and neither of them will say."

Jesse acted as the second at the lodge, so Todd certainly

LOVING HER COWBOY BEST FRIEND   **203**

couldn't advise Blake about what to do. He realized as he plodded along that Blake didn't need professional advice. He needed a brother for support. He needed an ear to vent to.

"I'll come over," he said. "See what I can do."

"Holly bustled Jesse out of the lodge, so it's diffused now," Blake said. "I just wish…I know we're all busy, and I'm trying not to be a jerk or whatever, but we need to get along."

Todd cocked his head, trying to hear the true meaning behind Blake's words. "How's Gina?"

"Fine, I guess," Blake said, sighing again. "She's never here anymore, so…fine, I guess."

Which meant that Blake wasn't fine. Todd had seen the shift in him since the Fourth of July, but once again, he didn't know how to help Blake with this particular ailment. "You're still dating, aren't you?"

"Yes," Blake said.

"Maybe you load up some pizza and drive in to see her."

"I don't have time for that," Blake said. "Kyle cut his forearm, and Daddy took him in to the clinic, so I have to introduce the band tonight."

Todd heard all of the stress and frustration in his brother's voice, and an idea sprang into his mind. "Okay," he said. "I'll get the pizza from the lodge and bring it to your house. You sound like you're out of the spotlight for now, so get out of there while you can."

"I can't—"

"Yes, you can," Todd said firmly. "I'm on my way in,

and I'll get the food and see you at your house in half an hour." He didn't leave any room for argument, and thankfully, Blake didn't try to give one for a second time.

"Good," Todd said. "I'll see you in thirty minutes." He made it back to the stable, brushed down Bronco and put the horse away, and then started toward his office. He could spare a couple of minutes to change his boots and wash his hands.

He entered his office and forgot everything he had yet to do that night at the mere sight of Laura standing behind his desk. His pulse boomed in his ears as he asked, "Laura?" He scanned the desk in front of her, but nothing seemed out of place. "Is everything all right?"

"We have a handful of chickens with fowl pox," she said. "I wanted you to know. I also checked all the dairy cows today, and they look great."

"Okay," he said, not sure how to talk to this woman. She'd been at the ranch for a couple of months now, and Todd's attraction to her hadn't lessened at all.

"I was just sitting here for a minute," she said, offering him a weary smile. "It's been—I haven't been sleeping super well, and my feet hurt."

He started toward her, and she edged out from behind the desk. "I know the feeling." He gave her a warm smile. "Sit. I don't care. I'm going to change my boots and wash my hands. Then I'm going to get dinner at the lodge. It's pizza night. Blake meant to text everyone."

Laura sat back down in his desk chair, and he wondered if her perfume would linger in the leather after she left. He gave himself a mental shake, because she didn't wear perfume to come to work on a ranch. If she did, it would be long gone by now.

"Do you stay for dinner here?" he asked, taking a seat on the bench against the wall. He pulled off his dirty boots, his toes getting instant relief. "I don't see you."

"Not usually," she said. "I've been nursing a couple of sick kittens for the past couple of weeks."

"No wonder you aren't sleeping," he said with a smile.

She returned the gesture. "I took them back to the vet this morning," she said. "So I'm planning to take something to help me sleep tonight since I don't have to be here until afternoon tomorrow."

"You're still good to run the milking demo?" He reached under his bench and pulled out a fresh pair of boots.

"Yes, sir."

He chuckled and shook his head. "Don't call me sir."

"Sorry, sir." She laughed too, and Todd dared to sneak a peek at her. She sure seemed like she was flirting with him, but he wasn't entirely sure.

"If you don't have the kittens tonight," he said, his throat dry as cotton by the end of that sentence, and he still had more to say. He cleared his throat and busied himself with pulling on his boots. "I'll get you a whole mess of pizza too, and you can join me for dinner."

Todd got to his feet but couldn't look at Laura. He stepped over to the tiny sink in the corner of his office, his back to her now. "I'm takin' dinner to Blake too. You're welcome to join us."

"The two of you?"

"Yep." He washed his hands, really soaping up and scrubbing up to his elbow before rinsing the day's work from his skin. He turned, and Laura stood only an arm's length from him, holding a towel.

She extended it toward him, and transfixed by those beautiful eyes, Todd took it. "Thanks," he murmured.

Laura's eyes fired emotion at him, but Todd wasn't sure which one. "I'd like to eat with you," she said, taking a step closer. "Is Gina going to be at Blake's?"

"I doubt it," Todd said. "She's been heading back to town to help with her momma."

Laura nodded. "Maybe another time then." She stood right in front of him, and she made no move to leave his office.

Todd's thoughts raced, trying to calculate the probability of kissing her right here, right now. If he did that, she'd know he'd been crushing on her—hard—since he'd met her. He reached up and ran two fingertips down the side of her face.

Laura didn't flinch and she didn't move. Todd watched the progress of his touch, the softness of her skin sending desire through him like lightning.

"Todd," Sierra said, and his hand dropped to his side.

"Yeah." He turned that way.

Sierra looked at him with both eyebrows raised, her gaze switching to Laura behind him. "Have you got a minute?"

"Not really," he said. "I'm taking dinner to Blake, and he's not in great shape." He silently begged Sierra to drop this. Leave it. "Can I text you later?"

"Yeah," she said slowly, her eyes sweeping the rest of the office. "Azure, come on, bud. You can't get up on my desk." She marched over to the dog, who carried a bright blue ball in his mouth. She took it from him and put it back on her desk. "That's not for you."

Properly scolded, Azure flopped to the ground, his tongue hanging out of his mouth.

Sierra tossed Todd another glare like it was his fault the blue heeler had an obsession with balls. "That's my therapy ball."

"Yep," Todd said.

"Tell Blake to call me," Sierra said. "I want to talk to him about the harvester."

She walked toward the door, and since the office was barely big enough for the two of them, she'd left already when he said, "You're not getting that harvester."

"Have him call me," she yelled back to him, and Todd shook his head and sighed.

"We don't have the money for a new harvester," he grumbled to himself, finally facing Laura again. He didn't know how to describe the moment that had been broken by Sierra. He swallowed, his throat working through how to say what blistered his mind.

"You sure you don't want to come to dinner tonight?"

"I'm sure," she said.

Before he lost his nerve, Todd asked, "How about this then? How about you and I go to dinner sometime?"

"Just the two of us?"

His fingers squeezed into fists. "Yes," he said. "Not

here at the ranch. Somewhere in town." He absolutely needed a whole bottle of water to say another word.

Laura's mouth twitched into a smile. "Are you asking me on a date, Todd?"

He blinked and swallowed simultaneously. "Maybe," he choked out. "If I was, would you say yes?"

Laura reached up and trailed her fingertips down the side of his face. His eyes drifted closed, and he realized that he'd given away too much by allowing himself to do that.

He opened his eyes again and looked straight into Laura's. "Laura, I'd love to take you to dinner off the ranch sometime. Maybe when things aren't so crazy around here." Which was never, but Todd could hope, pray, and dream.

Her hand fell back to her side, and her eyes searched his. Then she said, "I'd like that, Todd."

He grinned at her and said, "Great. Yeah, great." Pure relief rushed through him, almost making his knees weak.

"Great," Laura repeated, and then she moved to leave the office. "See you tomorrow, Todd."

"Yeah, tomorrow," he said. Laura left, and he stood there staring at the empty doorway, wondering what alternate reality he'd entered—and if the ranch had any rules or paperwork about dating an employee.

He could ask Blake about it tonight, over pizza, from the privacy of his brother's cabin.

CHAPTER
TWENTY

B lake finished a third piece of pizza, his stomach finally starting to feel full. Todd had shown up ten minutes ago with more food than the two of them could eat that night, but Blake liked leftover pizza straight from the fridge.

Eating cold pizza as he walked from his cabin to the lodge made happiness flow through him, but even pizza and sunshine couldn't replace the hole in his heart that widened with each passing day where he only saw Gina for a few minutes.

He'd tried calling her at night, but he couldn't predict where she'd be, and she sometimes sent him straight to voicemail with a quick, *I'll call you later.*

Later didn't come, and he'd see her the next morning only if he dared to poke his head into the kitchen after he'd eaten breakfast. The chefs didn't come out and eat with everyone else, but took a break after everyone else had eaten.

She did still sneak away with him at lunchtime, but she literally set a timer for thirty minutes and enforced her departure strictly. She did have a lot of cakes, pies, bread puddings, and more desserts to make.

He simply missed her. He wanted to be first in her life, and the fact was, he wasn't.

"It's fine," he muttered to himself, because he wasn't going to be the cowboy-jerk who demanded his girlfriend choose him over her aging parents and exhausted siblings. Every time he thought of Ella and heard her desperate voice, his guilt reappeared.

"You okay?" Todd asked, and Blake looked up.

"Yeah," he said.

"You forgot you weren't alone." Todd grinned at him and took an enormous bite of the ham and sausage pizza.

"Maybe," Blake said with a half-smile. "I am used to being alone at night."

His brother nodded as he chewed. After he swallowed, he asked, "Do you think things will balance out?"

"I sure hope so," Blake said, getting up to put his plate in the dishwasher. "This summer has felt intense, hasn't it?"

"It has," Todd agreed. "I'm not sure why."

"Gina's…competitive." Blake flipped on the faucet and looked out the window. The land spread before him, and the sight of all the green and then the blue above it soothed him. "I'm more intense when I'm with her. The cornhole with Sierra and Holly and Adam and Lowry—there's a lot of tension there."

"Then Jesse and Nash," Todd said. "You can feel it when you walk inside the lodge."

Blake turned back to him, leaning his back against the countertop. "That's not good."

"It's fine," Todd said. "I think the guests categorize it as excitement. Life."

The ranch had always possessed this electric power of life, and Blake hadn't had to work very hard to create that. Adam worked hard to provide authentic animal experiences for their guests, and Kyle outdid himself with every concert that got played at the Texas Longhorn Ranch.

The food coming out of the kitchen had never been better, and all of their activities filled every single day. Things were going so well at the lodge and ranch that Blake expected them to crash and burn at any moment now. He knew better than most that good things didn't stay that way forever.

"You sure you're okay?" Todd asked.

"Yeah," Blake said. "I'm just tired. Another month, and school will start again. We'll be less busy here. Maybe Gina won't have to sit with her parents every night."

"Have you asked if you can go sit with her?"

Blake gave his brother a hard stare. "No," he said. "Even if I did, she'd tell me no. I don't have time either." Blake hated the concept of time. He wished it didn't waste away as easily as it did, and he wished he could freeze it for the time it took him to drive to Chestnut Springs. If he could work during the drive, that might influence his decision to go or not.

"No, I know," Todd said. "I was just wondering. I'm not saying you're doing anything wrong, Blake."

"I feel like I am," he said, the dam of emotions he'd been holding back by sheer will threatening to break through his strongholds.

"Tomorrow night, give me anything you don't have done by five-thirty that has to be done, and go see her. Don't ask her. Just show up and sit with her and her parents if that's what you have to do."

Blake considered the idea. "I could answer emails on my phone."

"Yep," Todd said, stretching to reach for another piece of pizza. "I can see your mind working."

It was, yes. Blake didn't like this walking-on-eggshells feeling. He didn't want to have to ask permission to see Gina. He wanted to support her as she went through this trying time, and he did feel like he'd simply taken a step back.

She hadn't specifically asked him to do that, but that was the vibe he got from her whenever he offered to drive in dinner or have something delivered. She always said, "No, Blake, it's fine. I have something here," or "You don't have time for that, and I'd hate to make you come all this way."

He'd let her put him off, and perhaps he shouldn't have done that. "What time is it?" he asked.

"No idea," Todd said around a mouthful of cheese, crust, and pepperoni.

Blake turned and looked at the clock. It was after six already, and he didn't have time to go implement Todd's plan right now. He should think more about it anyway and really make a plan of his own before he just showed up on her mother's doorstep.

"All right," he said. "Thanks, Todd."

"Sure," he said. "I'll work on Nash and Jesse too." He dusted his hands of the cornmeal and finished his last bite of pizza. "Now, I have something I have to tell you, and I'd really like it if you didn't tell anyone else."

Blake found his old smile as it slid into position on his face. "Oh, I can't wait to hear this."

Todd shook his head, no smile or laughter in sight. "It's not gossip. It's…" He cleared his throat, his neck turning a shade of auburn Blake hadn't seen in a while. "I asked Laura to dinner."

Blake blinked, trying to figure out who Laura was. "Laura…the vet?"

"Yes," Todd said, his voice stuck way down in his throat.

"What did she say?"

"Is there some rule against me asking her out?" he asked.

"Rule?"

"Yeah, like a ranch rule. Companies have relationship rules and stuff. HR departments. That kind of thing."

Blake kept staring at him. "Todd," he said with a laugh in his brother's name. "This is a family ranch. There is no HR department."

"So I can go out with her and be her boss?" Todd

cocked his head, his frown growing deeper. "What if she claims I did something inappropriate? Or fears she'll lose her job if she doesn't go out with me?"

"Did she say she wouldn't go out with you?" Blake folded his arms, because the world wasn't always as simple as he imagined it to be.

"No," Todd said.

"She said yes."

"Yes."

Blake grinned at his brother. "Then I don't think we need to worry too much, Todd. Go have fun. Heaven knows one of us should be seeing the woman they like."

"Yeah," Todd said almost absently. He took off his cowboy hat and ran his fingers through his hair before he looked up at Blake with new clarity in his eyes. "By the way, I don't really believe what you just said."

"Why not?"

"You don't just like Gina, Blake. You're in love with her."

"No," Blake said, though he wasn't sure why he was denying it, especially to Todd. "Fine," he amended. "Maybe a little."

Todd laughed this time, the sound rich and full and filling the kitchen. "Can you be a *little* in love? I thought it was kind of like bein' wet. You're either wet or you're not. There's no in between."

"Oh, that's so not true," Blake said. "You can be damp. Clothes can be *almost* dry."

"If they're not dry, they're wet," Todd said, getting to

his feet. "Come on, that alarm on your phone's been goin' off for a good minute at least."

Blake reached for his phone, which lay face-down on the island where he'd been sitting to eat. He hadn't even heard the buzzing of the alarm, which told him it was time to leave the cabin and get over to the stage so he could introduce that night's band.

Todd walked with him over to the lodge, where they loaded up into a golf cart to go out to the huge open-air barn with a professional stage under the roof. Cowboys and cowgirls were already directing traffic and managing the parking situation, and Blake saw good people everywhere he looked.

"This is an amazing place," he said, wishing Gina was there with him. She'd told him she did love his family and want to spend time with them over her own, and a pang of sadness that she couldn't have that hit him right in the breastbone.

"It is," Todd said. "That it is."

Blake felt like he belonged right here, on this ranch and this land. He simply wanted Gina at his side forever and always, on this ranch and this land. He pulled behind the barn where the trailers and private area for the band had been set up, and he parked the golf cart thinking, *You'll make a plan, and you'll figure out how to get her back where you want her…and where she belongs.*

———

Blake peered through the windshield as he turned into Gina's parents' driveway. Her car sat there, and he pulled behind it. An empty lane ran up to the garage, which stood open to reveal the tools, boxes, junk, and the single car parked inside.

His chest tightened, and he tried to take a big breath to get it to expand. He'd texted her forty-five minutes ago to tell her he was on his way. She hadn't responded.

He told himself it would be fine, that she'd probably be happy to see him. She'd told him that afternoon that she appreciated him, and that seemed like a big thing to him. He wanted to be the anchor in a stormy sea for her and dealing with her parents was difficult for her.

Other than a few other sentences at lunch that day, Gina had been very quiet. Blake had let her eat and think about whatever she wanted, and he'd held her hand and walked her back to the kitchen door. He'd kissed her on the steps, and her job had stolen her away from him again.

He got out of his truck and turned back to get the plastic bag full of food he'd gone to town to get. The walk to the porch almost felt like walking toward a cliff, and Blake pressed his eyes closed as he raised his hand to knock on the door. Gina had told him the doorbell didn't work, and he mentally kicked himself for not bringing batteries to fix it.

Voices from the other side of the door met his ears, as well as quite a bit of barking, and Blake backed up a step. It took at least a minute for Gina to open the door, and when she did, she didn't smile and immediately invite him in. "Blake," she said, her eyes dropping down to the food he held. "What are you doing here?"

A little black and white dog that wouldn't hurt a fly peered up at him too, and Blake felt very on the spot.

"I texted you," he said, lifting the food. He'd gone to her favorite Tex-Mex place and gotten the sweet pork burrito she loved. At least she'd used to love it, and Blake's panic reared and splashed against his heartbeat. "I brought dinner, and I thought I'd just...do whatever you're doing tonight."

"I'm cleaning my mom's fridge."

Blake suddenly smelled the scent of bleach with a slight tang of lemons. "Okay," he said. "That's fine."

"We ate already."

"Then I can put this in the newly cleaned fridge," he said, his frustration starting to grow.

"Who is it, dear?" Sarah Barlow edged in next to Gina, who glanced at her. "Blake Stewart." Sarah gave him the smile he wished Gina would've and beckoned to him. "Come in, come in."

"Mom," Gina said, but Blake wanted to come in.

"I'll make coffee." Sarah turned and moved away from the door, the little dog going with her. He clearly belonged to her, and he wasn't that interested in Blake.

"You can't make coffee, Mom. I'm cleaning the pot," Gina called after her before turning to look at Blake.

He raised his eyebrows, not sure what would come out of his mouth if he spoke.

"Come in, I guess."

"Don't sound so excited about it," he said, stepping

past her. The house smelled like mothballs and old yarn, and Blake took in the living room, where Gina's parents obviously spent most of their time.

A hutch held all the yarn Blake could smell, as well as dozens of blankets that had been folded and stacked lovingly. A recliner sat next to a coffee table piled high with books, and her father obviously sat there.

"I haven't been here in forever," he said.

"It needs some work," Gina said from behind him.

He turned and looked at her. "Is this the worst thing imaginable? Me coming with dinner and to keep you company? Heck, you can even put me to work."

She softened, and Blake was glad he'd taken a moment to calm himself before he spoke. "No," she said. "It's not the worst thing imaginable." She nodded toward the wide, arched doorway that led into the kitchen. "That fridge is the worst thing imaginable."

A girl about ten years old appeared in the doorway. "Aunt Gina," she said. "Grandma went outside."

"Through the door or out to the sunroom?"

"The back door."

"Thanks, Daph." Gina brushed by Blake adding, "Put the food down, Blake, and come help me."

"Okay," he said, hurrying after her as she broke into a jog when she entered the kitchen.

"Mom," Gina called.

Blake paused to look at the little girl. "Where can I put this?"

"The kitchen is a mess," she said. "I'll take it to the

sunroom." She took the bag, her arm muscles straining against the multiple meals Blake had brought.

"Thanks," he said, entering the kitchen. He paused again, because it looked like a bomb had gone off. Two buckets sat on the floor; the kitchen sink overflowed with Tupperware and dishes; the table was covered with canned and boxed goods. Every cupboard door stood open, and they'd all been emptied.

Blake couldn't believe this was what Gina had been doing after work at the lodge. Pure exhaustion moved through him at the thought. An additional dose of guilt hit him hard, making swallowing difficult, and as she called for her mom again, Blake got himself moving toward the back door.

Outside, Gina had her arm linked through her mother's, and she was trying to turn her around. Blake went down the wooden steps from the small back porch, the whole structure swaying. No wonder Gina didn't want her mom leaving through the back door.

The sunroom sat to his right, and Gina's dad called, "Sarah, come get dinner."

Blake went across the lumpy lawn and arrived at Sarah's side, exactly like her little dog did. He met Gina's eyes, and she looked one breath away from crying. "Come with me, Sarah," he said. "I brought tacos."

Sarah Barlow looked at him, and her face lit up. "Blake Stewart," she said. "I haven't seen you in a while."

"I know," he said easily, though she'd literally seen him two minutes ago. "I brought your favorite—grilled chicken tacos. Aren't you hungry?" Gina dropped her mom's arm as Blake took over. He walked her in a wide arch while Gina stood in the same spot, her face hard and unyielding.

Blake kept talking to Sarah, telling her all about the new things at the lodge. He probably could've told her about the old things and she wouldn't have known. He took her to the steps leading from the sunroom, which didn't shake and wobble as they climbed them together.

"What's your dog's name?" he asked.

"Fox," she said, clear as anything.

"Thank you, Blake," Gina's dad said, smiling at him when they went inside the screened sunroom. "Look, Sarah. Blake brought dinner. Isn't that great?"

"It looks wonderful," Sarah said, allowing Blake to help her into a chair at the white metal table. "Daphne, dear, can you get the lemonade out of the fridge?"

"It's right here, Grandma," Daphne said, indicating the glass pitcher of pink lemonade in the middle of the table. She pulled out the last container of food and popped the lid. "This one is a burrito."

"That one's for Gina," Blake said. He looked through the screens and found her walking away from the house at a pace he'd have to run to catch up with. He didn't know what to do. Go after her? Sit down and eat with her family?

He hadn't known Daphne was here, and he'd brought four meals. Ben, Gina's father, put the container of tacos, refried beans, and Spanish rice in front of his wife. "This one's for you, dear."

"Thank you," she said.

"I got the burrito for Gina," Blake said. "Anything else is fair game."

"Thank you," Ben said with another wide smile as he took a container with shredded beef tacos. "Are the nachos okay for you, Daphne?"

"Yeah, I love nachos," Daphne said. She smiled at her grandfather and then Blake. "Thank you, Blake. This is real nice."

"You're welcome," he said, smiling back a her. She belonged to Ella, and Blake was glad he'd been able to help this family tonight. He looked back outside, and Gina had disappeared somewhere. "I'll take this out to Gina." He picked up the burrito, a set of plastic silverware, and a napkin. "We'll be right back."

"I'll make coffee," her mom said, and Blake didn't wait around to hear who would tell her that she couldn't make coffee because Gina was cleaning the pot. He left and went in search of Gina, praying he could find her quickly.

CHAPTER
TWENTY-ONE

G ina stomped through the weeds growing along the property's edge. The Allens behind her parents' house owned a small farm, but they hadn't kept it up for years. If she just kept moving, she wouldn't start crying. She wondered if she could walk and walk and walk until she simply collapsed from exhaustion.

She'd rather do that than go back to her parents' house and face the situation there. For the first week or two, she'd simply sat with her mom and listened to her talk as she knitted. She'd make dinner or bring a cake, and they'd sit in the sunroom. She'd tell them about her day and all the guests who came through the lodge, and she'd do the dishes.

"I don't know what to do," she said, her voice pinching as her emotions finally overcame her.

She'd mowed the lawn a few times, and that had been terribly difficult for her. She was used to being on her feet, working all day, but pushing a mower through shin-high grass, emptying that bag, and seeing all the work the yard needed had been too much for her.

Last week, she and Ella had sat down with their parents and gone over their finances. They had enough money to hire a landscaping company to come take care of the yard, and Gina had made the calls, met with the manager, and gotten her parents on the schedule. With that burden eased, Gina had turned her attention to the house.

Namely, the kitchen.

Simply sitting around and listening to the same stories over and over drove her crazy. Ella had agreed to send over one of her kids every day after school, and together, Gina worked with them to get something cleaned up or repaired. She had enjoyed getting to know her niece and nephews better, and she took pride in knowing that she was helping her parents and Ella at the same time.

"You're not a good daughter," she said next, because she hadn't even seen these needs until Ella had called Blake and told him how neglectful Gina had been. She hadn't meant to be; she didn't know how to deal with her mother's health challenges, and she'd been running from hard things like that her whole life.

Just like she was running from Blake right now.

She hadn't seen his text, but if she had, she'd have tried to get him not to come. Not because she was embarrassed of her parents. Not because she didn't want or need his help. Not because she didn't crave his presence in her life.

But because she didn't deserve it. Her selfishness had

been plaguing her for weeks, and she couldn't find a way to move past it.

"Gina," Blake called, and she spun back to him. He jogged through the thigh-high weeds, carrying an aluminum container that made her stomach roar. To add to her humiliation and unworthiness, she'd lied to him.

"Hey," he said, panting as he approached. He wore anxiety in his expression, and Gina couldn't handle making him feel that way.

She burst into tears, and Blake said, "Okay, come here." She didn't know what he did with the container, but he did take her into his strong arms and hold her close. He didn't try to shush her or reassure her, but he simply let her cling to him and let all of her unhappiness come out of her body.

After a few minutes, he stroked her hair and said, "Talk to me, sweetheart."

She released him, and he stepped away from her. He didn't let go of her completely, and Gina liked that. "Why are you here?" she asked.

"I miss you," he said. "I had no idea you were over here cleaning every night after the crazy days we have out at the lodge." He wore a frown above his eyes, and he indicated the house somewhere behind them. "I would've come to help. You don't have to do this alone."

"I do though," she insisted.

"Why?" He searched her face, and Gina didn't like how heavy his eyes landed on hers. "Why are you punishing yourself like this?"

"Because," she said, exhaling as a hiccup blipped through her chest. "Because I've never taken care of my parents. I'm literally the most selfish person alive, and I—I—" She didn't know how to explain a lifetime of her inadequacies to him. "I need to help them."

Blake dropped his hand from her arm. "That doesn't mean you have to do it alone."

"I feel like I do."

"You're not the most selfish person in the world."

"I feel like I am."

"Is Ella saying that?" he demanded. "Because that's not true, Gina. It's absolutely not."

"Ella doesn't need to say it," Gina said, looking down at her feet. "It's just true." She looked up into Blake's eyes. "I lied to you about dinner."

"I know," he said. "They're all eating, Gina. They just said thank you and dug in." He bent and picked up the aluminum container. "I brought you a sweet pork burrito."

She took it from him, her smile threatening to break through the sadness on her face. "Thank you," she whispered.

"I need you to tell me why you wanted to send me away," he said.

Gina turned and spotted a rickety fence. She took a few steps and sat on the top rung of it. "Because," she said with another heavy sigh.

Blake joined her and handed her a package of plastic silverware. "Because why?"

"Because I don't want you to see how pathetic I am."

"You're not pathetic."

"I don't know how to make time for you—us—and help my mom," she said, opening the lid. The spicy scent of the Tex-Mex food made her mouth water and her stomach roar. "I know I'm not being a good girlfriend, but it feels like if I am, then I'm not a good daughter. I don't know how to be both."

Blake didn't say anything, and Gina unwrapped her plastic knife and fork and cut off the corner of the burrito. "Did you get your nachos?"

"I gave them to Daphne," he said. "I didn't know she was here, or I'd have gotten her something."

"I didn't see your text," she said, then put a delicious bite of food in her mouth as she looked at him.

Blake nodded and looked over the dilapidated land and buildings surrounding them. "Gina, I...I don't want to make you feel like you're not being a good girlfriend. I don't care about that. I just..."

"You do care about that," she said. "We don't spend hardly any time together anymore. I know that. I feel it. There's this distance between us, and I don't like it, Blake. I don't." She focused on her food again. "I just don't know how to fix it."

"You could not lie to me."

She couldn't defend herself, so she didn't.

"You could let me bring dinner every single night," he said. "I'd help with the chores too."

"I don't want you to," she said.

"Why's that?" he asked. "We'd be able to see one another. Talk. Spend all that time together. I could get to know your nieces and nephews and your parents. You wouldn't have to do everything alone."

"I like—" She cut off before she could admit she liked

feeling powerful and like she'd done something all by herself.

"I know what you were going to say," he said.

"No," she said.

"I do," he said. "You were going to say I like doing things alone." He shook his head, obviously irritated. "I know you, Gina. You're independent and strong. I like that about you, I honestly do—except for in times like this."

He jumped down to the ground and turned back to her, dusting his hands together. "It feels like you're pushing me away on purpose. So you sit there and you cry and you say you're selfish, but it's not that. You say you've put distance between us, but you don't know how to fix it. You do, though. You just don't want to, because you're too proud."

Gina glared at him. "I'm not the one who needs help."

"Aren't you?" He cocked his head at her, his eyes narrowing slightly. All of the scrutiny dropped from his face. "You're the one who said you wanted to be in love with your best friend. This is me trying to be your friend, and you don't seem to want it. It's not about me being upset that you're not a good girlfriend—which *isn't* true." He folded his arms and gave her glare right back to her.

"A *friend* would come sit with you while you cleaned. They'd work alongside you. They'd bring dinner and offer all the coffee so you don't have to shoulder everything alone."

Gina's throat constricted, and she didn't know how to answer.

Blake shook his head, his frustration overflowing from him and filling the air around them. "All right, I've said everything I need to say. Enjoy your dinner." He turned and started back through the weeds.

Stunned, Gina could only watch him for several long seconds. Then she jumped down from the fence too, saying, "Blake, wait."

He'd gotten too far from her, and he didn't turn back. She followed him, silently, until they got back to tamer land. He moved faster than her, and she stayed by the back shed with her amazing burrito as Blake went up the steps and into the sunroom.

The screens blurred the scene, but she clearly saw him hug her mom, shake her dad's hand, and grin at Daphne. Then he left. Just like that, he left.

The sound of a truck engine filled the air from the front of the house, and then it drove away. Gina stood by the back shed, unsure about what to do now. Her pulse started to race through her body, because things between her and Blake had been tense before.

"Not tense," she said. "Stale. Distant. You've been distant with him." A relationship couldn't grow and bloom with a thirty-minute lunch each day, where she barely spoke. Now, though, she had no idea if she and Blake even had a relationship anymore.

He hadn't said he wanted to break up, and Gina looked up into the perfect summer evening sky. "I don't want to lose him."

Then don't. The words entered her mind in a whispered voice that could've belonged to anyone.

You're too proud streamed through her head as she

walked back to the house. *Aren't you?* he'd asked her when she'd said she wasn't the one who needed help.

In the sunroom, her family ate merrily at the table, and she sat down with them. They talked, and Gina listened while she ate. Back in the kitchen, with the mountain of work in front of her, Gina could acknowledge that yes, she very much needed help.

———

THE TEXAS LATE-SUMMER HEAT ASSAULTED GINA AS SHE LEFT the kitchen, her grab-and-go lunchbox in her hand. The picnic table wasn't empty, and while she'd go sit by Starla, she really wanted to be headed to Blake's.

They hadn't talked about lunch specifically, because they weren't talking right now. The day after he'd brought dinner to her parents' house, he'd texted her to say he had a meeting in town during lunch, and that had been the end of their lunchtimes together.

Only a few days had passed, but they felt like a lifetime to Gina. She could construct anything out of cake and frosting, but she didn't know how to build a bridge back to Blake.

She walked past the barns and across the gravel to Starla, sighing as she sat next to her on top of the table.

"Hey," Starla said, her voice far too nasally to be allergies. Starla didn't have those anyway. "You're here again."

"Yep." Gina opened her box to the croissant sandwich, potato salad, mint brownie she'd made herself that morning, and bag of veggies and ranch.

"Still not talking to Blake?"

"Who said I wasn't talking to Blake?"

Starla gave Gina a pointed look, her eyelashes clearly wet as she hadn't wiped her eyes yet. "Please," she said. "Everyone knows." She lifted her croissant to her mouth and took a bite.

"Well, that doesn't make me feel better about it," Gina said sourly. She stared at the bald cypress, the memories on the other side of it like poison in an already-open wound. She didn't feel like eating, and her lunchbox sat on her lap, open but untouched.

"Join the club," Starla said. She took another bite of her sandwich, sniffling as she did.

Gina set aside her own relationship problems and linked her arm through Starla's. "I thought Jesse was coming over last night."

"He did."

"And?" She was still crying, so it couldn't have gone well.

"And I don't know," Starla said in a whisper. She leaned her head against Gina's shoulder, and it just became the two of them there on that picnic table. "Things are very complicated between us right now."

"I'm sorry," Gina said. "What can I do? I can talk to Nash. He's still talking to me right now. I'll tell him to get over himself, that he's worked with you for five years, and if he was interested, he should've said something *before* Jesse asked you out."

Starla gave a tiny shake of her head against Gina's arm.

"No," she whispered. "Don't say anything to him. It'll only make things worse."

Gina watched the wispy clouds move through the distant sky. She wished she didn't feel the same way, like life just pushed her around and she went with it. She'd hated that growing up, and she'd left Chestnut Springs to make her own way in the world. She'd wanted a life she had created, and she had it.

"Look at it this way," Gina said. "You've got two of the hottest cowboys in love with you."

Starla giggled and sat up straight. "That's not true."

"I think Jesse's good looks must've blinded you then. The man is seriously hot."

Starla met her eyes, a hint of her former happiness there. "I didn't mean to make a mess of things. I thought Nash was dating Ashley, and I just wanted to play cornhole with someone."

"I know, sweetie." Gina wiped her fingers across Starla's forehead. "You've got flour up here."

"I'm always draped in some food product," she said, wiping her face too. "It's a miracle all the dogs around here don't attack me twenty-four-seven."

They giggled together, and Gina sighed again. "I need to talk to Blake."

"Are you two playing cornhole in the morning? I think you could beat Adam and Lowry."

Gina shook her head. "I don't know. We haven't talked about it." She looked at Starla. "Are you playing with Jesse?"

Before she could answer, someone cleared their throat.

Both Gina and Starla whipped around, and Starla scrambled to the ground. Jesse stood on the other side of the table, both hands gripping opposite sides of the brim of his cowboy hat.

His dark-as-pitch hair grew wild under that thing, and Gina wondered how long he'd been standing there. She hoped not long enough that he'd heard her call him "seriously hot."

"Starla," he said, shooting Gina a nervous look. "Can I talk to you for a second?"

"Yes," she said, her kitchen manager voice fully employed.

"I'm done with lunch," Gina said, picking up her box and sliding to the ground. She looked at the full array of her food. "I mean, I'll go eat somewhere else." She flashed Jesse a smile as she went past him, but he only had eyes for Starla.

"Good luck," Gina whispered under her breath when she knew Jesse wouldn't hear her. She sincerely hoped he and Starla could work through whatever was keeping them apart.

She needed to do the same thing with her and Blake, and she took her lunch toward the barn where Todd kept his office. Maybe he'd have some ideas she could use, and Gina started wishing herself good luck too.

CHAPTER
TWENTY-TWO

Jesse Stewart nodded to his left, indicating that Starla should start walking that way. She did, and he quickly fell into step beside her. He couldn't believe he'd been so blind and so stupid. Him, one of only two of the Stewarts who'd been married before.

Honestly, his own inability to see a situation clearly was one of his major flaws, one he'd thought he'd gotten past enough to see his feelings for Starla clearly.

His feelings weren't the problem. It was that Nash had feelings for her too, and Jesse had stomped all over them.

"Are you going to say anything?" she asked, her hands tucked neatly into the front pocket of her apron.

"Yes." Jesse cleared his throat, still not sure what to say. He paused in the shade of a tree lining the drive that led back to the guest cabins. In the other direction, behind the new barns sat the family cabins, out of sight from anywhere in the lodge and concealed by plenty of trees from the road.

He lived back there, in a cabin with two bedrooms and two bathrooms. Adam lived down the hall from him, and they still kept their place clean with the aid of a chore chart. Mama was so proud.

He sighed out some of his frustration. "Starla, I don't know what to do."

"You can't pick fights with Nash," she said, "I know that much."

"For the record," Jesse said, his blood already heating. "He's the one who goaded me. Ask anyone."

She gave him a hard look that only made him like her more. "I'm not going to ask anyone. I *know* what happened. I was there."

Then she knew, and Jesse hadn't sought her out and taken her from Gina to argue about this again.

"I don't know how to say this." He moved around the tree trunk to the side in the grass. The view from here softened the world, something Jesse had often needed in his life.

"If you want to break-up—"

"I don't *want* to," he said, staring at the fields as they rolled along, getting broken up by trees and fences.

She leaned against the tree too, and her fingers tapped his. She linked her pinky finger in his, and said, "Just say it."

He looked at her, because he could be mature enough to do that. "I really like you Starla. A lot. But there's something inside me that won't stop whispering."

She nodded, but Jesse knew she didn't understand. He barely did. "What does it say?"

"It says that maybe I should've been more careful. Maybe I should've asked questions before I bullied you into the walk-in and kissed you. Maybe I should've read the signs better." He shook his head and jammed his hat back onto it.

Literally everyone in the Stewart family and who worked with Nash and Starla knew Nash had a crush on her. It sure did seem like the only person in the whole world who hadn't known was Jesse, and he'd kicked his brother in the teeth unknowingly.

"He's never asked me out," Starla said, peering up at him despite his cowboy hat. "He still hasn't, Jesse." She pulled her fingers away from his and looked away. "You don't want to break up with me, but you're still saying you are."

"I'm saying maybe it's not the right time," he said slowly, trying to measure out the words before he said them. "I think maybe...maybe you and Nash should see if there's something better between the two of you."

Starla scoffed, and Jesse understood that. "I'm not just going to run to him from you," she said angrily. "The staff already talks about me unfavorably. Can you imagine?"

"They all know about this whole fiasco already," he said, feeling his chest hollow out and go dead. "It won't matter." He'd felt like this after his divorce too. Like nothing mattered, including him. With the help of his brothers and sisters, a good therapist, and a more active role at the ranch, Jesse had made it through some harrowing times.

"I sure do like you," he said. "Maybe we could try again in the future?"

Starla nodded, her jaw set. He'd seen that fierce look on her face before, and it sure did make him smile. "Tell me you're not going to march over to Nash's and punch him in the nose."

"I'm thinking about it," she growled. In the blink of an eye, she changed from the strong, fearsome kitchen manager to the soft, beautiful woman Jesse had gotten to know that summer. She stepped in front of him and ran her hands up his chest. "Why does he get to decide?"

"He doesn't," Jesse said, not daring to move for fear that when he did, it would be to take her into his arms and kiss her again. "Star-sweetheart, you two work together. You have a long history. I have to work with him—heck, we share an office—and he's…"

"Your brother," she said at the same time he said, "My brother."

She looked away, her hands falling back to her sides. "I'm upset with him," she said.

"I know, but that'll fade."

"I don't want to go out with him."

"You might, though," Jesse said, reaching to guide her face back toward his. Their eyes met, and he searched hers. "You told me once, way before I started texting you and bringing you dinner, that you had a little crush on him. Remember?"

She nodded, her eyes so big and so wide. Jesse loved looking into them and reading Starla's true emotions.

"I'm not saying we can never be together," he whispered. "I'm saying I don't think it's the right time right now."

Starla closed those eyes, nodding still, and moved into his embrace. Jesse took a deep breath of her hair and skin, getting that soft cottony scent mixed with the savory scents from the kitchen.

She sniffled and stepped back after only a few moments. Not nearly long enough for him, but he could corral his emotions and box them up until the time was right. If it ever was. "We can still play cornhole tomorrow, right? We're in fifth place, and I bet we can beat Todd and Kyle."

Jesse smiled at her though it hurt to do so. "Of course."

She nodded just once and looked back to the lodge. "Jesse?"

"Yeah?"

She met his eyes again, that fierce, strong warrior-princess shining through. "I just want you to know one thing before you go."

He swallowed, hoping *he* wasn't about to get punched in the nose. "Okay."

She took a step toward him, and he pressed his back into the bark on the tree. "You did not bully me into the walk-in and kiss me."

"No, ma'am," he said.

"If I hadn't wanted to kiss you, I wouldn't have let you kiss me."

Jesse grinned at her. "No? What would you have done?"

"There was a huge bottle of mayonnaise nearby," she said. "I would've cracked that over your head and left you to freeze in there." She grinned at him too, and Jesse tipped his head back and laughed.

She laughed with him, but the sound of it quickly turned sad. Jesse's did too, and they sobered together.

"I'll miss you," he said.

"You still work at the lodge," she said. "So do I. I'll see you everyday."

He cradled her face in both hands. "It won't be the same."

"No," she said. "It won't be. It'll be okay, though."

"Yeah," Jesse said, dropping his hands. "It'll be okay. I'm sorry, Starla."

She gave him a smile that sent pain into his heart, because hers held pain. "Me too, Jesse." She drew in a deep breath and looked back to the lodge again. "Okay, I have to get back to work."

She walked away just like that, and Jesse turned and leaned against the tree to watch her. He should get back to work too, but instead, he waited until Starla had entered the kitchen. Then he pushed away from the tree and headed for the stables.

He could talk to a few horses first, and maybe he wouldn't turn into a beast the next time he saw Nash. "Promises, promises," he muttered to himself.

————

LATER THAT NIGHT, HE LOOKED UP FROM HIS POSITION ON THE couch when the front door opened. He ran a lot of the activities and operations in the lodge, but he still got home far earlier than Adam usually did.

Tonight, his brother walked in with mud splattered from head to toe, and Jesse flipped off the TV with, "I made Gramma's mac and cheese. There's lots." He stood and took in his brother. "What happened out there?"

"Burst pipe," Adam growled. "Right on the route for the carriage rides."

"Yikes."

Adam glared at him as if Jesse had broken the pipe on purpose with his bare hands. "I'm going to go shower."

"I can heat up one of those pretzels to go with the mac and cheese."

"Sure," Adam said, clomping down the hall in his dirty boots. He usually left them at the front or back door—same with his hat—but Jesse suspected he'd wash everything up in the bathroom instead of leaving mud all over the house. That, or he'd throw everything away and start fresh.

That was more Adam's mentality. If something didn't work out the way he wanted it to the first time, he'd cancel and correct, but he really struggled to try again. He hadn't dated at all since his divorce, nor had he attended therapy or talked to anyone in the family about it. Not even Jesse.

He sighed and started toward the front door to close it. August wasn't a month to be leaving doors open, that was for sure. He'd just put his hand on the knob when Nash said, "Hey, Jesse."

He froze from top to bottom, suddenly feeling naked in his T-shirt and gym shorts inside his own house.

Nash swept his perfectly clean cowboy hat off his head. "I talked to Starla a little bit ago."

"Good for you," Jesse said, his voice as even and emotionless as possible.

"She's not real happy with me."

"We should start a club."

Nash actually smiled as he dropped his head. He lifted it slightly, really pulling his eyes up to look at Jesse. "I'm really sorry, Jess. Honest I am."

The rigidity inside him bent. Jesse was three years older than Nash, and his younger brother had been annoying him since age ten. He always wanted to tag along with Jesse and Adam, the two brothers older than him. Only Sierra came after Nash, and he'd never wanted to spend his time with his sister.

"I know you are," Jesse said, sighing. He stepped back and waved Nash into the house. "We can't be coolin' the whole world."

His brother came inside, and Jesse closed the door behind him. "There's mac and cheese, and I'm going to heat up a pretzel for Adam." Jesse went past him and into the kitchen. "Want one?"

"Sure," Nash said. "I—you didn't have to break up with her."

"Didn't I?" Jesse asked, twisting to look over his shoulder. "What would you have had me do instead?"

Nash lifted one shoulder, and Jesse bent to get the pretzels out of the freezer drawer. He set the oven and got out a tray, all while Nash said nothing. Jesse supposed he'd come to apologize, and he had, so there wasn't much more to say.

Jesse put three of the top-knot pretzels on a tray and looked at Nash. "I'm sorry too, okay? I didn't know you liked her. Honestly, I didn't. Blake thinks I'm stupid that I didn't know, and Holly lectured me for a solid twenty minutes about how obvious you are and how insensitive I am."

"You're not insensitive."

Jesse wasn't going to argue with Nash about his faults. The truth was, he was a bit insensitive. He had a job to do, and feelings weren't required. In matters of the heart, though, he had to learn to listen to his feelings and pay attention to those around him better.

"If I'd have known, I wouldn't have started anything with her." He turned and put the tray in the oven though it wasn't preheated yet. Looking back at Nash, he pressed his palm to his pulse. "I apologize."

"Thank you," Nash said quietly. He still hadn't come any further into the cabin, and Jesse indicated the bar. He moved toward it and took a barstool. "I'm not going to ask her out."

"Yeah, I'd give that a while," Jesse said. "I think she actually liked me." He chuckled, but only for a moment. "You know why I broke up with her, right?"

"So I wouldn't attack you in front of guests?"

Jesse shook his head, listening to the shower whine down the hall. "You're my brother, Nash. I can't...I can't have bad blood between us."

Nash nodded, his eyes so trusting. In a lot of ways, he was more than three years younger than Jesse. He'd never been married. In fact, he'd never even been in a serious relationship. He viewed the world through a different lens, and Jesse wouldn't be the one to discolor his optimism and zeal for life.

He rounded the counter and cupped his brother's head in his hand, bringing Nash's forehead against his own. "I love you, brother," he said roughly.

"I love you too," Nash said back.

Jesse stepped back and dropped his hand. After clearing his throat, he said, "If you could let me know next time you have feelings for a woman, that would be great. Then I won't ask her out."

Nash chuckled then, and Jesse cracked a smile. "Will do," Nash said just as Adam bellowed for help from the bathroom.

Jesse jogged that way and opened the door a crack. "Are you dead?"

"There's no body wash," Adam called back. "Can you get me some? It's like a muddy river in here, and I have it between my blasted teeth."

"Yep," Jesse said, smart enough to keep his laughter contained until the body wash had been delivered and the bathroom door had been closed. Then he chuckled to himself about Adam's predicament.

Jesse didn't want to live with him forever, but for now, he could. He couldn't know what the Lord had in store for him, but for now, he could take life one day at a time. He wasn't sure if he and Starla would ever get back together, but for now, he could live with that.

Back in the kitchen, he said, "Starla and I are still going to play the last round of cornhole tomorrow. What tips can you give me on Kyle and Todd? There has to be a way to get past them."

Nash grinned at him and leaned forward. "Kyle gets really rattled when it's too quiet…"

CHAPTER
TWENTY-THREE

Blake approached the front door of his childhood home, the noise coming from inside enough to make him pause. He should just go back to his cabin. If he did that, though, the party would move from this house to his, and he couldn't have that.

He continued across the porch and opened the door. Half of the people inside immediately stopped talking and the other half roared with welcome. Todd and Sierra rushed him, both of them hugging him at the same time while they clamored over his appearance.

Annoyance sang through him, and he frowned as he hugged his siblings. They stepped back and Kyle said, "Come get some of this cheesecake. It's phenomenal."

"Did Gina make it?" Blake asked, because he didn't want any if she had. He hadn't spoken to her for four very long days, and his patience with the whole situation was about to snap.

"No," Todd said. "Daddy ordered it from New York City."

"He knows it's a family breakfast, right?" Blake asked, but he couldn't stop the tide. Everyone who'd been lying in wait for his arrival in the living room pressed him into the kitchen, where his mother gave him a wide smile and reached up to hug him.

"Cheesecake," Holly said, handing him a plate with a delectable piece of cheesecake with whole blackberries decorating the top. His mouth did water, and Blake had never said no to dessert for breakfast.

"The bread pudding French toast will be ready soon," Mama said. "You boys get the table set." She started handing plates and utensils to her sons, and Blake dutifully did what she asked him to do.

"Are you ready to lose later today?" Adam asked Holly, who immediately scoffed.

"We're in first place, buddy-boy," she said, practically slamming the juice glass on the table. "Not only that, but you and pretty-boy Lowry haven't been able to unseat us for three weeks in a row."

"Fourth time's the charm," Adam said, his smile more predatory than playful.

"It's third," Kyle said from down the table. "*Third* time's the charm."

"Yeah," Sierra said, grinning as she put the salt and pepper shakers on the table. "Besides, Blake and Gina are so close to you, they might even take over second place."

All eyes swung to him, plenty of them with questions. He didn't confirm that he and Gina would be playing that day, because he honestly didn't know if they would be or not. He hadn't asked her about coming to the final round of the family tournament. She hadn't reached out to him at all.

He drew in a deep breath and continued putting out plates. He didn't have to tell his siblings anything about his personal life. If he could just make it through this family breakfast and then the tournament—and then the next three weeks until summer ended and families returned home so their children could go back to school—he might be able to pick up the pieces of the past few months and put them back together.

"Fresh juice," Daddy called, breaking the silence that had fallen over the dining room table.

"Great," Jesse practically yelled, tearing his eyes from Blake. "Come on, guys. Let's get our glasses full of this fine, fresh-squeezed orange juice."

Blake ducked his head and smiled, grateful for Jesse's attempt to get the attention off of him. Todd stood right beside Blake while a few others also made a big deal out of their daddy's new juicer, which could take the pulp right out of citrus fruits.

"You okay?" Todd asked.

"I'm still breathin'," Blake muttered.

"French toast," Mama said. "Adam, come get this bacon. Holly, put the butter and jam on the table. Nash, why are you riding that broomstick? Stop it."

Blake chuckled then, because meals with his whole family—all ten of them—could be loud and obnoxious. He did love spending time with them, and he had a relationship with each of them in a unique and different way.

Nash put the broom in the corner and grinned at Blake, who hadn't left the table to get juice. "Hey," he said, glancing at Kyle. The smile slipped from his face as he took in the hustle and bustle in the kitchen.

"Everything okay with you and Jesse?" Blake asked.

"Yes," Nash said with a sigh. "He broke up with Starla."

Blake nodded, because he'd heard. News traveled fast around the ranch, and faster through the family gossip grapevine. "As long as she doesn't quit, you don't punch him, and we don't lose him back to that end cabin where he doesn't talk to any of us for weeks," Blake said. "I don't much care what happens."

"She's not going to quit," Nash said.

"Jesse's here," Todd added.

Blake looked between the two of them. "No punching?"

Nash chuckled and shook his head. "I can commit to no punching."

"Great," Blake said as Daddy raised both hands above his head and started calling for silence so they could pray.

"Are you going to call Gina?" Nash asked.

"Go get her," Todd said. "You guys are in third place, and you really could beat Adam and Lowry."

"Why doesn't anyone want Adam and Lowry to win?" Blake asked.

"Your memory must be lacking," Todd said dryly just

as everyone finally stopped talking. Everyone looked at him, so he zipped his lips and didn't finish his thought.

Blake swept his cowboy hat off his head along with everyone else, and Daddy started to pray. Blake's heart pounded as he thought about calling Gina after the silence they'd put between them. He couldn't even imagine what she might say to him.

He felt like he'd laid everything out while he stood out in the weeds with her, and she hadn't said anything at all. She'd let him walk away from her, and she hadn't texted or called or stopped by his office or anything.

The prayer ended, and Blake stuffed his cowboy hat back on his head. He'd call after the family breakfast. Yes, that was what he'd do.

———

An hour or two later, Blake stood between Todd and Jesse, the two brothers who'd been at his side since the fallout with Gina. He hadn't exactly broken up with her, and she hadn't left town this time. His heart still hurt as he stood in the morning sunshine and waited for Todd to start the last round of the tournament.

Everyone would play this morning, and he shouldn't have eaten so many slabs of French toast. His stomach held bricks, and he glanced over to the lodge to see if Gina was coming. She'd worked the breakfast shift in the kitchen this morning, just like she usually did.

Instead of Gina, he found Starla hurrying toward the

cornhole area, and he touched Jesse's arm and nodded toward her.

"Praise the heavens," Jesse said, leaving Blake's side to go greet Starla. He'd seen them embrace and laugh before, but this morning, Jesse simply went to her, then turned and the two of them walked side-by-side back to the game-play area.

Starla looked at Blake, and he suddenly had so many questions. Starla shook her head, and Blake nodded. He had to accept that he and Gina weren't going to play this morning, and they weren't going to have any sort of future together.

Not even friends? he asked himself, and the helplessness and desperation he'd become well acquainted with over the past few days welled in his already full stomach.

Todd met his eye too, and said, "We've got to start, Blake."

"I know," he said, the words scraping his throat. "Go ahead. She's obviously not coming. We'll forfeit this round."

Todd wore a sympathetic look and took the microphone from Nash.

"Go get her," Jesse growled out of the corner of his mouth.

"I don't see how that will work," Blake said back. "Have you met Gina? She's stubborn and fierce when you try to boss her around." He glared at Jesse. "Just ask Starla."

"He's right," Starla said as Todd started announcing the first wave of players. "She has to come to him."

"Then text her and apologize and beg," Jesse said.

"He doesn't have anything to apologize for," Starla said, looking at Jesse and then swinging her gaze to Blake. "Don't do that. It'll only make her feel even more stupid. *She* knows she needs to come to you."

"Why won't she do it then?" Blake asked.

"Like you said," Starla said as her name and Jesse's was announced. The crowd cheered and Starla raised her hand in a friendly wave, the strength in her eyes melting into friendliness.

"Come on," Jesse said. "We're down here." He moved away, but Starla looked back at Blake.

"She's proud, and she's trying to figure out how to swallow that. It's a big bite, you know?" Starla nodded, her eyes earnest and sincere, and then she followed Jesse.

His name hadn't been announced as a forfeit, and Todd returned to his side. "I bought you however long it takes for this first wave of games," he said. "If she's not here when it's your turn to play whoever wins out of the girls and Adam and Lowry."

"Thanks," Blake said, the word barely leaving his mouth. He looked back to the lodge, but the only people he saw were guests coming to watch the tournament.

He didn't care about the leaderboard; he wanted Gina.

She cared about the leaderboard though, and Blake wondered if he could lure her out of the kitchen with the idea that they might be able to take second place.

He shook his head at himself. He didn't want Gina to come play with him because she might get second place.

He wanted her to come, because she wanted to be with him.

He folded his arms and watched Starla and Jesse play Todd and Kyle. He clapped on every good throw, no matter who launched it. He couldn't pick who he wanted to win the match, because everyone in it had been a great support to him the past few days. Longer than that too.

In the end, Starla and Jesse won, and she whooped as she ran across the distance to Jesse. He lifted her right up off her feet, both of them laughing, and Blake caught the way Jesse's eyes drifted closed in bliss.

His brother had shown strength and maturity by putting family above Starla. Blake wasn't sure he agreed with Jesse's decision, but he could respect it. He sure didn't want to get between Nash swinging his fists again, that was for sure.

"All right," Todd said. "We're going to do some quick calculations, and then we'll start the next round."

Holly and Sierra had beaten Adam and Lowry, so now it would be up to Blake and Gina to take their second place from them. Holly and Sierra had won the whole thing, and a large group of people surrounded them.

Blake didn't look toward the lodge, and instead, moved toward Adam. He didn't look happy, but when Blake told him he'd have to forfeit and they'd still get second place, that should cheer him up.

"Next round," Todd bellowed into the mic, making Blake cringe. "We've got Adam and Lowry in second place. They would play Blake and Gina, but they're going to have to forfeit."

All eyes moved to Blake, and he stood there, resolute. He should've slinked back to his office—or better yet, his cabin—so he wouldn't have to shoulder this humiliation in public.

"Wait," someone said, and his whole soul perked up. "We're not forfeiting."

He couldn't see Gina, but the crowd parted like Moses himself was coming through the Red Sea, and there she strode. She looked gorgeous, as always, her expression fierce and full of fire.

The closer she got to him, the more nervousness he noted. She went right up to Todd and leaned in to whisper something to him. He held the mic away from them, so Blake couldn't hear. He wasn't able to process much past the booming, echoing of his pulse anyway.

Todd grinned and passed the mic to Gina. She gripped it like she was trying to strangle the life out of it. Her eyes came straight to Blake's, and she took a deep breath as she lifted the mic to her mouth.

His heartbeat sounded like gunshots, and his fingers curled into a fist and released, over and over and over as he waited for her to speak.

CHAPTER
TWENTY-FOUR

Gina had done hard things before. Cleaning her parents' fridge had nearly brought her to her knees. She could tell Blake how stupid she'd been, beg for his forgiveness, and kiss him in front of all these people.

She could.

He took a step toward her, his expression full of compassion and love. He held up one hand and said, "You don't have to do this."

Gina took a breath and dove into the deep end. "I need you, Blake Stewart." He paused, his eyes going a bit wider. "I haven't wanted to admit it, because it made me feel weak, but that's just..." She shook her head, her eyes filling with tears. "I'm not weak because I need help sometimes. From my family, from my friends." She scanned everyone gathered there, catching Starla's eyes and watching her press a palm to her heart.

She looked back to Blake. "From you. You're my best friend, and I should be able to accept your help." She cleared her throat. "You're more than my best friend too. I've missed you *so* much the past few days, and I'm absolutely miserable without you in my life. I want to talk to you every morning, and sneak out to your cabin at lunchtime, and curl into your side at night."

Todd chuckled beside her, and joy filled Gina too. She looked only at Blake, who took another slow step toward her. A few more, and he could take the mic from her. The world beyond him swam, because Gina wasn't one to make big, personal speeches in large crowds.

"I want you to come read off the expiration dates on all those cans in my mom's kitchen, because no one should be eating those." She smiled at him, though he blurred through the tears in her eyes.

"I will," he said.

"I want you to bring burritos every night." Her voice broke, but she wasn't done yet, and she took another strengthening breath.

"Anything you want, sweetheart," he said, his voice low and gruff. Only three steps separated them now.

"I'd rather not forfeit, because I think we can beat Adam and Lowry, but this leaderboard doesn't mean anything to me without you. I'd rather be very last—way down at the bottom—than not put you first." She sniffled, as did a few others around her. She didn't know who; she could only see Blake.

He arrived in front of her, and she looked up at him

and lowered the mic. "I love you. I'm sorry I've been such a diva and pushed you away. I love you."

"I don't think we quite heard that," Todd yelled, taking the mic from her while Blake grinned at her, his joy and happiness blending with her own. She blinked, the tears running down her face now. "Why don't you say it again, Gina?"

Todd held the mic right in front of her face as Blake's big hands slid along her waist. She half-laughed and half-cried at this crazy family she so desperately wanted to be part of. She turned her head and said right into the mic. "I'm in love with Blake Stewart."

The crowd erupted into applause, and Gina laughed as she turned back to the cowboy who'd captured her heart. Not just once, but twice now.

He leaned down, kneading her closer, and whispered in her ear, "I love you too." Then he kissed her right there in front of everyone to much whooping and hollering—the kind only cowboys could do.

She could stand in his arms and kiss him forever, but he pulled away much sooner than that. He looked at Todd, and said, "I guess we're not going to forfeit."

Adam and Lowry groaned as loudly as the rest of the family cheered, and Todd said, "You're down on aisle two. Go on and get down there."

Blake held her hand and led her down to the cornhole platforms where they'd play. She snuggled into his side as Todd continued to announce the teams who'd be playing next. "Is it wrong of me to want to forfeit so we can just go back to your place?"

"Not at all," he said, peering down at her. He could make any moment more intimate by shielding them with the brim of that cowboy hat. "Do you want to do that?"

Torn, Gina looked to the leaderboard and then back to Blake. "Can I come over after this? Maybe stay all afternoon and into the evening?"

"You can stay forever," he murmured, placing a kiss against the side of her eye. Gina would like that, and she pressed her eyes closed and sent up a prayer of gratitude that she'd been able to get out of her own way for at least thirty seconds. That was all it had taken to get the words out and get Blake back.

As Adam arrived and handed Blake the red bags, Gina cleared her throat and her mind. It was game time, and that required a game face.

———

GINA LEANED INTO THE DOORWAY OF BLAKE'S OFFICE, grinning at him. He held up one hand as a signal that he'd be off the phone in a moment. "Yes, sir," he said a couple of times, clearly trying to hurry along the call.

He stood and leaned over. "I'll talk to you tomorrow." He practically slammed the phone into the cradle on his desk and looked at her. "Hey. What brings you by so early in the morning?"

Blake had stars in his eyes as he approached her, but he stilled the moment she held up the trophy.

"Are you behind this?" she asked, hoping her flirtatious teasing could be interpreted by the handsome cowboy.

"Maybe," he said.

She looked at it. "It's a coffee mug."

"I know what it is."

Her gaze locked onto his. "Mine's engraved with 'World's Best Girlfriend' inside."

"Is it?" he asked innocently. He turned back to his desk and retrieved something, then faced her again. He held an identical trophy cup in shiny, glittering gold, and he made a big show of examining every inch of the cup-slash-mug. "Huh. Mine doesn't have that."

"Blake," she said, laughing.

He chuckled with her as he approached. "I told Holly to get trophies for the top three teams. That's all." He wrapped her in his arms, and Gina never wanted to be anywhere else.

"You just didn't want Adam to sneak into your cabin in the middle of the night with shaving cream."

"I know how to sweeten up my brother," Blake said, grinning. "That's not a crime." He matched his mouth to hers, and Gina sank into the warmth and tenderness of his kiss.

"Some of us work here," Becks called, and Gina broke the kiss by ducking and burying her face in Blake's chest.

"Yeah, because I've never had to endure you kissing Luke," he called back.

By the time Gina looked, Becks had disappeared either into her office or down the hall. She looked up at Blake and flattened his collar from where she'd gripped it in her fingers. "Starla said she's making us a special lunch today."

"Is she?"

"You are so bad at playing dumb," Gina said.

Blake blinked innocently. "Am I?"

She laughed and ran her fingernails up the back of his neck. "My birthday lunch is going to be served at your house," she said. "At noon sharp."

"Perfect." He kissed her again but didn't carry on too long. "I'm bringing dinner to Ella's tonight too. Did she spill the beans about that?"

"Unfortunately, all of your surprises have been spoiled," Gina told him.

"Hmm," he said with a frown. "I need better accomplices."

She giggled and then gazed at him. "What kind of cake did you get me?"

"You don't know yet?" He mimed zipping his lips. "I'm not telling then. It might be the only surprise you get today."

"I don't really like surprises," she said.

"Don't I know it." He grinned at her. "Don't worry, Gina. I know what you like, and you're going to love the cake."

"Do I have to wait until tonight to have it?"

"Guess you'll find out," he said as his desk phone rang again. He twisted that way with a sigh. "Okay, I have a billion things to get done before noon." He released her and stepped away. "See you soon, sweetheart."

"Yeah," she said a little wistfully. She and Blake had

won their round of cornhole a little over a week ago. Adam and Lowry had not been happy, but Holly and Sierra had chanted and danced for a good minute before Blake warned them to stop.

Gina had spent every afternoon and evening with him, either here at the ranch or at her parents' place. Once, at her apartment while Ella went over to their mother's with her family and a full dinner.

School would start soon, and then Ella would be back to teaching. Her kids would all be in school next year, and Gina had decided she could find more balance in her life. No one had gone to sit with Mama every evening until Ella had called Blake and laid on the guilt. She didn't have to go every night, and she'd sat down with everyone who lived in town to make a schedule.

As she left Blake's office, a sense of pure happiness filled her. Not the kind she'd experienced when she'd landed a top position in a luxury kitchen. Not the kind she'd felt when she'd graduated from college with her pastry arts degree. Not even the kind she'd felt when she'd told Blake she loved him and he'd repeated it back to her.

No, this joy felt fuller and more real. It filled her from top to bottom and front to back, because Gina was happy with herself. She wasn't perfect, but she knew now that she could work on her flaws and make improvements, one day at a time.

That level of contentment and joy didn't come from external sources; it came from within her, and as she entered the kitchen to finish her morning baking, she thanked the Lord for leading her back where she belonged.

Home, here in Chestnut Springs.

"Gina," Starla barked. "Where have you been? Your timer went off, and we had no choice but to pull your bake."

"The timer went off?" Gina hurried over to her station, where Starla stood with some very brown peanut butter cookies. She looked from them to her boss and best friend. "I forgot about the cookies."

"Clearly," Starla said with that line of disapproval between her eyes.

"We can use them on the ice cream bar," Gina said.

Starla's eyebrows went up. "What ice cream bar?"

"Oh, please," Gina said with a giggle. "I know there's going to be an ice cream bar at Blake's house for my birthday lunch party." She rolled her eyes and shook her head like duh. "I'll crumble these up and you can pretend to sneak them out of the kitchen the way you have with everything else."

She reached for a cookie and had crumbled it to bits before Starla said, "It's confirmed, everyone. Gina has eyes in the back of her head."

The kitchen staff laughed, including Gina, and Starla stood at her side and broke up the over-baked cookies. "Happy birthday, Gina," she said.

"Thank you." She beamed at Starla. "Anything with Nash?"

Her friend's face turned a bit harder, and she shook her head.

"Want me to talk to him?"

"Only if you want to die."

Gina laughed again, and Starla even smiled. She paused for a moment, and then said, "What if Nash and I aren't going to be a thing?"

"What if?" Gina repeated, not following the question.

"Would I be terrible if I went out with someone else?"

"Why would that make you terrible?" Gina poured the mound of crumbs into a zipper bag. "You're single. You're allowed to date."

"Yes," Starla said. "I'm allowed to date."

"He hasn't asked at all?"

She shook her head. "I don't even know if I'd say yes."

"So asking him is out."

"Totally out."

"You don't like him?"

Starla sighed, the sound of a thousand years of oppression and irritation in the air. "I mean, I did. Once. Before he acted all psycho." She glanced over her shoulder. "He's cute. He's smart. I've always liked working with him." She attacked another peanut butter cookie, and Gina could only guess at what she thought it represented. By the way she mashed it nearly to dust, Gina guessed Nash's head.

"He just...I think he ruined it," Starla said. "I don't know how to get past that, and I miss Jesse."

Gina didn't know what advice to give her. Starla had been loyal and kind to her in the four or five days when she wasn't talking to Blake. She'd encouraged her to get over herself and talk to him before the cornhole game. She'd stood at the upstairs window and watched the first match, trying to find her courage and the way past herself.

In the end, she'd had to take a deep breath and take the plunge.

She did the same now. "Okay, so maybe you do what *you* want. You follow *your* heart, and if it's saying Jesse, who cares what anyone else says?"

They finished the cookies, and Starla looked at her again. Pure vulnerability swam in her eyes, and Gina wrapped her in a hug. "Come to the birthday party, and Jesse will be there. Then you can just see."

"Okay," Starla whispered. She stepped back and said in a much louder voice, "Now, get these made again, because we need them for the grab-and-go lunches."

"Yes, boss," Gina yelled, and Starla marched away like she'd suddenly joined the military.

Gina smiled to herself as she got started on a second batch of peanut butter cookies, her mind imagining the gift Blake might get her for her birthday—and it included diamonds.

CHAPTER
TWENTY-FIVE

Todd left his jacket hanging on the back of the chair. It wasn't cool enough to warrant wearing it yet, though autumn had arrived in Chestnut Springs and on the Texas Longhorn Ranch. A sigh of relief moved through him, though his work never really ebbed and flowed the way it did for those who worked in the lodge.

Animals always needed to be fed. Crops always needed to be tended to. Machinery was always breaking down.

Today, though, Todd wasn't going to deal with any of that. Today, Todd was leaving his cabin and going to one elsewhere on the ranch. He'd pick up Laura there, and their first stop of the day was brunch at The Sunflower Café.

He adored the eggs Benedict there, with country ham and an extra side of biscuits and gravy. His stomach hadn't been well for the past twenty-four hours, and he prayed he could calm it enough to eat by the time they arrived at the café.

"You're cool," he muttered to himself. Laura had seemed just as interested in getting together off the ranch as he was. They worked together well, and she'd brought up their date a couple of times before he finally picked a date and approached her about it.

Everything that was hard for him to say out loud was easy to text, and Todd had gotten the date on the calendar through typing instead of talking. Laura didn't seem to mind that, because they still talked plenty.

He saw her every day around the ranch, and he couldn't wait to see what she'd wear to leave it. His heart thundered in his chest, the kind of thunder that hung in the Texas sky and grumbled for a full minute. He'd probably need to have that checked if it continued.

Outside, Azure lay on the porch, and the dog got to his feet as Todd came near. "Morning, bud." He bent down and scratched Azure's face and head, all the way behind his ears. "You're gonna stay here today. You can get over to the barn and go out with Sierra. She's runnin' things today."

He'd had to tell his youngest sister about the date, but he hadn't disclosed who it was with. Sierra wasn't stupid, though, and she'd guessed Laura on the first try. He did share an office with her, and he did text Laura quite often from the safety of his desk.

"How did you know?" he asked Sierra.

"You smile when she texts," Sierra had said wearing her own smile. "It's cute. You clearly like her."

"Yeah." Todd hadn't seen any reason to deny it, and he told himself not to be too obvious as he drove past the family cabins and out onto the main ranch road. He went past the main lodge, the concert barn, the road out to the guest cabins, and finally turned onto another dirt road that led out to cowboy cabins. Two or three of them usually shared, and Laura currently lived with a woman named Josie Ross. She worked in the lodge as a Guest Relations Specialist, and she helped out in the evenings with any events that required parking or ushering.

Todd knew her well enough, as she'd been at the lodge about a year now. He pulled up to Laura and Josie's cabin, wishing he could see through logs. He couldn't, so he got out and made the quick walk up the steps to the door. He knocked, suddenly worried that it sounded too aggressive.

Only a few seconds later, Laura opened the door. "Howdy, stranger," she said with a wide smile. She wore a pair of clean jeans, cowgirl boots, and a blouse the color of ripe strawberries. In fact, it had little black seeds all over it, and Todd could only stare at her.

Her hair had once again been clipped back on the sides, and she wore something on her face he'd never seen before: makeup.

"I must have two noses," she said, stepping out onto the porch. "For how hard you're staring at me."

He blinked and backed up. "Sorry," he said with a little shake of his head. "You look so great this morning."

"Thank you." She scanned him from hat to boot and said, "So do you."

He turned, and they faced the world together. He

suddenly felt strong with her at his side, and he said, "I thought we'd go to brunch at The Sunflower Café. Have you been there before?"

"Nope," she said.

She wasn't from Chestnut Springs, and Todd actually liked that. He'd get to share his town with her over time, and he held her door while she got in the truck. "It's about twenty-five minutes," he said.

"I have driven to town before," she said.

Todd chuckled and got the truck moving. "Yeah, so I'm a little nervous."

Laura turned fully toward him. "Why is that, Todd?"

He glanced at her. "Why am I nervous?"

"Yeah."

"Because." He tightened his fingers on the wheel and refused to look at her again. "You're beautiful and smart, and honestly, Laura, you're out of my league. I'm just waitin' for you to realize it and prayin' you don't at the same time."

She didn't laugh the way he expected her to, and he finally glanced over to her. "I'm just happy to be going out with you," she said. "You're handsome and smart too, Todd. Maybe I'm the lucky one."

"There's at least four women in my past who would disagree," he said.

"Their loss."

Todd didn't know what else to say to that, and as he hit the highway, he said, "Tell me about your family."

"Oh, boy. Going for the jugular."

"I didn't mean to."

Laura took a moment to answer, and Todd regretted asking until she said, "I've got an older brother named Eddie. He lives with his wife and family in Hidden Hollow —that little farm town I told you about."

"Hm mm."

"My parents still live there. It's about an hour from here. My daddy had a hip replacement about a week before I started here at Longhorn, and Mama makes jams and syrups and honeys—the most delicious honeys ever."

She spoke with pure love for them, and Todd smiled at her. "Sounds like you get along with them."

"I miss them," she said, looking out the passenger window.

"You've never left to go visit."

"You didn't tell me summer at Longhorn was like one long marathon." She cocked one eyebrow at him, and he laughed.

"Fair enough." A few minutes later, he pulled into the parking lot at The Sunflower Café. "Wow," he said. "Looks busy."

"I'll run in and see," she said, and just like that, she hopped from his truck and went jogging toward the entrance. She was petite yet powerful, and Todd couldn't help the swooping in his stomach.

She texted a minute later with, *They said an hour wait.*

He frowned. What were they going to do for an hour? He quickly tapped out, *We can go somewhere else. I'll circle around and pick you up.*

As he did that, he tried to think of somewhere else to take her. His heart and stomach had been set on Sunflower, and he cursed himself for not making a reservation on a Saturday morning. Duh.

Laura climbed back into the truck, and he said, "We can head over to this little place in the next town over. It's pretty good."

"Sure," she said. "We can wait here too."

"They won't be as busy at The Live Oak."

She told him about her fear of zip-lines as he drove from Chestnut Springs to nearby Franklin, and then she asked, "What would be the worst gift someone could give you?"

Surprised, Todd had to think for a few seconds. "I'm gonna go with oranges."

Laura burst out laughing, and Todd enjoyed the sound of that. He grinned too and slowed as the speed limit dropped going into town. "Why's that so funny?"

"Who would give oranges as a gift?"

"We get a whole heap of them at Christmastime," he said. "Honestly, it's not a gift. It's a punishment."

She let out another string of laughter, and Todd joined in this time. Pride filled his chest, and he told himself this wasn't so bad. No, they weren't going to his favorite café. He'd made her laugh, though, and that had to be good.

"A punishment," she said, still chortling. "That's terrific. I'm going to tell my mom and dad that."

"Let me guess," he said dryly as The Live Oak came into view. "They give oranges to their neighbors at Christmastime."

"You got it." Laura beamed at him, her pretty eyes like dazzling diamonds.

Todd dang near drove off the road but managed to make it seem like he meant to pull into the parking lot a little erratically. Inside, The Live Oak wasn't exactly empty, but they managed to get a table after only a minute.

"I will never get your oranges as a gift," she said. "When's your birthday?"

"Next month," he said. "You?"

"It was in July."

A hot slice went through his chest. "Why didn't you tell me?"

She shrugged, and he didn't like the sudden apprehension in her expression.

"You didn't go home, and you didn't have a party." He studied her face. "Do not tell me you did nothing. That not a single person wished you happy birthday."

"My momma called," she said in a small voice.

"Laura."

"What?" She lifted her eyes to his, and they held challenge now. "What was I supposed to do? I'd been at the ranch for six or seven weeks. I was still learning where I stood and who I could trust."

Todd blinked, sure he'd heard her wrong. "You can trust everyone at the ranch."

She shook her head. "You can't trust everyone, Todd. That's ridiculous."

He tilted his head, trying to see and hear things she wasn't showing or telling. "That's...interesting."

"It was fine," she said. "Daddy sent me a card, and they called."

"I would've had Gina make you a cake. We could've

sung to you at breakfast. It wouldn't have had to be much, but it would've been something."

"I was fine."

"You're part of the ranch now," he said. "Unless..."

"Unless what?"

He stared straight at her. "Unless you don't want to be."

Laura opened her mouth, then closed it just as quickly. "I...don't know what I want."

Todd understood that well, and he sighed. Glancing around, he noticed the tables nearest to them didn't have food. "Where's our server?" he asked. They hadn't even been greeted yet.

Just his luck. The phenomenal place he wanted to take Laura on their first date was too busy, and this place had terrible service. All he could do was pray they could laugh about it someday, because right now, all the situation caused inside him was dread.

———

A FEW HOURS LATER, HE SAID, "WE SHOULD JUST GO BACK. Everything's been a bust."

"It's fine," Laura said, and he noted that she said that a lot.

"Sure," he said. "Fine. In the amount of time it took us to drive to The Live Oak and then wait literally an hour for our food, we could've stayed at The Sunflower Café." He gripped the wheel at nine and three, pressing a little too hard on the gas pedal. He just wanted to get back to the ranch.

"The food wasn't even good," he said. "Then, there were no tours at the gardens. It's just…dumb."

Laura didn't respond, at least verbally. She did reach over and take his hand in hers, and once again, Todd very nearly ran the truck off the road. He looked at her delicate hand in his, his skin cells shooting fire up into his arm.

"It's fine," she said again. "We got to spend some time together where we weren't talking about pinkeye or fungus, so I'm calling that a win."

He squeezed her hand. "I know that pimento sandwich wasn't even good. You can admit it."

She smiled at him, and the heavens could've opened and beamed down heavenly light and it wouldn't have held a candle to that smile. "Fine," she said. "It wasn't good."

"I knew it." Todd shook his head, caging his anger in the process. "We can stop in the kitchen and see what there is to eat."

"I'm not even hungry," she said.

"You could come over to my place later," he said. "I'll raid the kitchen at the lodge or my mother's and haul it all to my cabin." He looked at her with hope, because he didn't want this day to be a complete waste of time. To him, it felt like it was, and he had to do something to fix that.

Laura nodded and said, "Okay, Todd. You've got yourself a second date."

"Hallelujah," he said with some sarcasm. He slowed to

make the turn onto the ranch. "Honestly, I should get a medal or something. *Terrible first date, and he still gets a second.*" He laughed, relieved when she did too.

In front of her cabin, she looked over to him. "Honestly, Todd, I had fun."

He didn't see how, but he nodded and said, "Me too."

"Can I bring a surprise tonight?"

"I wish you would," he said, and they got out of his truck. He walked with her up to the door, and it felt odd to have so much sunshine flooding his eyes as he dropped off his date. He didn't draw out the good-bye, because Todd hated awkwardness. He leaned into her and swept his lips along her cheek. "I'll see you later. Come by anytime. I'm not goin' back to work today."

"Okay," she said, pushing her hair off her face and reaching for the doorknob. She went inside, and Todd turned to get back to his truck. He couldn't believe things had gone as badly as they had today, and he felt like his momma as he shook his head and mentally recounted all that had gone wrong.

At the same time, a new flutter of excitement stole through him at what Laura's surprise would be that evening. He couldn't wait to find out, and he thought he might just stop by the barn office to see how Sierra was getting along. That would pass the time until Laura came over, and he wouldn't have to stare at the clock and count minutes.

CHAPTER
TWENTY-SIX

Laura laid on her bed, her ankles crossed, and waited for her mom to answer the phone. A specific type of giddiness ran through her, but she wouldn't let it go too fast. She'd let out a bit too much on her first date with Todd, namely that she didn't trust anyone.

She could still hear him telling her she had a place on this ranch if she wanted one, and Laura honestly didn't know what to do with a statement like that.

"Call me," she said to her mom's voicemail, because her phone would alert her with a different type of notification that deafened everyone within a mile.

Laura smiled at the thought and let her phone fall to her chest. She closed her eyes and let herself go backward through the past several hours. No, nothing had really worked out. They'd gone into the botanical gardens, only to learn the tours were sold out. Todd had asked for his money back, and they'd left fifteen minutes later.

They'd sat for at least twenty-five minutes at the second diner before their food had come, and no, it hadn't been good. She giggled as she remembered the sour look on Todd's face when he tasted the sweet tea.

"That is not good," he'd said.

Laura hadn't cared where they ate or what they did. Just being with him was a big step for her, and she'd enjoyed the day so far.

Her phone rang, and she lifted it to answer her mom. "Momma," she said. "I went out with Todd today." She giggled before her mom even said hello.

"My goodness," her mom said. "Today? I thought you said he was never going to set a date."

"We've been busy," she said, regretting that she told her mom that. "We just went to brunch and then to some gardens. Well, that didn't really work out, so we walked around the park a little."

"Sounds lovely in this weather," her mom said, and Laura giggled again. It had been hot, but Laura was used to heat. "You sound happy."

"I am," Laura said.

"I'm glad to hear it."

"I'm going to come home next weekend," Laura said.

"Really?" Her mom's voice held hope, and Laura felt the hot slice of guilt.

"Yes," she said, committing to it. "I'm sorry I didn't come for my birthday."

"Did Todd say something about it?"

"Yes," Laura said, wondering how her mother had known that. "He couldn't believe I didn't say anything to anyone."

Her mom waited a beat and said, "I can believe that, Laura. I didn't understand why you wouldn't come home."

"It just felt…too hard," she said with a sigh. "I'm sorry, okay? Will you make the coconut cream pie for me?"

"Of course," her mom said, her forgiveness one of the greatest blessings of Laura's life. She'd had to focus on the tiniest of blessings in her life, and her mother had always been her biggest one.

"How are you holding up?" her mom asked next, and Laura let her eyes close again.

"Okay," she said.

"Did you tell Todd about Hans?"

Laura sucked in a breath, which was all the answer her mother needed. Laura needed to talk about him though, and she hadn't realized it until right this moment. "No," she said. "I haven't told him yet. It was our first date, Momma."

"When are you seeing him again?"

"In a couple of hours," she said. "I'm going to dinner over at his place, and we're going to fly a kite."

"How very country," her mom said with a laugh tacked onto the end. "It really sounds nice, Laura."

"I like it here," Laura said. "When he said I should've told him about my birthday so he could have the chef at the lodge make a cake, I told him I didn't want to be a bother. He said I was part of this ranch now…if I wanted to be."

"Do you want to be?"

Laura opened her eyes and looked up at the ceiling in her bedroom. She shared this cabin with another woman, and this single bedroom was the only purely private space she had. "Yes," she whispered, not quite strong enough to vocalize the word louder than that.

"Good," her mom said. "You deserve everything good after what you've been through."

"Thank you, Momma."

"Call me after tonight's kite-flying date."

Laura knew she was teasing her, but she didn't care. "I will," she said. "I love you."

"Love you too, dear."

She once again let her phone rest on her chest, and now her thoughts only brought forward memories of Hans and the amazing thirteen months she'd had with him. She didn't know how to bring him up, how to explain who he was and why he'd been so important to her.

She and Todd weren't to the stage in their relationship where they talked about previous boyfriends and girl-friends anyway. Hans hadn't only been her boyfriend either.

She exhaled as she sat up and then stood. She liked to stay busy so some of the things she'd endured didn't over-take her life and make her spend too much time in the past. She'd learned that was no way to live, and she'd rather focus on today than relive yesterday.

Besides, today with Todd had been pretty spectacular,

and she couldn't wait to see him again.

––––––––

WHEN THE FRONT DOOR OF HIS CABIN OPENED LATER THAT day, Kyle stood in front of her, not Todd. "Hey," she said with a smile. She'd changed her clothes for a reason she couldn't name, and she now held up the bag where she'd carefully folded her kite after getting it out and testing it an hour ago.

"Is Todd here?"

"I haven't seen him," Kyle said, backing up. "C'mon in. I'll call him."

"I can call him," she said, stepping into the cabin. She looked around, seeing Todd clearly in the décor of the house. She didn't know Kyle as well, but the parts she couldn't attribute to Todd, she assumed came from him. The bright blue rug in the living room, for example, as well as the ornate mirror above the mantle.

This cabin was much more spacious than hers, and she smiled at the soft beige walls in the kitchen and the real wood ones in the living room and dining room.

"Hey," Kyle said, and she turned to him. He spoke into his phone. "Laura's here Where you at?" He nodded a couple of times and said, "I'll tell her."

Azure laid down on her feet, and Laura bent at the knee to pat him. "Howdy, heeler," she said to him, giving him a good scratch. "How are you feeling today?"

Azure looked at her with his bright blue eyes, and she smiled back at him. He seemed to grin at her too, and they'd always gotten along really well. "Why aren't you with Todd, huh?"

"He stopped by the barn for a minute," Kyle said. "I think we both know what that means." He also smiled at her, and Laura rose to her feet.

"I brought a kite," she said, hoping it wouldn't be a lame surprise for Todd. "Do you want to come outside and fly it with me?"

Kyle's eyebrows went up, and he shook his head. "I think Todd will shave my head in the middle of the night if I do." He chuckled and nodded for her to go ahead. "Azure will come with you."

The dog already trotted for the front door. He went right out, and Kyle added, "Don't tell him I let the dog in the house. I might lose more than my hair if he finds out."

Laura giggled and agreed to keep it their little secret. Outside, she took her kite out of the bag and attached the dual strings to it. She moved into the field in front of Todd's house so they wouldn't miss one another when he got home, and laid the kite on the ground.

Backing up, she kept the lines separate, and then she slipped her hands into the bracelets, gave them a sharp pull simultaneously, and jogged backward as the kite lifted up and caught the wind.

It sailed up into the sky, and Laura tipped her head back to watch it. She laughed, because there was something so freeing and amazing about flying a large stunt kite. She loved the way she could pull on the right string and it would swoop, and she could give a slight tug on the left, and it would dive.

Such tiny movements which caused such big reactions. She loved it, and she loved knowing that she wasn't the only thing being pushed to and fro by forces she couldn't control. She knew now that a minute adjustment could put her on a completely different life path, the same way that slight tug could cause a dive in the kite.

The wind, which had been blowing steadily all day, died, and the kite began to drift. Laura backed up again, pulling the lines tight, trying to get it to stay up. Kite flying required wind, and gusts weren't her friend right now. They only pushed the kite for a moment, and it lilted upward only to wilt again.

"Come on," she said. "This can't be happening." Not today, where everything else had gone wrong. Mother Nature always blew across the Hill Country; why not right now?

The kite landed on the ground, and Laura exhaled again, made sure the lines were straight and not tangled in anything, then she pulled again. The kite refused to catch any breeze at all, because none existed.

Laura turned as the sound of a truck's engine met her ears, and she slipped her hands out of the wrist bands of the kite. It wasn't going anywhere, because there wasn't a stitch of wind on the entire ranch right now.

Todd parked in front of his cabin and got out of the truck. She waved needlessly, and he came across the road and into the field. "Sorry," he said. "I got busy in my office."

"It's fine," she said, indicating the downed kite. "This is the surprise. I had it up for a minute, but the wind's died."

Todd looked at the parachute-like kite in an array of colors, then back to her. "I think that about sums up our whole day."

She grinned at him. "It's been windy for hours. I even flew this thing out at my cabin for a good half-hour to make sure it wasn't ripped."

He looked up into the sky. "Figures." He sighed and shook his head. "I'm also late with dinner, and maybe we should quit while we're ahead." He toed the ground, his head down.

"Are you asking me to leave?"

He looked up, his face flushed. "I guess not."

"Do you have any food at your house?"

"No."

"We could eat at the lodge." Laura turned when the barest tickle of a breeze tousled her hair. "Or wait out the wind and see if we can fly this thing."

"I haven't flown a kite in forever," he said.

"I find it relaxing," she said. "I love watching it sail through the sky, playing with the wind and the current." She was sure she'd just revealed too much, because Todd would ask her when she'd first flown a kite and liked it. Then she'd have to tell him about Hans.

"It's pretty," he said. "Like a rainbow-butterfly." He grinned at her. "I don't mind waiting for the wind." He slipped his fingers between hers, and Laura's whole body shivered, bringing that zing of excitement to her brain. "I'll call my mother and ask her what she's got in her fridge, and we could walk down there and get it."

"Okay," she said.

"Wait. I changed my mind." He turned back to his cabin. "I'll send Kyle. Otherwise, Mama will be bendin' my ear for a month, askin' about you."

She slipped her hand out of his and started to roll up the lines. "You don't want her to know?"

"I usually tell her last, yeah," he said. "She's great, but she's a little...overeager when one of us starts dating."

"Mm." Laura finished with the lines and picked up the kite. "I don't think the wind is coming back, and I actually am hungry now."

"I'll call my mom." He pulled out his phone to do that, and Laura walked back to his cabin with him. Kyle didn't protest about going to get the food, and Laura folded up her kite and put it back in the bag.

"I'd love to try flying that another time," he said. "I could use some relaxation."

She faced him, struck once again by his handsomeness. "I'd like that," she said.

"If it's a third strike, you won't have to go out with me again."

Laura smiled and shook her head. "We're not goin' out tonight, so technically, I think next time—*if* it's bad—will only be strike two."

He chuckled, cutting off the sound only a moment later. He cocked his head as if listening for something, and Laura copied him. She heard the howling of the wind as it whipped around the corner of the cabin, and she shook her head in disbelief.

"That's *wind*. I'm cursed," Todd said. "You might as well know it now. Get out while you can."

"I wish you'd quit trying to convince me to leave," she said, surprised at her own boldness. At the same time, she wasn't. She'd had to be brave and bold for a lot of years in veterinary school.

Todd blinked at her, obviously surprised. She slid her hands up his chest and wrapped them around the back of his neck. "I'm a big girl, Todd. If I want to leave, I'll leave."

"Okay," he said simply.

"Do you dance?" she asked, starting to sway in front of him.

He put his hands on her waist and brought her closer, the scent of his cologne filling her nose and head and making her a little drunk. "I can," he said. "A little."

"Mm," she said again, closing her eyes and leaning her head against his shoulder. Maybe the surprise was this dance and not the kite. She didn't know. What she knew was this gentle swaying to the song of the wind was the absolute perfect end to a date that had gone wrong after wrong after wrong. "I like this," she whispered.

"Me too," Todd said in a throaty voice, and Laura hoped they would end every date with a slow dance, even if it only lasted for a few seconds.

She pulled back on her thoughts that had moved too far into the future and focused on just him right now. Moving with him. Listening to him breathe. The feel of his hair along her fingertips, and the weight of his hands on her waist.

Yes, this was simply perfect, and for the first time, a tiny piece of Laura truly felt like she wanted to be a part of this relationship and this ranch.

The cabin door opened, and Kyle walked in with, "Dinner's here."

Todd stepped away from Laura and went to help his brother. They pulled out barbecue, mashed potatoes, sweet pea salad, and then Todd opened the freezer and got out a carton of ice cream.

"Did she send brownies?"

"Right here, bro." Kyle took them out of the bag last and set them with the rest of the food. "I'm going to go eat at the lodge."

"Okay," Todd said, already getting out bowls. He looked at Laura, his eyes lit from within. "Dessert first." He put a brownie in the bowl and scooped a big dollop of vanilla ice cream on top of it.

He opened a drawer and picked something from it. A candle, which he stuck down into the ice cream.

"Todd," she said, her heart beating against the cage she'd put it in so long ago.

"Happy birthday to you," he started to sing, his voice smooth and rich and wonderful. He lit the candle and continued the song, having no idea that he'd just clipped the strings holding Laura's heart inside her chest.

He finished the song and indicated the flame. "Make a wish and blow it out."

She did, and he clapped for her. Then he dished himself a brownie and ice cream, got out two spoons, and handed her one.

"Thank you," she said, taking the spoon and then throwing herself into his arms. She wouldn't cry, and she told herself not to over and over and over again.

He held her tightly and whispered, "Of course," again. "Like I said earlier, everyone deserves something, even if it's small, on their birthday."

She stroked her hands down the side of his face, her gaze landing on his mouth. "Thank you," she said again, and she did the thing that felt the most natural to her.

She kissed him. He pulled in a breath, obviously surprised, then kissed her back. Laura's brain caught up to what she'd just done only a few moments later, and she pulled away. She kept her head down as embarrassment heated her from her face down to her toes.

"Sorry," she said when Todd said nothing.

His fingers brushed against hers, then took them into his hand. "You'll tell me what's got you so...emotional about your birthday, won't you?"

She looked up, her heartbeat growling at her like a big tractor engine. She told herself she could trust him, but she wasn't entirely convinced, even if that kiss had shifted everything in her life in only three seconds.

"Yes," she said. "One day." She let out her breath, the tension in his cabin too much for her right now. "Can we just eat and...I don't know." She swept her gaze across the spread of food on his countertop. "Talk about lighter things?"

"Sure," he said. "We can do that."

"Thank you," she said again, knowing she'd just bought herself some time but that it would run out eventually, and she'd have to tell him everything.

CHAPTER
TWENTY-SEVEN

Blake stood on his parents' front porch, his eyes trained down the dirt road. Gina should be arriving any second now, but he'd been telling himself that for fifteen minutes. His heart skipped a beat, then raced to catch up.

He gripped the banister and turned away from the road. After walking to the edge of the porch, he turned and went back the way he'd already come. Behind him in the house, pots and pans boiled and bubbled with everything his family would eat for Thanksgiving dinner.

They'd already served it at the lodge an hour ago, and his parents invited everyone who lived and worked on the ranch to their house for a traditional turkey feast in the afternoon. All activities were paused from noon to six p.m., and then his family would go over to the lodge and serve a simple dinner of soups and sandwiches.

Everyone would perform for the guests, and they'd all clean up together and be done and home by eight.

Blake did love his family and his ranch, even though he had to work on holidays like Thanksgiving. He also loved Gina, and he wanted her to live out here with him full-time. It had been over four months since she'd shouted into the microphone that she loved him, and today, he wanted to ask her to be his wife.

He would, if she ever showed up.

He looked back down the road and still didn't see her. She'd said she'd stop and get her parents and bring them out to the ranch by three-thirty. The Stewarts ate at four p.m. on the dot, which allowed enough time to consume copious amounts of food, nap for a half-hour, and then get over to the lodge for the dinner and entertainment.

The door behind him opened, and Starla asked, "She's still not here?"

"No," Blake practically barked.

Starla came out onto the porch with him, closing the door behind her and sealing the noise inside, at least partially. "She's going to say yes."

Blake wiped his palms down his shirt. "I know. I mean, I guess she will."

Starla went to the pillar at the top of the steps and leaned against it, a sigh slipping from her mouth. Blake joined her, staring at her and willing her to look at him. She wouldn't, and Blake sighed too.

"I'm fine, Blake."

"Me too," he said.

"You're pacing like a caged tiger," she said, nodding to the house. "Everyone in there keeps asking about you. Your momma almost called the police to find out if she's been in an accident."

Blake rolled his eyes. "That's just Mama." She could be intense, but she was probably as nervous as he was.

"Involving all of them probably wasn't your smartest move," Starla said with a grin.

"Probably not." He jerked his attention back to the road as he finally heard the crunching of tires over the dirt. Gina's car came toward him at an astronomically slow pace, and he went down the steps saying, "Get them ready, Starla."

"Yes, sir," she said behind him, and he heard the laughter from inside increase as she opened the door, then silence when she closed it behind her.

Gina pulled into the driveway, a murderous look on her face. Blake grinned at her, hoping she could disappear in the crowd inside and let someone else take care of her parents. He would, and his had been ecstatic when Blake had asked if they could host Sarah and Ben in addition to everyone on the ranch.

Her dad rode in the passenger seat, and her mom rode in the back, so once the car had come to a stop, Blake opened the back door, and said, "Happy Thanksgiving, Mrs. Barlow."

She looked up at him, and he knew why Gina had been late. Her mother wore makeup, and it…didn't look great. It looked like she'd put it on with shaking hands and someone had tried to fix it. His chest squeezed as Sarah said, "Hello, young man."

"It's Blake, Mom," Gina said.

"Yes, Blake, of course." Sarah reached her hand out, and Blake helped her stand from the back seat. Gina's dad had already gotten out, and Gina followed last. She shouldered her purse and met his eyes.

"Hey," he said again, his voice filled with fondness. "You look amazing." She wore a sweater with geometric patterns on it, in shades of cream, beige, tan, and brown, with one tiny patch of orange. "Very festive." Her skinny jeans disappeared into knee-high boots, and Blake couldn't wait to sneak away with her during nap time and kiss her. There were plenty of trees to hide behind out here in the family row.

"Thank you," she said with a sigh. "The pies are in the trunk."

He leaned down and kissed her quickly, keeping his face close to hers. "Everything okay?" he whispered.

"Sorry we're late," she murmured, keeping her eyes closed and touching the tip of her nose to his.

"You're fine," he said. "Plenty of time before we eat." He put proper distance between them and went to get the pies. She'd brought six, all of them sitting in a single layer inside a huge lettuce box. He picked it up easily, and he walked after Gina, who'd started herding her parents toward the cabin.

He'd designed it for him to enter last, and Nash should be waiting right beside the door to take anything he'd carried in for Gina. Kyle, Adam, and Jesse better have their guitars out already. Mama should've turned down burners and gotten things out of the oven so he wouldn't have any timers going off during his proposal. She didn't want to miss it, and both Holly and Sierra were recording it so they could get all angles.

It was probably far too big of a show, but Blake had seven siblings and involved parents. If Gina wasn't ready for a public spectacle for everything, she should probably tell him she didn't want to be his wife.

His throat turned numb, and he tried to swallow past it. What if she said no?

"Gina," he said, intending to stop her, but she'd already stepped past her father to open the door.

"You just go in, Daddy," she said. "You don't need to ring the doorbell." She pushed the door open and turned back to let her parents pass first. She met Blake's eye and said, "They're going to be the death of me."

Blake tried to smile, but his nerves probably made it look like a grimace. He nodded into the house and said, "My mama will take them from here. Go on. I'm right behind you."

She entered the house, and Blake noted there was no noise. No chatter. No arguing. No laughter. The scent of roasted meat and butter hung in the air, and his mouth watered.

He followed Gina into the house, handed the huge box of pies to Nash, and nodded to Sierra.

"What's going on?" Gina asked, turning back to him. "They're all standing there, still and staring at me."

He swallowed, and the sound of Kyle's acoustic guitar

filled the air. He could make the instrument sound like angels singing from heaven, and it relaxed Blake enough to keep him inside his head and inside this situation.

Jesse and Adam joined Kyle after the first several notes, and Blake noticed the lights on his sisters' phones. They were recording.

"Blake," Gina said, plenty of warning in her voice.

Before he could answer, his family started singing. Kyle had written the song several years ago, and he'd taught it to everyone. It was a welcome song the Stewarts sang at the lodge on special occasions, like the anniversary of when they'd opened, his mama and daddy's birthdays, their wedding anniversary—and apparently today.

Anyone who worked at the Texas Longhorn Ranch for very long knew it, and Starla, Baby John, Lowry, and Sammy Boy knew all the words. Blake was tempted to join in on the chorus, which picked up in volume and speed and said, "Welcome, welcome, we welcome you today," but he didn't.

His parents' house opened up just past the front door into a big living room that extended from wall to wall across the front of the cabin. The kitchen and dining room took up the back two-thirds, and Blake moved his eyes from Gina to his mom as she came toward him. She held a single red rose in her hand, and she handed it to him with a smile and tears in her eyes.

His daddy came next, and he carried a sunflower almost as big as a dinner plate. Anyone who wasn't film-ing, holding a pie box, or playing the guitar continued to bring Blake flowers until he held over twenty of them in a huge bouquet.

Starla stepped between him and Gina, still singing, and wrapped a huge blue bow around the stems while he held all the flowers still for her. She smiled at him with such friendliness and love, and that gave him the last bit of courage he needed.

He looked at Gina, who stood six feet from him, tears running down her face and both hands pressed to her chest. Todd edged closer to Blake, and he nodded at him.

Blake took a step closer to Gina and then another one. Right in front of her, he grinned at her and waited until the singing faded. Only Kyle kept playing, a low-range tune as background music.

"I love you, Regina Barlow. I've loved you since I was fifteen years old. If I'd have known then I'd have to wait twenty years to ask you this question, I probably would've been so frustrated. But now..." He smiled, his own emotions rising up and cutting off his voice.

He cleared his throat and looked at the flowers he'd carefully chosen for this woman he loved so much. He looked back at her, everything so clear and so perfect when it was just him and her. "Now, all I see when I look at you is someone who needed an opportunity to learn and grow and fly somewhere else. I'm so glad the Lord brought you back to me, and that I didn't mess things up too badly this time."

She shook her head and wiped her eyes.

He smiled and chin-nodded to the flowers. "I chose

each of these specifically because they mean something to me about you." He extended them toward her, and she took them with trembling hands.

Todd handed him the diamond ring and faded into the background, and Blake got down on both knees. "You'd make me the happiest man in Texas if you'd say yes to bein' my wife."

Gina leaned into her flowers and smelled them, and Blake asked, "Gina, will you marry me?"

Her eyes met his, and she said, "Yes," without a moment's hesitation.

The crowd gathered at his parents' house for Thanksgiving roared, whooped, and hollered, and Blake got to his feet, slipped the diamond onto Gina's ring finger, and she held the flowers to the side as he wrapped her in his arms and kissed her.

He didn't make a show of it and pulled away after only a few seconds. He kept his forehead right next to hers though, creating an intimate space for the two of them amidst all the chaos of his family. "I love you."

"I love you too," she whispered just loud enough for him to hear.

Then they got separated as her mother wanted to hug her. Blake turned to his brothers and hugged Todd and then Nash. He and Jesse, Adam, and Kyle had a four-way-group hug, where he said, "That was perfect, you guys. Thank you so much."

He lifted Starla right up off her feet, and laughed with her as she squealed. He then raised both hands and called for quiet. As the congratulations and good wishes silenced, he said, "Thank you, everyone. I know my mama and daddy are thrilled to have everyone here at the house for Thanksgiving, and Daddy's asked me to pray." He beamed at his parents, who stood back in the kitchen, arm-in-arm.

"Since Mama runs a tight ship, right on schedule, I think I'll get that done now, and then she can tell us how the food is going to go and where y'all can sit to eat." He raised his eyebrows at her, and she nodded.

He looked at Gina, and extended his hand to her. She came toward him, having handed her flowers off to someone. He couldn't stop smiling as she slipped her fingers between his, and then he looked around at all the good men and women he either worked with or was related to.

"All right," he said, giving everyone a chance to remove their cowboy hats. Then he bowed his head and prayed, asking the Lord to bless them all and thanking Him for the great bounty his family enjoyed.

At the end of the prayer, the noise from earlier immediately resumed. Blake stayed by the door with Gina's hand in his. "How'd I do?" he asked.

She looked at him with stars in her eyes. "Blake, that was seriously the most perfect proposal in the whole world. Sierra said she recorded it."

"Holly too," he said.

"I'm going to need to learn that song," Gina said.

"I'll teach it to you," he said. "It's how we welcome everyone to the ranch."

"I can't wait to live here with you." She stretched up and kissed him, and this time Blake didn't keep it to a couple of seconds. She was the one who broke the kiss as she said, "I love you, Blake."

"I love you too, sweetheart."

———

Keep reading for the first couple of chapters in the next book in the series, **KISSING HER COWBOY BOSS**.

SNEAK PEEK - KISSING HER COWBOY BOSS CHAPTER ONE:

Laura Woodcross bent her head into the wind, her spirits as low as the temperatures had been falling this December. It wasn't exactly what she'd classify as cold, but it wasn't warm either.

That was about how everything in Laura's life had become. Neutral. Stale. Boring.

Her father had had hip replacement surgery several months ago, and he was doing okay. Just okay. Not great, but not in as much pain as he'd been in before.

She lived with another cowgirl, and they hadn't become best friends, despite Laura's attempts to talk to Josie and get to know her. They existed together, and Josie basically left Laura alone to live her life.

After her bust of a first date with Todd Stewart, which Laura had actually enjoyed, things between the two of them had been good. Fine. Okay. She saw him every day.

They spoke in person and on the phone, through texts, all of it.

He'd asked her out again, and they'd gone to dinner a few times. She'd celebrated his birthday with him, but she'd gone back to Hidden Hollow for Thanksgiving.

Laura's relationship with Todd had cooled as the work around a cattle ranch never really slowed or stopped. Deep down, she knew it wasn't work keeping them apart.

It was her.

Every time she thought about kissing Todd, her cells lit up and her brain told her to get the job done. She'd kissed him once, but it had been a very emotional moment triggered by an event in her past she still hadn't told him about.

He hadn't tried to kiss her again, and Laura wasn't sure she'd even let him. The single time she'd lost her mind and touched her lips to his had caused so much guilt to fill her. She'd been tripping over it since, and he seemed to know it.

The only saving grace was her job here at the Texas Longhorn Ranch. That presented her with a new challenge every single day. Or at least some variety.

They'd moved into birthing season, and that meant Laura had to check her pregnant cows every single day, multiple times throughout the day. Morning, noon, night, midnight. They didn't seem to care about her sleep schedule when it came to giving birth.

She took a deep breath and looked up into the shrouded sky. She didn't talk to Hans anymore, and she wasn't going to start today. He deserved to Rest In Peace, without her constant chatter to him about how she missed him and wished they'd gotten more time together.

The people she had time with right here on earth she'd started to shut out again. She didn't like this version of herself, but she didn't know how to change it.

She'd thought the Longhorn Ranch would be the answer to all of her prayers. For the first few months there, it had been. The people were nice, the job nothing she couldn't handle, and that handsome Todd Stewart...

Laura pushed him out of her thoughts as she swung into the saddle, but he simply galloped right back in. "All right, Miss Dolly," she said to the horse. "None of the momma cows are gonna have their babies in the next little bit. Let's go check the tree line."

Dolly didn't move too fast or too slow, just another medium in Laura's life. To be honest, she could use a runaway bull or a lightning strike only ten yards from her. Something to jolt her out of this funk and back to the land of the living.

The growl of a truck approached, but she wouldn't know if it was Todd or someone else until they rounded the bend. By the throatiness of the engine, it wasn't Todd. His truck purred like a kitten, and this one sounded like it could cough, sputter, and die on the next turn of the tires.

Sure enough, Little Nick came around the corner in a beige ranch truck. When he saw her, he gunned the engine and flashed his lights.

"Whoa," Laura said to Dolly, because Little Nick clearly needed to talk to her.

"Laura," he called out the open window. "There's been an accident at the demo. We need you."

Her brow crinkled. "The demo?" She didn't memorize all of the activities that went on at the ranch, especially the commercial side of it. She enjoyed the free breakfast and dinner every day of the week, and she'd signed up for the monthly grab-and-go lunches too. She definitely didn't want for food.

"Yeah," he said. "It turned into a pig stampede, and we've got someone who's bleeding."

"Okay," she said, still not getting it.

"Switch me," he said, coming to a stop. "I'll take Dolly in. You take the truck." The sandy blonde cowboy got out of the truck, but Laura's mind couldn't quite keep up.

"I'm a veterinarian," she said. "I don't patch up people. Isn't there a first aid kit at the lodge or something?"

"It's a little girl," Little Nick said. "He's here with his mom and gran, and they're deathly afraid of hospitals. Won't go." He took the reins from her, and Laura saw no way out of this.

She also knew exactly how that girl and her family felt. She'd spent so much time in hospitals, she wouldn't feel bad if she never had to step foot in one again.

"All right," she said, sliding from the saddle. "I still need to check the pasture out at the treelike."

Little Nick frowned, but he nodded, swung into the saddle, and said, "Yah, Dolly. Let's pick up the pace."

Above them, the sky grumbled with thunder, and Laura realized what a blessing she'd been given. If she'd stayed out here, she'd have been caught in the coming rain for sure.

As it was, she got behind the wheel of the truck, rolled up the window, and enjoyed a drama-free return to the ranch.

The outdoor demo area sat to the east of the main lodge, in the barn next to the one where Todd kept his office. Quite the crowd lingered there, as it sure seemed like people possessed a morbid streak and accidents and pain attracted their attention like nothing else.

If that were really truly, everyone would be staring at her all the time, not just right now as she pulled up in the rickety ranch truck.

"There you are," Adam Stewart said, pulling open her door before she'd even put the vehicle in park. "She's freaking out, and none of us can calm her down."

Laura gave him a calm smile. "Species?" He blinked at her, his eyes widening, and Laura shook her head. "Sorry," she said. "Bad joke." She joined him on the ground. "How old is she?"

"Four, maybe," Adam said. "I don't know. She's little."

"What happened?"

"Our huge six-hundred-pound sow stepped on her foot," another man said, and Laura came face-to-face with Todd Stewart. The man took her breath away, though he frowned with everything inside him. At least she'd never seen his face this unhappy before.

Face-to-face was a stretch too, as Laura usually had to look up to see everyone. The downfalls of only being five-foot-two.

"Hey," he said, sliding his hand along her hip. "Thanks for comin' in."

"Did you text?" she asked.

"Several times," he said, glancing up as the first drops of rain splattered the windshield with fat, splashy sounds. "I figured you were out too far, and this storm isn't helping anything."

Todd slid his hand away, and Laura's whole body went cold. How he did that so casually, she didn't understand. Because of his touch, she also couldn't quite figure out where their relationship stood.

She followed him as he turned and strode back the way he'd come. "We're under the demo roof, so we should stay dry."

Laura jogged to catch up to him, his longer legs covering so much more distance than hers. "So it's her foot? Her calf? Her whole leg? What?"

"I don't really know," he said, sliding her a look. Something burned hotly in his eyes. "She's hysterical, and her mother's not much better."

"Someone should get all these people inside," Laura said, and Todd lifted his hand. Two of his brothers came straight to him as if he was their king and they his servants.

"Get everyone inside the lodge," he said. "They don't need to be out here in the rain."

Adam nodded, immediately calling for everyone to follow him into the lodge to wait out the rain. Laura once again bent her head against the weather, this time to keep her face dry as the rain increased.

She and Todd went under the roof a moment later, the sound of the droplets on the metal above soothing to her. Beyond soothing. It meant she was outside, on a ranch, and she'd wanted this life for as long as she could remember.

A flicker of new light and extra life entered her heart and mind, and Todd got his brother Blake to move aside, revealing the little girl down on the ground.

Laura sucked in a breath at her dark, richly-colored hair. She looked like she'd been dipped in tar, her hair was so dark. She sat on the ground, her shoulders shaking violently as she cried.

"Honey," Todd said in a careful, gentle voice. "She's here." He looked up at Laura, who got herself moving again.

Her heart had lodged itself in the back of her throat, where it bobbed with every beat. Keep it together, she told herself as she dropped to her knees beside the girl.

Her eyes swept her from head to toe, catching the blood and the injury on her lower leg, just above her ankle. Maybe below it too.

"Hello, baby," she said in a calm quiet voice. She smiled at the little girl, who looked at her with wide, teary eyes the color of earth that had just been plowed under in preparation for planting.

"Her name is Ally," Todd said as a woman sobbed nearby. "Blake."

His brother moved over to the mother, and Laura shifted her body to shield the little girl from her mother's hysterics. A first aid kit sat on the ground beside her, and Laura reached into it to pull out a pair of gloves.

"My name is Laura," she said. "Do you like animals, Ally?"

The girl couldn't be more than four, and Laura guessed she was more like three. A pang of sadness hit her hard, the reverberations in her ribcage like that of a gong.

She didn't answer Laura, but Laura didn't need her to. "Once," she said as she finished putting on her gloves and reaching for the wet washcloth laying on top of the kit. "I knew a girl just like you."

She offered Ally a smile, never taking her eyes from the girl's. "Her name was Letty, though. She could speak another language. Can you do that?"

She stroked the cloth down the girl's leg softly, glancing there to see what wounds she was dealing with. Some of the blood had started to dry, and she quickly saw the enormous scrape that extended a good three or four inches along the front of Ally's leg.

The shin bone could be so sensitive, on all kinds of mammals.

"Do you have any pets?" Laura asked.

Ally looked around as if just now realizing her mom wasn't there. When she didn't see her, her teary eyes came back to Laura. "A cat," she said.

"My momma loves cats," Laura said. "Is it your cat or your momma's?"

"My gran's," Ally said, sniffling. "She named it Moonbaby."

Laura gave a light laugh. "Moonbaby. I like that." She

nodded to Todd, who took the cloth from her and handed it to someone she couldn't see.

Laura put her hands on her thighs and kept smiling at Ally. "Miss Ally, you've got a scrape here. Scrapes aren't that big of a deal." She took a fresh cloth from Todd and started on the back of Ally's leg this time, the heat from the cloth seeping into her fingers.

Ally's chin shook, and she turned to look at Todd. "She needs a blanket."

"Shock," he said, getting to his feet with a groan.

"Hold her," she said to him as he called for a blanket. He got back on the ground, and he pulled the little girl into his lap. He hummed to her in a quiet, low voice, and Laura blinked, seeing Hans and the life she'd once had right there in front of her.

Her anxiety tripled, and she swallowed against it. Nash arrived with a blanket, and Laura used the movement as Todd shifted Ally to get the last of the blood cleaned off her leg. She pressed the cloth right over the wound and Ally didn't even make a noise.

She curled into Todd's chest so much the way Hans's little sister had only a few days before he'd died. Laura couldn't look away from the sexy cowboy holding that little girl, and every nerve in her body screamed at her to get out of there.

Finish, she commanded herself. Focus. Flee.

She quickly dabbed some anti-bacterial ointment over the open wound, then bandaged it all up, saying, "All done, Miss Ally." She grinned at the girl, and Ally smiled back.

Laura got to her feet too and turned to go talk to the girl's mother. Todd joined her, and she gave the directions as quickly as she could. Todd transferred Ally to her mother, both of them calmer now.

Laura stepped away and peeled her gloves from her hands, her chest vibrating in a horrible, violent way. She had to get out of here. Now.

She spun and strode away, not caring that the rain hadn't let up, not even a little bit. Her hair and skin got soaked within a few seconds, and behind her, Todd called, "Laura, wait up."

She didn't. She couldn't.

She'd come here to get a fresh start after the ordeal of losing someone she loved so very much. Why did she have to see reminders of him literally everywhere?

A sob wrenched its way from her stomach, and it was going to come out of her throat.

"Laura," Todd said again, his voice closer.

She couldn't face him. Not right now. She broke into a run, praying the Lord could give her winged feet just this one time. She'd never ask Him for anything again, if she could just get away from everyone and find somewhere to cry her soul empty again.

SNEAK PEEK - KISSING HER COWBOY BOSS CHAPTER TWO:

Todd Stewart slowed his step as Laura broke into a run. Confusion struck his mind the way a snake did. Quick and without warning.

Every time he watched her work, she amazed him. She was always calm in the face of the stormiest of seas, and he'd seen her calm hysterical horses with a simple touch of her palm along their spines, deliver breech lambs, sew up a gash on a goat's side, and deal with all manner of diseases with their chickens and turkeys.

Now he'd witnessed her calm, beautiful spirit comfort a child, and she had never been more attractive to him than she was now.

He looked behind him, surprised how far from the demo arena he'd gotten in just a few seconds. Facing forward again, something told him to go after Laura.

He could barely see her through the rain anymore, and he didn't move as wild indecision raged through him.

"Where'd Laura go?" Blake asked as he came to stand beside Todd. "They've gone inside." He sighed and wiped his brow. "I told them I'd have Doc Hanson come out and look at her leg in a couple of days."

"Okay," Todd said, still not sure what to do. Laura had run off in the direction of her cabin, and he'd often seen her walking the road between the cowboy cabins and the barn where he divvied up the ranch responsibilities each day.

She owned a car, but she only drove it to town or home to Hidden Hollow. So many things about her intrigued him, and he disliked that he'd let her talk about simple things and not what really mattered.

He'd seen the pain on her face just now, even when she'd been smiling, and that got him moving across the gravel in the direction Laura had gone.

He took shelter under the eaves of the ice cream shop they opened and ran in the summer months and pulled out his phone. Laura didn't answer, and his frustration now was as sharp as it had been when he hadn't been able to get in touch with her when that little girl was screaming.

His phone tucked safely back in his pocket, Todd headed out into the rain again. He didn't care about being wet. Like he'd told Blake once, if he wasn't dry, he was wet, and whether that was a lot or a little didn't matter.

Laura lived in a cabin close to the front of the row of them, and he spotted her car parked out front. That didn't mean anything, and he climbed the steps and knocked on the front door.

He realized that he should've called all his men and women in off the ranch the moment the first drops of rain fell, and he got his phone out again to do that.

If you're still out on the ranch, come in, he tapped out. *The rain's not supposed to stop for a while.*

Only a moment after he'd sent his text, one came in from Starla. *Hot chocolate bar in the dining hall. Come one, come all.* She'd included an emoticon of a steaming cup of cocoa, and that screamed Starla.

Todd could see why both Jesse and Nash liked her, as she had the strong personality Jesse liked, with the brains and the beauty. Nash had a crush on Starla, and had for some time, but to Todd's knowledge, he hadn't asked her out in the five months since Jesse had ended his fleeting relationship with their kitchen manager and head chef at the lodge.

Todd's mouth watered for chocolate and mint, whipped cream and marshmallows, but his heart yearned for Laura Woodcross.

No one had come to the door, and he raised his fist to knock again. She still didn't come, and neither did Josie, the other cowgirl who lived here.

Frustration filled him, and Todd tried his phone again. He turned away from the door, his phone pressed to his ear, and went to the edge of the porch. The rain fell only a couple of inches in front of his face, and he saw something light up in Laura's car.

His pulse jumped and skipped through his veins, and while he feared he might be overstepping his bounds and drive her further from him, he jogged down the steps and toward her sedan.

Sure enough, he saw her sitting in the front seat now, and he bent down and peered in her window. She cracked it a few inches, and he asked, "Can I join you?"

"The doors are unlocked," she said. The window went up a moment later, and the thunder crashed through the sky with a noise great and terrific.

That prompted Todd to move, and move fast, around the car and into the passenger seat. He had to slid the seat back to make room for his longer legs, and he took off his cowboy hat, which held about as much water as the ground outside.

"It's really coming down," he said, hating himself for talking about the weather.

Laura had gathered her hair into a very low ponytail at the nape of her neck, as it wasn't long enough to do much more than that. She raked her fingers through it, pushing it back off her forehead. She usually clipped it on the sides, but Todd saw no evidence of barrettes this afternoon.

"They're doing hot chocolate at the lodge," he said in a lame attempt to make conversation.

"I got the text." She didn't look at him but leaned her head back against the rest, her eyes drifting closed.

Todd's frustration moved up a rung, and he considered what to say. He prayed for the right words, in the right order, but nothing came to mind.

"Laura," he started, his mind whirring. When he didn't continue, she turned toward him and opened her eyes. "You look tired," he said.

"Just what every woman wants to hear." She offered him a small smile that sent a teaspoon of joy into his heart.

"What can I do to help you?" he asked gently.

"Who says I need help?"

"I do," he said, adding some oomph to his voice. "I can see you're in distress, Laura. Even when you're smiling and working miracles with little girls, I can see the abso-lute...pain in your eyes."

Those lovely eyes filled with tears, and the last thing Todd wanted was to make her cry. "I'm sorry," he said quietly. "I—I wish you'd talk to me though."

He swallowed, now committed down this path. "I've enjoyed our dates, but I can feel the distance you keep between us." He gripped the brim of his cowboy hat, kneading it with his fingers until it was bent all out of shape. "And blast me, I let you, because I don't know how to make you talk to me. I can barely say what I want to say—and usually I can't at all. That's why I let you."

His lungs felt like someone had wrapped them in rubber bands, and they couldn't expand enough to get him the air he needed. He really didn't do well in talking to women. He could say hard things to any of his siblings. Anyone who worked for him—except Laura.

She reached over and took one of his hands away from the misshapen brim. "You're ruining your hat."

"It's just a hat," he said. "I have others."

Sunshine filled her face on this very rainy day in December, and Todd found himself returning the smile.

Her fingers wound around his and then slipped in

between them. She curled them and squeezed, and Todd liked this soft, quiet connection between them.

He dropped his hat completely and reached over with his other hand to tuck her hair behind her ear. "I've missed you, Laura."

"I know," she said, her eyes drifting closed with his touch. "I miss myself right now."

"Where does she go?" he asked.

"To things in the past," she said.

"I wish you'd tell me about it."

Her eyes opened, and she searched his face. "You can trust me," he said, remembering that she'd said it was ridiculous to think everyone could be trusted.

"I do trust you, Todd."

He let his hand come back to his lap and waited. Laura maybe needed a few moments to find her words and her voice, and he'd been pushing her too soon, or jumping in with his own thoughts when she needed the silence.

"I had a girl like that one once," she said, her smile made only of sadness now. "She wasn't mine, but she belonged to my fiancé." She gave a light laugh that carried no joy. "We were to be a family."

Todd's neck throbbed with his rapid pulse, and he had no idea what to say. Something—maybe the Good Lord Himself—told him not to say anything at all.

He just needed to be here with her, so Laura knew she didn't have to weather everything alone.

Laura's smile dissolved into a sob, and Todd wished they weren't seated in a car so he could take her into his arms and hold her tight. "Come on," he said, not caring about the rain. They both wore soaking wet clothes already.

He got out of the car and rounded the hood to get her out. She let him, and Todd swept the waif of a woman into his arms easily. He couldn't help the way his hormones fired, but he told himself now wasn't the time to be attracted to her.

Laura obviously had some serious things she was dealing with, and Todd wanted to be her safe place should she need one. In his opinion, she definitely needed one.

"Is the door unlocked?" he asked.

"Yes," she said, her voice hardly her own. "Who locks their doors out here?"

"Fair point." He opened the door and took her inside. As wet as they both were, he didn't dare sit on the couch, so he used his foot to kick a dining room chair out from under the table and he sank into that, cradling her on his lap.

She curled into his chest, sniffling. Todd once again felt prompted to give her time, and he stroked her hair back with one hand and kept her securely on his lap with the other.

His phone rang, but he ignored it. His jeans started to itch, but he didn't move a muscle. His throat turned dry, but he didn't ask for a drink.

Finally, Laura sat up and got to her feet. "I'm okay now."

"You're always okay," he said, watching her walk into

the kitchen and get a towel. She wiped it over her hair and faced him. "You're strong, Laura. You've always been a ray of sunshine on this ranch, and I want to help you get that back."

She smiled, and this time, it did hold some remnant of its old luster. "So I was obviously engaged," she said.

"I know what a fiancé is," he teased.

Thankfully, she didn't take offense to that, and she nodded to show her appreciation of his barb.

Her face crumbled, and she turned away from him. "His name was Hans, and he took care of his four-year-old half-sister after his dad passed away."

Todd got to his feet as Laura wiped her eyes. He approached her slowly, not wanting to overwhelm her or scare her back into silence.

"Ah, so that little girl reminded you of her."

"Yes." She looked at him, tears clinging to her eyelashes. "Hans was very ill, and he died before we could be married. I was supposed to still have Letty, but his aunt —who'd said she wouldn't take her from me—did exactly that."

She shook her head, smiling and half-scoffing as she tried not to burst into a sob. "It's okay. I went back to my veterinary program, because Hans hadn't wanted me to quit in the first place. I couldn't have done that with Letty."

"Doesn't mean you don't miss her." Todd ducked his head and watched her, her pain so raw and so real, he could almost feel it as if it belonged to him.

He opened his arms, a clear invitation for her to seek

refuge with him. She did, practically flying into his embrace. "I'm sorry," she said.

"You don't need to apologize to me." He pressed his lips to the top of her head. "Like I said before, you belong here, and I want to help you if I can."

"I love this ranch," she said. "I love my job here. Everyone has been so nice. Maybe not Josie, but it's okay. We get along okay."

The news that Josie wasn't nice surprised him, but he said, "I'm glad you like it here."

She ran her hands through his hair, her fingernails drawing shivers from him. His cold clothes probably helped with that, but he didn't try to still them.

They breathed in together, and Laura touched her nose to his cheek, and his mouth sought her jaw, then her earlobe. She pressed into his touch, the passion between them suddenly heating everything in his body.

Their lips caught for a moment, and then she ducked away. Todd wasn't sure if he should stop, step back, or stay. Laura looked up again, and he witnessed the conflict in her expression.

She'd kissed him last time, after he'd sung to her for her birthday and presented her with brownies and ice cream. This was different. This was attraction and desire—and pain.

This time, he lowered his head and kissed her, the fireworks just as loud in his ears, and the fire just as smoking hot as last time.

He could kiss her all day and never tire of it, but she

pulled away far too soon. Last time they'd kissed, she'd wanted something lighter and easier after that.

This time, Todd asked, "Okay?"

She looked up at him, her eyes full of a sexy softness, edged with fear. She didn't tell him the kiss was okay, and the longer the silence stretched, the more doubt filled him, until he was practically choking with it.

———

TEXAS LONGHORN RANCH ROMANCE

Book 1: Loving Her Cowboy Best Friend: She's a city girl returning to her hometown. He's a country boy through and through. When these two former best friends (and ex-lovers) start working together, romantic sparks fly that could ignite a wildfire... Will Regina and Blake get burned or can they tame the flames into true love?

Book 2: Kissing Her Cowboy Boss: She's a veterinarian with a secret past. He's her new boss. When Todd hires Laura, it's because she's willing to live on-site and work full-time for the ranch. But when their feelings turn personal, will Laura put up walls between them to keep them apart?

CHESTNUT RANCH ROMANCE

Book 1: A Cowboy and his Neighbor: Best friends and neighbors shouldn't share a kiss...

Book 2: A Cowboy and his Mistletoe Kiss: He wasn't supposed to kiss her. Can Travis and Millie find a way to turn their mistletoe kiss into true love?

Book 3: A Cowboy and his Christmas Crush: Can a Christmas crush and their mutual love of rescuing dogs bring them back together?

Book 4: A Cowboy and his Daughter: They were married for a few months. She lost their baby...or so he thought.

Book 5: A Cowboy and his Boss: She's his boss. He's had a crush on her for a couple of summers now. Can Toni and Griffin mix business and pleasure while making sure the teens they're in charge of stay in line?

Book 6: A Cowboy and his Fake Marriage: She needs a husband to keep her ranch...can she convince the cowboy next-door to marry her?

Book 7: A Cowboy and his Secret Kiss: He likes the pretty adventure guide next door, but she wants to keep their relationship off the grid. Can he kiss her in secret and keep his heart intact?

Book 8: A Cowboy and his Skipped Christmas: He's been in love with her forever. She's told him no more times than either of them can count. Can Theo and Sorrell find their way through past pain to a happy future together?

BLUEGRASS RANCH ROMANCE

Book 1: Winning the Cowboy Billionaire: She'll do anything to secure the funding she needs to take her perfumery to the next level...even date the boy next door.

Book 2: Roping the Cowboy Billionaire: She'll do anything to show her ex she's not still hung up on him...even date her best friend.

Book 3: Training the Cowboy Billionaire: She'll do anything to save her ranch...even marry a cowboy just so they can enter a race together.

Book 4: Parading the Cowboy Billionaire: She'll do anything to spite her mother and find her own happiness...even keep her cowboy billionaire boyfriend a secret.

Book 5: Promoting the Cowboy Billionaire: She'll do anything to keep her job...even date a client to stay on her boss's good side.

Book 6: Acquiring the Cowboy Billionaire: She'll do anything to keep her father's stud farm in the family...even marry the maddening cowboy billionaire she's never gotten along with.

Book 7: Saving the Cowboy Billionaire: She'll do anything to prove to her friends that she's over her ex...even date the cowboy she once went with in high school.

Book 8: Convincing the Cowboy Billionaire: She'll do anything to keep her dignity...even convincing the saltiest cowboy billionaire at the ranch to be her boyfriend.

ABOUT EMMY

Emmy is a Midwest mom who loves dogs, cowboys, and Texas. She's been writing for years and loves weaving stories of love, hope, and second chances. Learn more about her and her books at www.emmyeugene.com.

Printed in Great Britain
by Amazon

20032704R10189